BLAIR DENHOLM

POINT BLANK

By Blair Denholm

The Fighting Detective

Fighting Dirty

Kill Shot

Shot Clock

Trick Shot

Shot to the Heart

Drop Shot

Point Blank

Moving Target

Cold Shot

To all the people who have tried to master the infuriating game of golf and have failed.

Vinci Books

vinci-books.com

Published by Vinci Books Ltd in 2026

1

Copyright © Blair Denholm 2022

The author has asserted their moral right to be identified as the author of this work in accordance with the Copyright, Designs and Patents Act 1988. This work is a work of fiction. Names, characters, places and incidents are the product of the author's imagination or are used fictitiously. Any resemblance to actual persons, living or dead, places and incidents is entirely coincidental.
All rights reserved. No part of this publication may be copied, reproduced, distributed, stored in any retrieval system, or transmitted in any form or by any means, including photocopying, recording, or other electronic or mechanical methods, nor used as a source for any form of machine learning including AI datasets, without the prior written permission of the publisher.
The publisher and the author have made every effort to obtain permissions for any third party material used in this book and to comply with copyright law. Any queries in this respect should be brought to the attention of the publisher and any omissions will be corrected in future editions.
A CIP catalogue record for this book is available from the British Library.
Paperback ISBN: 9781036708283

The EU GPSR authorised representative is Logos Europe, 9 rue Nicolas Poussion, 17000 La Rochelle, France
contact@logoseurope.eu

Chapter One

THE LIE of the golf ball was perfect for the next shot. Never mind it took seven strokes to get here from the tee. Detective Sergeant Jack Lisbon of the Yorkville Police Central Investigation Bureau was sure he could put all the preceding muffed shots behind him and nail this next one. He was as rusty as an old barbed-wire fence when it came to golf, but at least he was doing better than his partner. Constable Aden Trevarthen had needed ten strokes to make it onto the green, where his ball sat tantalisingly close to the pin.

Jack cast a quick look back to the tee, about 300 metres distant in a straight line. A quartet of golfers were waiting for the two cops to finish the first hole and move to the second. Jack didn't need a degree in body language to know their rocking from side to side, pacing and foot tapping meant the other players were running out of patience. But he wouldn't let that rattle him. He and Trevarthen had paid their green fees and were entitled to take the time they needed to complete the hole.

The DS rubbed his craggy nose thoughtfully as he reexamined the ball in its little nest of kikuyu. The tuft of grass was the ideal launching pad – a bit of length, spongy and soft and easy to swing through. A gentle stroke with a pitching wedge to the lip of the green and the ball should slowly roll down the slight incline and pull up somewhere near the flag. Perhaps even in the hole. Only one problem. Jack didn't have a pitching wedge in his bare-bones hired golf bag. His request to borrow one from Constable Aden Trevarthen was met with a blank stare.

'Which one's that?' The large-framed officer leaned over the bag, eyes darting from the head of one club to another. 'I haven't played in that long I can't remember much about the equipment.'

'Not sure either,' said Jack. 'I think it's got the letter P imprinted on the top, innit.'

'Wouldn't that be the putter?'

Jack wiped a runnel of sweat from his brow. Even autumn in tropical Far North Queensland generated enough heat to make a body warm. 'Nah. The putter doesn't have a letter on it. Even a novice like you should be able to tell which one's the putter.'

Trevarthen, ten kilos lighter since Christmas thanks to regular running and gym work with Jack, as well as disavowing his favourite sugary snacks, placed his hands on his new slimline hips and gave a lopsided smile. He then reached into the bag, handed Jack a long club with a bulging black head on it. 'Like this?'

'No, you pillock. That's a five wood.'

'But it's made of plastic.'

'Still called a wood. Tradition 'n that.'

Trevarthen blew out a breath of exasperation. 'Then I can't help you.'

A hand darted out and snatched the club from

Trevarthen's grip. 'Tell you what, I think I remember using one of these around the green before.' Jack hadn't played the game in at least fifteen years, so his memory was fuzzy. 'It's got a bit of loft on the face of the club so you can use it like a wedge.' Jack paused. 'Probably.'

'Well, make up your mind. That group up there,' Trevarthen pointed towards the first tee, 'don't look very happy.'

'Tough luck,' said Jack. 'The more they carry on, the longer I'm gonna take. I espouse the same philosophy when it comes to tailgaters. The closer they get, the slower I go. But it don't matter. I'm taking the shot.'

After rehearsing the shot in his mind, "visualising" like the professional coaches advise, Jack was sure he'd figured out how hard to hit the ball. A deep breath, eyes focused on the small white object on the ground, a swing...and the ball sailed over the top of the flag before disappearing into a bunker on the other side of the green. Chattering green parrots in bushy trees that lined the fairway seemed to be mocking his poor play. 'An effin' sand trap on the first damn hole!' Jack flung the club towards the electric buggy they had rented, then shook a fist at the avian spectators. 'Who designs these courses? The Marquis de bleedin' Sade?'

'Careful, Jack!' Trevarthen blurted. 'I paid for that buggy with my credit card, if you damage it by throwing...'

But Jack wasn't listening. He reefed a sand wedge from his bag and stomped around the side of the elevated green. He wasn't sure if he could hear Trevarthen chuckling or if it was the birds again. Then the noise got louder. A buzzing sound like a thousand mosquitoes heading straight towards him. He squinted into the sun as the object skimmed over his head. The thing stopped, hovered in the air two metres or so directly over the brim of Jack's baseball cap. He heard

Trevarthen yelling out garbled words, then sensed the vibrations of his approaching footsteps as he ran towards his boss.

'What on Earth is it?' Trevarthen extended an arm towards the levitating object.

'A drone. But I've not seen one like this before.' The flying machine was an elongated H-shape with four arms bearing whizzing rotors. Black struts, visible red and green wires, with a stumpy, angular object crudely attached at the front end with what appeared to be grey gaffer tape. 'I reckon that's a jerry-rigged camera hanging there, look.'

'Yep. I'd say so.' Trevarthen squinted. 'Actually, no, I think that's an inbuilt camera under it. I can see a flashing light.'

'What's that then?' Jack pointed at the L-shaped blackness.

'Not sure, could be some kind of data logger,' Trevarthen replied. The machine's buzzing noise increased, now loud enough to make the two men wince and put fingers to their ears. The volume then dropped by half, rose again, before the device elevated to a height of about five metres. It waggled from side to side a few times, then zoomed off. It followed the path from the right of the green that led to the next tee and disappeared behind a stand of pandanus palm trees.

'That's a bit intrusive, don't you think?' said Jack.

Trevarthen shook his head. 'I reckon some kids are having a laugh. Frightening golfers and filming them. We'll probably end up being YouTube sensations by tonight.'

Jack pursed his lips. 'It's an effin' menace, that's what it is. I'm going to investigate this and kick up a stink.'

Trevarthen chuckled under his breath and returned to the far side of the green. Jack glanced up, mentally calculating the distance to the pin. He wriggled his feet into the soft sand to get purchase. This shot was going to be a Hail Mary. He had no idea how far behind the sand he was supposed to hit the ball. Should he give it a full swing or a stiff-armed jab? No, the "golden middle" in between was what was required.

He paused a moment to curl his bottom lip and blow an annoying fly away from his nose. A deep breath and a couple of practice swings beside the ball. Yes, Jack was pretty sure he'd get this one in the sweet spot and the ball would land a metre or so past the pin and then, with the gentle backspin he'd impart, it would roll back towards the hole. Too easy.

Then, all hell broke loose.

Chapter Two

THE IMAGES on the 10-inch first-person-view monitor shook about annoyingly. Sweat beaded on the skin between his nose and top lip. The pads of his thumbs worked on the thin black control sticks as he guided the device onward. The slightest touch impacted on the drone's flightpath. Nudge the left joystick for up and down and rotating side-to-side, the right one for forward and back. But there'd be very little back movement – just ploughing relentlessly forward to reach the target.

More sweat formed, trickled down the back of his neck. Eyes narrowed as he focused on the job. His heart raced like a freight train. Swirling sounds of blood rushing inside his head. Like the sound of the sea when you hold a shell to your ear. Except it was in both ears at once.

He blinked a droplet away, closed his eye and quickly wiped the lid with his upper arm, never letting go of the controller. Then, eyes quickly back to the FPV monitor. The tricky terrain of the golf course, plus the five kilometres separating him from the target, didn't make a hard job easier. On the plus side, he was safely tucked away. His location was comfortable, remote and secure, with practically zero likelihood of being disturbed. The signal to the drone was strong – the communications facilities in the area perfect for maintaining a steady flight path without the signal dropping out and derailing the mission.

Six months of intense training had gone into this plan. Practise, practise and practise some more, until it became a matter of muscle memory. Like driving a back-hoe or a ride-on-mower or a forklift, until you could make all the right moves without even thinking about it. Most people had no idea of the technical skill required to manoeuvre a complex machine in three dimensions. It was damned difficult and he was proud of the hard work he'd put in – hours and hours of boring drills, recharging batteries countless times, the odd crash. No one had a clue what he was up to. Once this task was completed, he'd drop the hobby with more enthusiasm than a kid freed from after-school piano practice. He'd carried out all his training in a supremely clandestine fashion, away from curious eyes. And ears – this bad boy made more noise than he would have liked. But hey, that was the current state of technology and, as he was fond of repeating to himself – *it is what it is.*

And that was just the flying part of the operation.

There was also the gun part to nail down. A video he'd found on YouTube proved the set-up was not only possible, but functional and effective. Mount a semi-automatic pistol on a drone and fire it remotely. He'd had to practice long hours, hovering and shooting at tin cans on a fence, working out how to keep firing after the flight path was altered by vicious recoil. At last, after three months of practice, he was satisfied. His skill levels were good enough to execute the plan and bring the fucker down.

The cream on the cake was the addition of a megaphone, attached with Velcro and activated via a dedicated transmitter unit. That sucker could blast sound a distance of 1200 metres, had three hours of talk time and 24 hours stand-by. Not that anything like that would be required for this mission; this would be an in-your-face announcement followed by a clean execution from a distance of less than two metres. In total, the modified quadcopter capable of carrying the required payload, including the semi-automatic pistol – nearly a kilogram with a full clip – and the loudspeaker, had cost over a grand. But the result was going to make it all worth while.

At first, when he watched the online video, it all sounded and looked easy. But that was a two-minute long news report, not a step-by-step guide. So he had to figure it out himself. And to be extra careful, his research had been carried out at a library, logging onto the Internet anonymously, even reading old-fashioned printed books. And not a local library either; he made several trips to Cairns to gather the information he needed to buy the right drone and turn it into a killing machine. A lot of slog, sure. But it would all be worth it once the target was neutralised.

Despite the practice and drills, though, the danger of a collision or a mechanical failure was ever-present. A bird could swoop on the drone, a wayward golf ball could knock it out of the sky. Or he could do what humans often do in stressful situations – simply fuck up. If the craft crashed, the chances of him being discovered increased by an order of magnitude.

And so, at this most critical moment, his concentration was at peak level.

He hunched his shoulders, one more left turn at the back of the 18th hole and he'd be on the way to the first tee.

Exactly where the trio would be hitting off at – he checked the convenient digital clock in the corner of the screen – 09:30. And if people filmed it all, so what! The drone would be ditched out to sea where it would sink to the bottom, never to be found again.

The drone cruised at a height of fifteen metres to clear the tallest trees on the course. He piloted the machine to a position vertically above the first tee, panned the camera down. And there they…wait, what?

Shit! It's not them. Instead of the expected party, it was a quartet of pensioners. He knew the prime target was a stickler for punctuality – could they have cancelled the round? Maybe they weren't even on the course at all… Or, maybe they'd gotten off to an early start. Yes, that must be it!

A mental recalculation, a toggle of the sensitive controls, and he was – virtually – down at the first hole putting green, levitating above two guys mucking about in a bunker.

Again, not the target! The man with the weather-beaten face and craggy nose, shielding his eyes as he stared directly into the camera, was annoyingly familiar. It was the face of a violent man best not to mess with. He might view the footage later and try to ID him. No time to waste, though. The hunt was becoming desperate.

One more hole. If the target wasn't there, he'd abort the mission. If the course managers got wind of an unauthorised drone buzzing about…anything could happen.

He flew to the second hole tee block. Vacant. And then the camera picked them up, standing in a bunch halfway up the fairway. *The plan would be carried out to completion.*

Under a cloudless, clear blue sky, the drone and its deadly cargo raced up the middle of the neatly mown fairway. Three pairs of curious eyes turned up to observe. Smiles of wonder on their faces.

He took a deep breath as he set the device to hover, aligned the camera's cross hairs to a point exactly above the target's head. He pressed a button to turn on the megaphone. His voice would be scrambled by software – none of the party would recognise who was speaking. *This is it, no turning back now.*

'Come a step closer please, sir. We're taking photos of our favourite members for the Country Club yearbook.'

Oh my God. The egotistical prick's doing it. He's actually doing it. He's grinning like an idiot, saying something to the two people with him. The drone only carried a loudspeaker, not a microphone. Sadly, his last words won't be recorded for posterity. What a shame. Now he's laying his five iron on the turf. The vain bastard's even taking off his cap and smoothing his mane of black hair. A beaming smile. The drone dropped to be level with the man's forehead, inched forward towards the beaming fool.

'Say cheese!'

A press of another button and the gun jerked the drone backwards with the recoil. BANG! Right on target. A split second to realign. Another shot to finish him off. BANG!

Now, time for the old man...

Chapter Three

THE BARKING gunfire erupted a microsecond before Jack's club drilled into the grit. Another botched shot. The ball travelled barely a metre before it hit the rim of the bunker and plopped back into the soft sand. But Jack couldn't care less about that.

The fearsome racket was unmistakable. A semi-automatic handgun. The repeated firing sounded exactly the same as Jack's rarely used service pistol, a .40 calibre Glock 22.

A woman screamed, and then the shooting started again. Jack guessed close to an entire magazine had been emptied in the two bursts.

Amid the sensory overload, Jack's legs and arms were pumping like pistons. Trevarthen had reacted first, and was haring across a small wooden footbridge towards the second hole. The source of the noise seemed to be somewhere behind the trees ringing the first-hole green.

Both men were over the bridge now, Jack hot on Trevarthen's heels. Up ahead, the DS spied a small group of people in the middle of the fairway of the second hole, halfway to the compact green at the top of a small hillock. Two on the deck, one kneeling.

From 50 metres distant, the grass around the trio appeared to bubble and boil, crimson and slick with blood. A woman rocked back and forth on her haunches, convulsing. Her clothes were spattered with red dots and streaks and blotches. She leaned all the way forward, mumbling something, placed her head across the blood-soaked chest of a man who lay motionless, arms and legs akimbo. Fifteen metres from those two lay a second man. Grey-haired and thin-limbed, he was curled up in the foetal position, a shiny iron club and his wide-brimmed hat a metre away. Blood pooled around the man's stomach area. He made slight, jerky movements.

Jack and Trevarthen were now upon them. The DS pointed at the older gentleman, turned to his friend and colleague. 'Go and check him, Aden. I'll call an ambulance. Keep your wits about you. The shooter could still be in the area.'

'Got it,' Trevarthen said calmly. *A good man in a crisis*, Jack thought to himself.

Fingers jabbed at the emergency number, triple zero. His call was directed to the Police Communications Centre in the nearby city of Cairns. 'Detective Sergeant Jack Lisbon speaking. I'm at the scene of a shooting. People have been hit multiple times.'

'Location?' asked a woman.

'Yorkville Country Club,' Jack blurted. 'Second fairway. Get a chopper here ASAP. I don't care how you do it, just do it! I'll take care of the police side of things.'

'Roger that. Hang tight and help should arrive soon.'

A quick call to Inspector Batista. The boss gasped in

horror at the news, agreed to send all available troops to the scene. He'd join the effort himself once he'd concluded a video-link conference with Jennifer Landacre, Assistant Commissioner for Far North Queensland.

'Sir, we need someone up at the clubhouse to stop curious souls from wandering down for a look. It's not pretty here.'

'Constable Wilson's attending a reported break and enter not far from there. I'll tell him to drop it and head your way.'

'Cheers.'

'I'll also call the club president, see if he's at the course this morning. He's a good man. He might be able to instil calm if people get panicky.'

'Thanks, sir. I…' The swaying rear end of a goanna lizard crossing the fairway caught the corner of Jack's eye, distracted him for a moment.

'Yes, DS Lisbon?'

'Sorry, sir. Just some wildlife.' He drew a deep breath. 'The woman's in deep shock, two men down. Gotta go. Make sure Wilson and the rest of them get here ASAP.'

Jack disconnect the call and yelled out to Trevarthen. 'What's his status?'

'Alive, barely, but unconscious. Breathing's weak.' Trevarthen stood and whipped off his polo shirt, revealing the beginnings of a six pack that two months ago was a blob of jelly. He tourniqueted the shirt around the man's upper arm, tied a knot and pulled it tight. Then he bunched up a small towel he'd been carrying in the back pocket of his shorts and pressed it hard against the man's torso. 'There's so much blood it's hard to tell, but I'd say there's three bullets in him. One in the shoulder, one seems to have gone through the fleshy part of his upper arm. Those wounds don't look too bad. One's gone into the lower stomach. That's a genuine worry, blood's gushing. Yours?'

Jack shook his head. 'Not looking too good, sunshine.' He crouched down next to assess the victim. It was immediately clear, the man the woman was clinging onto was stone cold dead. Two bullet holes the size of dollar coins through the front of the skull; the circumferences were neat, the shots taken from point blank range. Most likely the projectiles had exited through the back of the man's head. Eyes wide open in terrified surprise, but also the hint of a fading smile on his lips. A scan of the rest of his body revealed no other visible injuries.

Jack prised the woman's fingers apart and pulled her away from the dead man. 'What the hell happened here? How many of them were there?'

She blinked a pair of icy blue eyes, the brightest Jack had ever seen on a dark-haired person. Her face was as white as the golf ball he'd abandoned in the bunker. 'None,' she croaked.

'What?'

'It was the feckin' drone.' Her accent was Irish, pure County Cork. That helped explain the unusual eye-hair combination. There were no tears, no histrionics. Not yet. 'It...just...appeared...out of...nowhere. We all...stared at it...and then it spoke like a ghost...oh, my God!' Her bloodied hands went to her cheeks, left a smear like the Nike swoosh.

Now it made sense. Jack had a suspicion the flying box must have had something to do with this atrocity. The angular object slung at the front of the drone was a gun, not a data logger. It sounded like an entire clip had been fired, but perhaps there were a couple of bullets left in the chamber. He and Trevarthen were unarmed, so shooting it out of the sky if it returned was not an option. His heart accelerated thinking about the possibility of another attack.

'There're players ahead of us,' said Trevarthen with a restrained urgency. 'The course has been open since early this morning. There could be people on every fairway and green for all we know.'

'Dammit, Aden, you're right.' Jack scratched his crown through his cap. How could they alert players and direct them away from the possible danger? He pulled the unused scorecard from his top pocket, located the Country Club's main phone number in the corner. A woman with a childlike, nasally voice answered the call. 'Country Club reception. Ruby speaking. How can I help you?'

After introducing himself at record speed, Jack poured out the details of the shootings. Except for the bit about the fatality. That would come later.

'Holy shit!' the woman cried. Jack heard a sharp intake of breath. 'There are dozens of people out there. What'll we do?'

'Remain calm, for one thing. We need to remove people from the course without creating panic. Is there anyone on hand who can quickly drive a vehicle around the course taking the most efficient route?'

'Yeah, me. There's a Yamaha quaddie and a couple of motorbikes in the shed.'

'What?'

'I'm the greenkeeper's daughter. I help dad out sometimes when one of his workers gets sick. The trail bike's too big for me, but I've been riding the old Honda step-through for years. The keys are in the office. I'll head out now.'

'Not sure I should be letting you do this…'

'What, because I'm a girl?'

'No, no…of course not… I…ah…don't like using civilians in this way.' Piss weak reasoning, Lisbon. It *is* because she's a girl, and she sounds like a young one at that.

'Look, there's a bunch of pensioners out there, sitting ducks if that drone comes back,' Ruby reasoned. 'Not all of them have electric buggies, either, so it'll take them a while to get back to the clubhouse.'

'Shit, shit, shit,' Jack muttered.

'Didn't you say not to panic?'

The girl's got a cheek. 'I guess I did.'

'I know the layout like the back of my hand. Should take me less than half an hour to burn around the course. See you.'

'Wait!'

'What?'

'You may as well skip the first and second holes, if that'll make the job easier. Tell everyone you see to hug the edges of the fairways, stay as close to the tree-line as possible.'

'Righto.'

A flutter ran through Jack's stomach. He could be putting an innocent woman in danger. The trade-off was potentially saving more lives. The gunshots were loud, but there was no guarantee everyone heard them. And if they did, the sounds could have been interpreted as something harmless, like groundskeeping machinery backfiring. One last confirmation. 'You sure you're up for it, Ruby?'

'No dramas, Detective. I'll keep my eyes peeled.' The woman's gung-ho attitude was both a blessing and a curse. If she got hurt, Jack would never forgive himself.

'And wear a bloody helmet!'

He hung up and glanced across to Trevarthen, diligently pressing on the injured man's wound. Satisfied the constable was doing his utmost, Jack turned his attention back to the

Irish woman, breathing sharply and staring straight ahead. 'Hey, you still with us?'

'What?'

'Did you see where the drone went?' The question was idiotic, but it jumped out of his mouth automatically. Like you'd ask where a human suspect had run to. A drone was a different proposition. It could fly off in one direction, then head in another and be miles away in no time. Knowing its initial trajectory was next to useless.

'No, I ducked and covered my head when it started firing. Oh Mary, Mother of Jesus, is he alright?'

'Sorry?'

She pointed at the body. 'Paul. Is he going to be OK? He won't answer me.'

No point skirting the obvious and unpleasant. 'I'm terribly sorry, love. He's gone.'

She nodded, like she'd been waiting for verification of a nasty suspicion. 'What about my husband?'

Jack blinked hard. 'This isn't your husband?'

'N-n-no. That's h-h-him over there.' She turned her head and waved towards the prone figure under Trevarthen's care. 'This,' she whispered, 'is the man I love.'

Chapter Four

'HELLO! IS EVERYTHING ALL RIGHT?' A faint, nervous voice drifted down the fairway from the second tee. Jack recognised the man's ridiculous pink plus-fours. It was one of the foursome playing behind Jack and Trevarthen. Then there were three more of them, shaking and huddled together like frightened sheep.

Jack stood to his full height, cupped his blood-stained hands to his mouth and yelled at them. 'I'm a police officer. People have been shot. Get back to the clubhouse and wait. If you see anyone, tell them to go there too! No one is to come down here. I repeat, no one is to come down here!'

No sooner were the words out of Jack's mouth than the golfers vanished behind the trees. A quick check of his watch. *Where was the helicopter?* So far, no sign of the deadly drone returning. Still, he didn't like it. An eerie silence hung over the golf course. Then it was split momentarily by the mosquito whine of Ruby on the motorbike. Good lass, she'd wasted no time. He guessed she was tearing along the third fairway behind a knoll that edged the second-hole green. The engine of the bike faded into silence.

Jack left the Irish woman for a moment to check on the older man. Hard to credit this was her husband. He was still breathing shallowly, and he'd lost a lot of blood. Trevarthen was keeping a close eye, but there was only so much he could do apart from hold a soaked handtowel to the geezer's forehead and keep the pressure on the stomach wound with his sodden shirt.

Where were the paramedics?

Jack had a quick hunt around for spent cartridges, found three about a metre to the right of the dead man. Also the two bullets that must have traversed his cranium, about half a metre away at 2 o'clock relative to the man's right eye. Next to the shells and bullets he placed bright orange marker discs, the kind golfers use to indicate where a ball has been temporarily removed from the putting green to allow others an unobstructed shot at the hole. Better to bag the evidence up when forensics arrive than to handle things now. Jack knew there must be more brass casings at the scene, bullets on the ground or embedded in trees, but the woman's distressing sounds made him suspend the search.

She was moaning softly now, perhaps drifting closer and closer to a catatonic state. Jack returned to her, led her to a thick eucalypt with large overhanging branches that provided an awning of shade. He helped her sit, propped her back against the tree. 'Wait here, love.' Again, meaningless words. She was going nowhere. He fetched a clear drink bottle from the buggy several metres away. It was labelled "Dervla", a traditional Irish girl's name.

'Here, drink this.' Jack handed her the opened bottle of water, she took it in shaking hands. 'I take it you're Dervla?'

'Yeah, that's me. Ta,' she whispered. She tilted her head

back and drained the bottle, tossed it to one side like it was trash, and stared straight ahead again. She'd be needing something stronger than water soon. *Where were the paramedics, dammit?* Jack took another look at the woman. He estimated Dervla's age at mid 20's to early 30's. One thing was sure, she was much younger than her shot-up spouse. Jack wouldn't harass her now with tough questions about her personal relationships. All that and more would happen once the immediate crisis had been dealt with. Now that her lover was history, the priority was to save her husband's life.

Jack brushed pieces of recently mowed grass from his shorts, gave Dervla a reassuring pat on the wrist, and went to see how Trevarthen was doing with the unconscious man. The constable produced a brown leather wallet he'd extracted from the victim's back pocket, gave a rundown of what was inside. A driver's licence stated the bearer was Lachlan Troy Morris, aged 69, ticked off as an organ donor and requiring visual aids to drive. No spectacles nearby, perhaps he wore contact lenses. A platinum Amex card stood out among the usual assortment of plastic rectangles – loyalty cards, Medicare, the local library, auto club. 'I did a quick Google search while we're waiting for the cavalry,' said Trevarthen.

'Good work, sunshine. And?'

'He's a retired mechanical engineer, currently the president of the Rotary Club of Yorkville. A pillar of the community.'

'Right.' Jack rubbed his chin thoughtfully. 'I think I've heard the fella's name before. Rumours about him using his position to his own advantage. We'll have to look into that further. A bloke like that could've trodden on the wrong toes and set himself up as a target.'

Trevarthen nodded. 'Maybe the dead guy's influential, too. Have you ID'd him?'

Jack shrugged and gave a guilty smirk. 'I must be getting soft as I get older. He fell on his back and I guess... I dunno, perhaps I thought it disrespectful to roll him over and examine him like that.'

'That's one way of looking at it, I guess,' said Trevarthen. 'Or perhaps you just hadn't got around to it yet.'

'Yeah,' Jack sighed. Trevarthen's generous spirit was on display again. 'I'll run with that version.'

He sat with Dervla once again for a moment; she was mumbling incoherently now, sweat beading profusely on her brow, her fingers clenching and unclenching. PTSD would haunt the poor soul for many years to come. Considering her state of bewilderment, it was unlikely she'd be bothered by − or even notice − Jack rummaging around in Paul's pockets. The DS grunted as he reached a hand under the body's left hip and tried to raise him. Huffing and straining, Jack elevated the body just enough to slide a hand under and have a feel. No wallet in the back left pocket. Repeat from the other side. Again, nothing. Maybe his personal items were in the golf buggy? A quick search in the rear storage compartment turned up the required item along with three mobile phones.

There was the man's C class Queensland driver's license. Paul Sterling Keenan. His dark hair was much shorter in the photo taken three years ago. The man was a handsome specimen, no doubt. Not unlike a famous American actor whose name eluded Jack for the moment. Then there was the Irish surname. Perhaps a commonality that brought him and Dervla together? Forty-one, older than Dervla, but the gap was much narrower than between her and her still-alive spouse. Address was in a well-to-do part of town. Jack knew the street, Hagan Avenue, one of Yorkville's most prestigious locations abutting the CBD. Another assortment of cards, plus a sum of cash that was rather large for the digital age, exactly $1000 in fifties. What could that be for? Friendly wagers as they played the course? A membership card for the Yorkville Country Club. Looked like he was a full member. Jack knew that cost a packet, so Paul must have a good job. Taking a leaf out of Trevarthen's book, he quickly consulted the Internet on his own Samsung. Good job indeed. Keenan was manager and franchisee of the central Yorkville branch of the Trust Bank of Australia, and also a member of the same rotary club presided over by Dervla's husband. Quite a tangled situation, Jack mused.

There was no time for more reflection on the trio; Jack's thoughts were interrupted by the throaty, reassuring throb of the approaching chopper. The underbelly of the red and white AW139, known locally as Rescue 510, cast a broad shadow over the fairway as it slowly descended. The noise of the engine dropped as the machine settled onto the ground, sending ripples through the longer grass either side of the fairway. A side door on rollers slid wide open, revealing the team of first responders, eager to get amongst it. Behind them were saline drips, woollen and foil blankets, and assorted medical equipment.

Two paramedics in helmets and fluoro gear leapt from the chopper; its still-spinning rotors created a pummelling rush of warm air. Trevarthen waved his arms desperately while Jack made hand signals like an airport marshaller on the tarmac. *Him first!* was the unspoken order. Another paramedic appeared and, head bowed, darted towards Jack and Dervla. In a flash, the woman had escorted a trembling

Dervla inside the aircraft. Jack could see inside a window; the ambo was trying to get Dervla to talk, but the only response was staring stillness. He trotted over to where the Irish woman's husband was being strapped into a stretcher, ready to be loaded aboard.

'What can you tell us?' said Jack to a tall medical officer endowed with more wrinkles than someone his young age ought to have. 'Will he live?'

'It'll be touch and go.' The man spoke rapidly. 'He's lost a lot of blood, so he'll probably need a transfusion. Listen, we have to hurry. You got more questions, head to the hospital, OK?'

Jack nodded; unnecessary delay would put Lachlan Morris at more risk. Within less than a minute, the paramedics and cuckold Morris were inside the chopper and tracking for Cairns Base Hospital in a mighty hurry.

Chapter Five

AS THE STRUTS of the helicopter disappeared beyond the canopy of waving tall eucalypts, the Yorkville Station's white Ford Territory pulled up on the fairway. Two uniformed officers, Constables Noah Semmens and Kylie Smith alighted, followed by a civilian from the back seat.

'And you are?' said Jack, ignoring his own troops for the moment. The man, lean and tall, shaved head, dressed in a lemon polo shirt and tan slacks, exuded officiousness. As he extended a hand, the DS caught a hint of lavender soap confused by a musky cologne.

'Wayne Fletcher. I'm the managing director of the golf club.'

'Is that the same as the president?'

'Ah, no. That's Jeff Bloomberg. He's in Sydney for the weekend. Why do you ask?'

'Because the Inspector said he was calling the president, not you. Now, if you don't mind, sir, I'd rather you went back to the clubhouse and gave us some space. You can make yourself useful up there by telling the punters to remain calm.' Jack couldn't believe his team had allowed the man onto the scene. 'Semmens, why is he here?'

'He was most insistent, DS Lisbon,' said the constable. 'Claimed he was concerned about the welfare of his members. He also said he'd lay a complaint with Inspector Batista if we kept him in the dark.'

'Did he now?'

'He said Batista's a respected member of the club and a good mate of his.'

'I don't care if they're effin' best buddies, which I strongly doubt. This bloke's got no business being here impeding our investigation.' Jack tossed a nicotine gum in his mouth and bit down hard. 'And where the hell is Wilson? He's supposed to be keeping everyone back.'

'He's up there, DS Lisbon.' Semmens pointed in the direction of the clubhouse. 'He's doing his level best. But this gentleman shoved his way past Wilson when he spotted our vehicle and made a beeline for us.'

Fletcher gave Jack a hard stare. 'I'll return if you order me to,' he said, as if doing so would be a noble sacrifice. 'But you have to understand, there are people back there eager to tee off. I need to explain to them what's going on.'

'Didn't you take my officers' word for it? Or the word of the party I sent back with a message there'd been a shooting on the course?'

The man adopted a challenging pose, hands on hips. Jack knew the type. Always wanting to be at the centre of attention. Micro managers. 'A shooting?' His eyebrows scaled the heights of his broad forehead. 'I was told there'd been an *incident*. The people you mentioned hurried off, jumped in their car and then they were gone.' He blinked a couple of times. 'I must know exactly what happened.

Keeping the details from me isn't acceptable. I've made complaints against the police before, you know.'

'Really?' said Jack, quirking an eyebrow. 'Good for you.'

'Look, I saw the chopper arrived and left pretty quickly.' Fletcher's tone reached new levels of annoying. 'So I assumed we'd be OK to proceed with the important business of running a golf course.'

'You are *not* OK to proceed. Play is cancelled for the day. Maybe for the next couple of days.'

'You're joking!'

'I most certainly am not. As we speak, your receptionist Ruby is racing over the golf course on a motorbike, telling whoever she sees to haul arse back to the clubhouse.'

'I beg your pardon? She had no permission to abandon her post on reception. She'll be lucky to keep her job after this.'

'Sack her and you'll have me to deal with.' Jack squared his shoulders. 'Ruby was acting on my instructions.'

The man let out a sigh of exasperation. 'If you can't offer me a proper explanation, I'll be left with no choice but to tell the members they are right to play.'

'Do that and I'll arrest you for failing to comply with a reasonable instruction. Now, get in the car, please, sir. The nice officer will take you back to the clubhouse.'

Fletcher puffed out his cheeks, about to air more grievances. If that's the way he wanted it. 'Right, come with me.' Jack grabbed him by the crook of the arm, marched him to the motionless lump on the ground. 'See that?' Jack lifted the blanket so Fletcher could see the bullet holes in Keenan's forehead, the vacant dead eyes. 'You think the golfers can play around him like he's a…what do they call it…a temporary hazard?'

'Oh my God, It's Paul! Is he…?'

'Yes, he's dead.'

Fletcher's face went whiter than chalk, his mouth opened and closed but no sound came out. Jack beckoned to Semmens. 'Take Mr Fletcher back to his office. Call a doctor for him if he needs one, and then get back here ASAP.

'Sir,'

'And take Constable Smith with you to assist Wilson. Sounds like these golfers are an entitled bunch of so-and-sos.'

'Roger that,' said Semmens. The Territory ripped up a section of turf as it sped away creating the biggest divot in the course's history, the managing director in the back seat cradling his head in his hands and muttering incoherently.

'You sure you should've showed him the body, Jack?' said Trevarthen as the vehicle bounced along the fairway. 'Could give the man nightmares.'

'Nightmares are a part of life, innit. Besides, it was the only way to get the message across. Stuffed shirts like him grind my gears.'

A minute later Jack's mobile buzzed. He read the text. More troops were on their way. The Inspector and Detective Constable Claudia Taylor. That meant only rookie Constable Damien Wells was left at the station to handle enquiries. Jack called Taylor. 'How far away are you?'

'We're turning into the car park,' she said in a clipped tone. 'I can see Noah Semmens assisting some guy bent double; he's got his arm around the man's waist. Was he shot, too?'

'No. But I wouldn't mind...' *Don't say it.*

'Sorry?'

'Talk to him, Claudia.'

'Who, Noah or the bald guy?'

'The bald guy. Wayne Fletcher. He's the bloke who runs the joint. He ID'd the dead victim straight away. He might have some insight into this mess.'

'He looks distressed. You sure about this?'

'I'll leave it to your discretion. And try to get statements from anyone who might have seen the drone from up at the clubhouse. Or from wherever they were at the time. Come down to the crime scene when you're done.'

'Will do.'

'Get someone to give the Inspector a lift down to the second hole. And one more thing.'

'Yes?'

'Send a couple of cold cans of soft drink down, will ya? Me and Aden didn't bring any 'cos we were only planning a quick nine holes, after which we were supposed to be going fishing. Instead, we get World War III. In short, we're effin' parched.'

'Is that all?'

'No, actually. Can you buy Aden a clean shirt from the pro shop? Anything in a large.'

'What does he…?'

Jack had already hung up.

Chapter Six

SATURDAY MORNING in early autumn was the perfect time for catching up with girlfriends over brunch, reading a spicy romance novel on the front veranda or taking a relaxing walk in the rainforest. It definitely *wasn't* the time to be chasing after crazed killers, DC Taylor thought to herself. Not counting the usual assortment of low-grade felonies and misdemeanours, Yorkville had been virtually crime free since the sensational murder of international tennis star Roderick McAdam three months ago. That homicide had grabbed the world's attention by the throat and kept Yorkville in the spotlight for an uncomfortable couple of weeks. This strange drone slaying could become just as infamous. *Please, not again.*

Bright-eyed Constable Ben Wilson greeted Taylor and Inspector Joe Batista at the elegant French-doored front entrance. She kept half a pace behind the boss as they made their way inside, between parallel rows of brightly coloured flowers in terracotta pots. Batista had earlier regaled Taylor with details of a heated argument he'd had with his wife. A minor matter over clearing the table after dinner that escalated into a row. He'd hoped to smooth things over with Marjorie this morning but she remained incalcitrant and was giving him the silent treatment. His mood was sour enough without having a grisly homicide to contend with. Taylor thought it prudent to give him plenty of space.

'Where's Fletcher?' said Batista.

'Semmens took him to his office,' Wilson replied. 'DS Lisbon gave Fletcher a peek at the victim and he took it rather badly. I'd say he's unfit to be questioned.'

'I'll decide that. Is Semmens with him now?'

'No, sir. He's outside in the Territory waiting to drive you down to the crime scene.'

'He'll have to wait a little longer, until I've got things sorted here first. Where's Smith?'

'Kylie's watching over Fletcher at the minute.'

'Excellent.'

'Semmens called the bloke's GP to come and give him the once over. ETA fifteen minutes.'

'What a softie that Fletcher must be,' Taylor remarked offhandedly. 'I can't stand the sight of blood and corpses, but I put up with it.' Remembering the chief's abrasive attitude, she instantly regretted voicing the gripe, but it was too late.

'You're a cop. It's your damn job to put up with it,' Batista snapped before turning back to Wilson. 'I want this place sealed tight as a drum. Get out in the carpark and turn away anyone trying to get in. And don't let anyone leave who's already here. We need their statements. Direct them upstairs to the bar area. Think you can manage that?'

'Yes, sir. What should I tell people arriving at the course, sir?'

'To bugger off. I don't care what reason you give, just keep them out.'

'What about the press?'

'I doubt they've caught wind of it yet, but these days you can never be sure. Someone could've posted or tweeted about an emergency at the country club. If any journos turn up at the gate, tell them an official statement will be released later. This entire golf course is a crime scene until I say otherwise.'

Wilson hustled out of the clubhouse, the heels of his highly polished black leather boots squeaking on the tiled floor. Batista swapped places with Smith in the operations manager's office, ordered Taylor to direct potential witnesses upstairs and wait there until they could be questioned.

Taylor ushered eight elderly golfers upstairs to the bar area, while Smith stood at the door leading off the eighteenth green waiting for another party. Many were out of breath, like they'd sprinted to the safety of the clubhouse building. Taylor squinted through a huge window that offered a panorama of the course, and a clear view of three fairways. Dots scurrying like ants were players keen to avoid being hunted down.

Taylor glimpsed a small red motorcycle whizzing across a fairway at breakneck speed. It flew over the lip of a bunker and landed with a spinning rear wheel before it headed for an industrial shed. Whoever was riding it must have delivered a warning to the golfers. With a crowd of potential witnesses to process, there was no time to waste. Her eyes fell upon two males in their late teens, the only people now left in the downstairs foyer. They were leaning with adolescent attitude against a drink vending machine. Both broke into broad grins as Taylor reached them, notebook in hand. Ignoring Batista's command to immediately direct all witnesses upstairs, she thought she might get more out of them on their own. Maybe they held no promise at all, but she knew from experience that the least likely can occasionally lead police in the right direction.

One lad was nearly as tall as Inspector Batista, the other met Taylor at eye level. She quickly introduced herself, with her ID outstretched for emphasis. 'Morning. You two fellas see anything unusual today? Objects in the sky?'

'Nope,' said the taller one, sporting a bright red peaked cap with Ping emblazoned across the front. 'Just bright sunshine and small fluffy clouds, perfect for a round of 18 holes.'

'Hear any unusual noises?'

'Like what?' said the second teenager, strikingly good looking with wavy black hair and a slight gap between his front teeth.

'Like a drone, or gunshots.'

'No, nothing like that.' He rested a hand on his slim hip. His head tilted and brown eyes simmered as he looked Taylor up and down. A cocky teen thinking he can flirt with the older lady copper. 'We got here when all the panic started and they refused to let us onto the course. You said gunshots. What happened out there today?' He paused and flashed a gleaming smile. Taylor imagined the boy would be rather successful with a certain type of female: the vacuous kind fond of tattooing eyebrows and pumping their faces full of chemical enhancements. 'My name's Jasper, by the way. And this is Darren.' He extended a hand to Taylor, which she ignored by folding her arms across her chest. The adolescent's eyes dropped, the hand darted back into his pocket.

'People have been badly injured by firearms, that's all I

can say at this point.' Taylor blinked twice. She hated withholding information, almost equated it to telling small fibs. Jack called it detectives' privilege. But a death by armed drone on a public golf links is kind of a big deal.

'Must have been real bad to have all you cops swarming about the place.' Darren posed the observation like a question. 'I'm guessing the drone you asked about has something to do with it. This is like something out of a spy movie. Please tell us what happened.' He attempted a puppy-dog face which only succeeded in giving him the appearance of a sad clown.

'Like I said, my hands are tied for now.' She drew a deep breath. 'Are you sure you didn't notice anything around 10:00am?'

'We were still at Jasper's place. Getting ready for a day on the course. Looks like we'll have to find something else to do.'

'When did you arrive here?'

The teens exchanged a look. Jasper said, 'Maybe 10:30 or so. I drove us here in my dad's ute. When we arrived, me and Darren nearly got sideswiped by a carload of people tearing out of the carpark in a real hurry. Did they see the incident?'

Taylor had no idea who these people were or what they had seen. 'I'll have to check with my colleagues about that. You didn't happen to recognise the people inside the vehicle, did you?'

Jasper placed his thumb and forefinger in an V-shape under his chin and made a humming sound. A flash of recollection in his eyes. 'I think...hang on...let me check.' He wandered to a large corkboard behind a sliding glass panel. Inside were photos pinned to the board with thumbtacks. Perhaps a hundred or so, all crammed in tight with barely any cork between them. Some were old black-and-white snaps, and a collage of coloured ones spanning the decades. Taylor guessed they went back to the early 2000's when the market dumped film in favour of digital cameras. The more recent images were cut from coloured glossy paper spat out of a printer.

'Quite a history of the club on this wall,' Taylor observed.

'Yep.' Darren tapped the glass against a large colour photograph a third of the way down and slightly to the left of centre. 'I'm pretty sure the guy behind the wheel was this bloke. Hubert Johnson, the only player from this club to graduate to the pros. He managed one season before he got the world's worst case of the yips and dropped out.'

'The yips?'

'Yeah. It's when golfers lose their nerve and can't play their shots like they used to. Anyway, this bloke had his short time in the limelight. Everyone calls him Bert. I'm positive he was the driver.'

Taylor stood close to the display cabinet, her breath creating a little circle of condensation that she wiped away with her index finger. The man in question was a handsome, lithe, dark-haired gentleman. Against a background of porcelain-blue sky and surrounded by a group of smiling people with their hands in the air, Bert held aloft a trophy. Their tight clothes and outmoded haircuts suggested a time when disco reigned supreme.

'He's a lot older now, probably in his mid-seventies,' said Jasper. 'But those bushy eyebrows and hooked nose are unmistakable. I hear he still plays off a reasonable handicap.'

Taylor surmised the carload fleeing the scene were the people Jack had mentioned, playing one hole behind him and Trevarthen. She turned back to the young men. 'Are you both members of the club?'

'We sure are,' said Darren. 'Me and Jasper here have golf in our blood. We play most weekends, sometimes during the week after uni.'

'Right,' said Taylor. 'Well, at least I've got old Bert to chase up.' She went to close her notebook, realised she'd forgotten to get the boys' details. Pen poised, she asked for their full names and contact phone numbers. Darren Kovacs and Jasper Keenan. *Surely not...please no.*

'Uh, Jasper. You aren't by any chance related to Paul Keenan, are you?' She heard her voice wavering. There was going to be a scene, no doubt.

'Yeah, he's my uncle.'

A wavelet of mild relief washed over Taylor, her heart rate slowed a fraction. Not his father, at least. 'OK,' she drew concentric circles on her jotter. 'Wait here for a moment while I speak to my boss.'

'What's the matter? Is Uncle Paul hurt?' The flirtatiousness was gone. Anxiety dilated the young man's pupils.

Taylor parted her lips, no sound came out.

'Why won't you tell me, for fuck's sake!'

'I think...no...I'll get the Inspector. Please, don't go anywhere.' She offered a wan smile that she was sure told the lads everything she was unable to say with words.

Taylor scurried off, found Batista standing behind a man with a hopeless combover examining Fletcher. The manager, chest rising and falling, lay on a couch, the end of a stethoscope snaked underneath his shirt. Taylor tapped lightly on the door frame. 'Sir?'

Batista spun around. 'Yes?'

'There's someone here I think you're going to want to speak to.'

Three minutes later, Batista, Taylor and the two young men sat on white plastic chairs at a round table on the upper floor of the clubhouse. Other golfers, told to remain on site until addressed by the Inspector, sat in small groups or pairs at tables dotted around the bar and bistro. Floor-to-ceiling windows offered a panoramic view of the first tee and the 18th green, parts of other fairways dotting the landscape. The tropical idyl was garnished by lush green treetops busy with birdlife, glimpses of the deep blue Pacific Ocean and the sky melding into the distant horizon. Kylie Smith had headed outdoors; Taylor could see her directing a trio of golfers towards the clubhouse. The Inspector told Taylor that Smith would remain there until the last of the players had made their way off the course. He also relayed Jack's message about the courageous receptionist, which elicited a nod of appreciation from the DC. Looking back at the trickle of wobbly-legged players taking instructions from Smith, even from a distance of 50 metres Taylor could make out the worried expressions in their eyes.

The way the guests had been herded into this space on the upper floor reminded Taylor of makeshift shelters set up for victims of natural disasters. She had volunteered as a marshal at one such venue three years ago when a cyclone tore through Yorkville and left dozens of families homeless. Hundred-mile-an-hour winds ripped roofs and walls from buildings, flattened vehicles, floods destroyed small businesses, three people drowned.

A burly ruddy-cheeked man stood behind the bar. Sleeves rolled up, in between cleaning glasses he took orders for drinks and snacks. Taylor admired a patina of intricate grey-wash snake tattoos on his muscled forearms, light hairs caught and highlighted by sun streaming through the windows. She had this thing for men's forearms. Turning her attention back to the room, Taylor sensed tension in the air. Conversations were conducted in hushed voices and whispers, the occasional uncomfortable laugh rang out. They all knew something terrible had happened. How would they react when Batista described the incident in all its ghastly detail?

Before that could happen, though, the tragic news had to be broken to the victim's nephew. Batista cleared his throat, leaned in, which encouraged the others to follow suit. 'I'm afraid the news is of the worst kind, Jasper. Your uncle Paul has sadly died out on the course.'

'What?' The blurted response caused heads to turn. 'No way. We're meeting up with him for lunch. It's a mistake!'

Taylor reached across and grabbed Jasper's wrist as he cradled his head in his hands. He began to blubber, tears quickly cascading down his arms and splashing on the tabletop. 'I'm sorry,' she whispered. 'But it's the truth.'

Darren reached an arm across his mate's shoulder, gave it a squeeze. Jasper dropped his hands, his eyes glistened. 'Did he have a heart attack or something? He's got a stressful job. I've been telling him to give up the smokes, but he never listens.'

'No,' said Taylor. 'We've been advised that your uncle Paul was shot at close range. We're very sorry for your loss.'

'Shot? On the golf course? In Yorkville? No way! What...'

'That's why I asked you about the drone, Jasper,' Taylor continued, keeping her voice as low and gentle as possible. 'I know this is going to sound insane, but we believe a gun was mounted on the drone and someone has fired it at your uncle remotely.'

'It *does* sound insane,' said Darren. 'Who'd want to kill him? I'm finding it all hard to believe.'

'I'm afraid it's exactly what happened,' said Batista. 'We've got witnesses. Mr Keenan was playing with a Mr Lachlan Morris and his wife Dervla.' He turned to Jasper. 'Since you had plans to have lunch with your uncle, I'm assuming you also know the Morrises. Correct?'

A slow nod. 'Yeah. I know them. Long-time friends of the family. Well, old man Morris is. His wife is fairly new on the scene.'

'Mr Morris was also shot. However, he miraculously survived the attack. He and Dervla are recovering in Cairns Base Hospital. She's in deep shock.'

'So am I! This is…oh my God…' The blubbering combined with racking breaths continued for a minute before Jasper brought himself under control. 'He's got kids…my little baby cousins…oh, geez. What happens now?'

'What happens, Jasper,' said Batista, 'is Yorkville CIB will move heaven and Earth to find out who's behind this. Do you have any ideas who might have had it in for your uncle Paul?'

A rapid head shake. Taylor poured a glass of water from a jug, passed it across the table. Jasper took it in trembling hands and guzzled it down. He refilled the glass himself and drained half of it before setting it down unsteadily.

'What about you, Darren,' Taylor ventured. 'Do you know Mr Keenan and the others?'

'Of course. I've visited his house with Jasper plenty of times. He and Paul are more like good friends than uncle and nephew. As for his personal life, all I know is he separated from his wife about two years ago.'

'Eighteen months, it was,' corrected Jasper, wiping his nose with a serviette. 'Hey, do you think I could go home? I'm feeling…' He had no time to complete the sentence as he projectile vomited over the table. All conversation ceased as the waiting golfers turned to the source of the sickening sound. Jasper excused himself, said he'd be back in a minute. He marched unsteadily towards a door at the back of the room marked with the universal WC signs, Darren close behind.

'Taylor,' barked the Inspector, standing and grasping at the napkin dispenser. 'Find something to wipe this up, will you.'

'Sir? Are you serious?'

'Never more so. Get onto it!'

Taylor stood, looked about, unsure what to do.

'No need to trouble yourself, ma'am.' It was the beefy barman with the arms. He approached with a bucket full of sudsy water. 'I keep this under the bar for emergencies. I've done this a few times.' He set to cleaning with a flourish of sponge and towel. 'When some of our wilder patrons over-imbibe.' He shared a smile with Taylor; she felt heat rise in her cheeks. He was a handsome specimen, around the right age. Her eyes involuntarily did a wedding ring check. Single. In less than a minute the barman had cleaned up the mess and left the table smelling like a hospital corridor. Hips swivelling, Taylor thought for her benefit, he returned to his station behind the bar.

Batista's bony finger beckoned towards Darren, who was returning with his rubber-limbed, ashen-faced friend. 'Hang fire for a moment, son. I'll arrange for the two of you to be taken home shortly.'

'No need,' said Darren, waving the offer away with a shake of the hand. 'I'll drive Jasper home in his dad's ute. I'd like to be the one to tell his parents about what happened.'

'Nice of you to offer,' said Taylor sympathetically. 'But

I'm not sure that's such a good idea. We can arrange for a social worker to be there. What do you say, Inspector?'

Batista held his bottom lip between his teeth for a moment. 'Yes, I agree.'

'What about Uncle Paul's wife?' said Jasper. 'Who'll tell her? They're separated, but…'

'Don't worry about that,' said Taylor. 'Unless they're divorced, she's still next of kin, so a police officer will inform her.'

As if reading Taylor's mind, Batista pulled out his phone. He called Smith, confirmed the last of the registered golfers had arrived back at the clubhouse, and directed her to track down – he held his hand over the mobile's microphone – 'what's her name and address, Jasper?'

'Sabrina Keenan. 28 Lang Street Yorkville West.' The lad fished a shiny silver Samsung from his pants pocket, finger scrolled for a moment and turned the screen to show his aunt's number.

Batista offered a friendly smile of thanks, relayed the information to Smith, whom he entrusted with the task of informing Sabrina Keenan of her sudden change of status from estranged wife to widow. 'Take Semmens with you. Wilson's got the keys to the Stinger.' The Inspector disconnected the call and tugged sharply on his cuffs. Taylor knew he often did this before making a long-winded lecture. True to form, he stood, cleared his throat and banged a spoon on a beer glass as if he were about to make a speech at a wedding.

'Ladies and gentlemen.' The crowd went silent. 'If I could have your attention please. What I'm about to tell you is distressing. You could not have failed to observe the intense police activity at the club and I'm sorry for keeping you in the dark for so long. However, I'm sure you've joined the dots and realised something very serious has happened. I would implore you to remain calm.' He took a long sip of water before continuing. 'A member of the Yorkville Country Club has tragically been shot and killed on the golf course, another is on life support in hospital.' He paused to let the news sink in. Reactions varied from stunned silence to loud gasps and coughs accompanied by scraping chairs.

'Who was it?' A male voice cried out.

'The name of the deceased victim is Paul Keenan.' More gasps this time. It seemed the name meant something to many people. 'In his company was another gentleman, Lachlan Morris, and his wife Dervla. Mr Morris was also shot several times and, as I said, is in a critical condition. His wife was not shot but she is, understandably, in a state of shock.' Taylor felt the oxygen being sucked out of the room when the Inspector paused again. Those names were even more familiar. 'Fortunately,' Batista continued. 'It seems everyone else who signed the book for today's play is accounted for. Detective Sergeant Jack Lisbon, who was playing one hole behind the victims, described the attack as a cowardly one – a gun mounted on the front of a drone was used to murder Mr Keenan and wound Mr Morris.'

A middle-aged woman stood from her seat. 'I think I saw a drone.'

'I also saw it,' said the man next to her, who chose to remain seated. 'And heard it. We were putting out the third hole when the drone disappeared behind a stand of palms, back in the direction of the second hole.'

More voices chimed in with "so did I" and "me too". Taylor and Batista exchanged a glance of optimism. Civilian witnesses in addition to Jack, Trevarthen and the victims was a positive development. Perhaps one of them had had the foresight to take a video on their phone.

'Excellent,' said Batista with gravitas. 'To those who witnessed something, please come forward and provide your contact details to Detective Constable Taylor after I go. If anyone else has theories as to why Paul Keenan and Lachlan Morris would be targeted in this fashion, we'd like to talk to you. Finally, I would appeal to your collective conscience and ask you to refrain from contacting the press or posting anything about today's incident on social media until after we've released an official statement.'

Batista shook hands with the two young men before Darren guided Jasper Keenan down the stairs. Taylor had seen drunk-and-disorderlies walk with more assuredness than the dead man's nephew.

Chapter Seven

'YOUR DAD DOES A MARVELLOUS JOB. The course is in mint condition, as always.' Inspector Joe Batista smiled grimly. He savoured the cooling breeze on his face as the greenkeeper's daughter steered the golf cart confidently around a bunker filled with blindingly white sand. He wasn't sure whether casual chat was appropriate in the circumstances, but the words spilled out. He was in a weird headspace, he hoped – temporarily. The stupid and pointless argument with his wife was playing on his mind, affecting his thought processes, exactly when he needed to be on the ball. The woman had a way of getting into his brain and taking up residence like a squatter.

Ruby, teeth gritted, didn't seem inclined to respond to Batista's words, so he decided to abandon the conversation. She tugged the steering wheel down to the left, took them along a well-worn track between the elevated putting surface and a reedy pond buzzing with dragonflies, then over a red-arched Japanese-style wooden bridge. Next, a sharp right turn at the tee block of the second hole. The electric motor hummed as Ruby stepped hard on the accelerator to coax the cart up a sharp incline and then onward to the crime scene.

'He's not always appreciated for his efforts, though.' Ruby's long-delayed and unexpected answer to his question made Batista jump in his seat.

'Sorry?'

'Some of the members have been giving him a hard time about the reconstruction work on the back nine. Dust and rocks and shit like that. They reckon it's taking too long, but that's nothing to do with dad. He's doing his best working around all that. I guess it's easier to blame the lowly greenkeeper for any problems.' Ruby Brownstone shook her head.

'I find that hard to believe. The course is one of the best I've ever played on. Reg is a master of his craft. The redevelopment is disruptive, sure, but that's hardly Reg's fault.'

'Damn straight,' she said through narrowed lips before taking a deep breath. 'I hate to speak ill of the recently dead,' she continued. 'But Paul Keenan was the worst of them.'

'What do you mean?' The Inspector's ears pricked up.

'A month ago it was. Mr Keenan was playing in a charity pro-am tournament, had a shocker of a round apparently. Double bogeys galore.' The cart took a sharp dogleg to the right, driver and passenger leaned to the left. 'When he gave a speech at the clubhouse dinner that night he said…'

'He said what, Ruby?'

'Never mind. It's not important.'

Batista studied the girl's face, eyes squinting underneath her sunglasses. She'd realised telling a story about the victim deriding her dad in public could implicate him – or even her. The Inspector wouldn't press her about it. Taylor could question her, give her a gentle prod. Batista had known Reg Brownstone for over a decade. He'd held the position of head greenkeeper – or superintendent as the job was called these days – through a couple of changes of management and board members. Always held in high esteem. The Country Club course was rated by many experts as the best in Far North Queensland. Could Keenan publicly calling Brownstone's abilities into question lead the man to organise a fatal drone shooting? Or could Reg's doting and proud daughter have sought revenge for the public insult? Both scenarios were laughable. At least on the surface.

'But what does any of that matter today, huh?' She pointed at the scene looming up ahead. 'You've got that to deal with.'

The forensics team had arrived. The white van was parked about 20 metres to the left of the centre of the action. DS Lisbon and Constable Trevarthen were speaking eagerly to the chief scientist. All were surrounded by a vast square enclosure of blue-and-white police tape attached to star pickets. Batista recognised the imposing frame of pathologist Margaret Proctor. With assistant Clara Littlejohn capering beside her, both dressed in head-to-toe Tyvek suits and shoe covers, the Inspector was reminded of a mother polar bear with her cub.

The golf cart came to a sudden stop 50 metres from the edge of the closed-off area. DS Lisbon gave an urgent wave, Batista acknowledged his officer with a nod that said *Be with you as soon as I can*. 'I'm gonna drop you off and then head home, if you don't mind.' Ruby sniffed and rubbed the back of her wrist against her nose. 'I'd rather not get too near...that.' She pointed at the spot where Keenan lay under a white sheet.

'Sure,' said Batista. 'You've done plenty to assist the police already. Thanks for rounding up the players earlier. We didn't know what we were dealing with. You were rather brave.'

'No worries.' Her cheeks reddened. 'Glad to help out. It can get pretty boring on reception.'

The Inspector nodded. 'Today's been anything but boring.'

'Damn straight.' She chewed a fingernail absently. 'Horrible.'

Batista took a long, sympathetic look at the young woman. He was unsure of her age, but he guessed late teens to early twenties. She was tanned and slim with sinewy arms, a proficient golfer herself with potential to become a professional in time, or so the word was around the club. Her face now was flushed, but a grim stoicism glowed in her hazel eyes. God knew what was going on in her head. The Inspector wanted one last word before he disembarked from the cart. 'Ruby, another favour if you don't mind.'

'What?'

'I'd like you to speak with one of our detectives. DC Claudia Taylor.'

'What for?' Her tone sharpened. 'I don't know anything about what happened.'

'You seem to have a firm opinion about the victim.'

'Only 'cos he badmouthed my dad.' Quick to get on the defensive, the Inspector noted. A petulant frown dragged her lips down in an arc. 'In public too!'

'Were you there?'

'No. Dad neither. It was an event for the fancy-pantses, not the common people.'

'Then how do you know what was said?'

'Dad's got good friends in the club. Most of the

members love him. One of them let him know what… Keenan…said.'

'Tell me.'

'Can't remember the exact words. No doubt someone filmed it. Look online.'

'Surely you've had a look.' She turned her head away. 'You have, haven't you? Is it on social media somewhere?'

No reply.

'At least tell me who passed the word onto Reg.'

'I'm not a tattle-tale. Ask dad if you need to know. It's up to him, hey?'

'OK. You're not obliged to say anything. But—'

'Look. I wouldn't want to see Keenan dead over an insult, no matter how bad. And neither would dad. What kind of people do you think we are?'

'You totally misunderstand me.' *She understands all right*, thought the Inspector. 'I'm wondering if you might know more than you think you do.'

'What do you mean?' She closed one eye as she grasped the steering wheel tighter. 'Look, I'm too tired to answer all these questions. I wanna go.'

'Do you agree to speak with DC Taylor?'

'Sure. But I want dad or someone else there with me.'

Batista smiled. 'Agreed.'

'I'll ring the station later and give you my address.' Her expression blank, she tipped the Inspector a finger-to-forehead salute, turned the cart around and zoomed away. She had already disappeared from view when Batista realised he'd forgotten to retrieve the soft drinks for his officers, and bring down a clean shirt for Trevarthen from the pro shop.

Chapter Eight

JACK CAUGHT the movement in the corner of his eye. He jerked his head to the right as the Inspector, casual almost to the point of incognito in jeans and a checked collared shirt, reefed up a section of police tape. He bent his long insect-like body under the tape, stood tall and strode purposefully towards the DS, hand extended. Jack took it, admiring the boss's firm grip. Not bad for a desk-bound administrator whose main functions seemed to be attending events and giving speeches. The same greeting was offered and laconically accepted by Trevarthen, shirtless, arms and upper body splattered with blood.

'Sir, glad to see you,' said Jack. 'What an effin' mess, hey? We've got our hands full with this one.'

Batista shook his head. 'Absolutely shocking. I can't believe something like this can happen in broad daylight. What can you tell me about the victims? I've already got some preconceived ideas about these men.'

Jack quickly explained what they'd learned after finding

their IDs and talking to Dervla. 'A love triangle, influential people in the community. Plenty of potential for things to go pear shaped. I've got a feeling we're going to dig up some bad shit during this investigation, sir.'

'We're dealing with a devious killer,' said Trevarthen. 'Jack and I stared at the damned drone hovering above us, like kangaroos in the headlights we were. The victims would've been caught by complete surprise.'

Jack rubbed an itchy patch of skin behind his ear. He looked at his fingertip – a crushed mosquito oozing blood. *Fitting*. 'Aden's right. The technical know-how to implement this assassination would seem to limit the amount of suspects. Unless it was, like, a contract job.'

Batista thrust his hands in his pockets, looked into the sky as if half-expecting the killer craft to return. 'Some of the golfers back there reckon they saw the drone. Did either of you notice anything identifiable?'

'Nope,' said Trevarthen. 'Black struts and rotors and that's about it. Oh, and the black pistol, which we didn't recognise as a weapon at the time.'

'Never mind, Aden,' Batista said in a soothing tone. 'You couldn't have guessed what was about to happen. However,' he tapped the pistol strapped to his hip, 'if it comes back I'm prepared.'

Jack nodded. 'And the last time you shot that was…?'

'Never you mind about that. What do we know from the scene?'

Before Jack could answer, the head pathologist Dr Margaret Proctor was alongside the two men holding up a brass casing. 'Carla and I found eight of these in the vicinity. In addition to the six found by DS Lisbon and Constable Trevarthen, that makes up a full clip for a semi-automatic minus one shot. Two bullets went through the dead man's head; DS Lisbon found those prior to our arrival. Additionally, three bullets are lodged inside Lachlan Morris.'

'Where are the rest?' said Jack. 'Fourteen casings and only five slugs?'

'Clara's retrieved six that dug into the turf around where you found Mr Morris. That leaves three, assuming we found all the casings. The missing bullets could be wedged in trees or lying somewhere else in the grass. I'll have a hunt around with a metal detector, but I'm not going to waste too much time on it. Finding bullets that missed isn't likely to aid the investigation.'

'Quite right,' said Batista with a frown. 'How do you reconstruct the murder in your mind, Margaret?'

'I reckon the situation played out more or less as follows.' She paused for a moment, the three officers craned their heads forward. 'The remotely based pilot has positioned the drone very close to the vic. How they did that, I have no idea. How the killer knew exactly where to find them? Again, I'm clueless. Keenan obviously suspected nothing when he met his doom. I must say, it would have taken extraordinary skill to get off an accurate shot and then readjust the drone's position for a second one.'

'Recoil?' suggested Trevarthen.

'Exactly,' said Proctor. 'To get that second shot into the middle of the head, extraordinary, even considering the rapid fire capability of a semi automatic pistol.'

'OK,' said the Inspector. 'What about Morris then?'

'Let me put forward my thoughts, see if Margaret agrees,' said Jack.

Proctor made a be-my-guest gesture with both hands.

'There's a distance of 15 metres between where Keenan lay dead and Morris copped the three bullets. I'm guessing it was one to the shoulder and another to the upper arm as he's fleeing; those shots spun him around, then, as he falls, he cops one in the guts. As for the sprayed shots, well, even the best prepared killer's going to send a few wide of the mark.'

'Very good, Detective Sergeant,' said Proctor. 'My thoughts exactly. Which leaves the unharmed woman, Dervla Morris.'

'Not a target, obviously,' said Jack. He fished a packet of nicotine gum from a pocket and started chomping to get some saliva working in his dry mouth. He turned to Batista. 'Chief, I can't believe you forgot the drinks in the golf cart.'

'Head's all over the place,' he said with a shrug. 'Sorry.'

'You thirsty, DS Lisbon?' said Proctor. She jerked a thumb towards the forensics van. 'There's a cooler in there with bottles of water.'

'You what? Why dincha bleedin' say? You can see me and Aden are about to perish from heatstroke.'

'Don't be ridiculous.' She called out to Littlejohn to fetch drinks for the police officers. A minute later and Jack was quaffing the welcome cold water, Trevarthen the same. Water drunk and empty bottles removed, Proctor cleared her throat. 'Now, as for the ammunition used, I'd venture to guess the casings are from Luger 9 mm shells. No clue what the weapon was. Could have been a Glock, Smith and Wesson M&P maybe.'

'Hang on, sunshine,' said Jack. 'Where did all this specialist ballistics knowledge come from?' In Jack's four years as a detective in Yorkville's CIB he'd never seen spent shells at a crime scene with his own eyes until today. Most murders he and the team had solved — with a couple of cold cases still unsolved — had been committed with knives, ropes, bare hands, even nylon stockings and a gym weight.

This was only his second death-by-shooting case. To Jack's knowledge, the Queensland Police Service only employed half a dozen dedicated forensics ballistics experts, and Dr Proctor definitely wasn't one of them.

'You'd be surprised what fields of science I'm interested in, DS Lisbon,' she said, straightening her shoulders. 'I like to keep abreast of all areas of forensics.'

Jack whistled under his breath, then said, 'We're lucky to have someone as dedicated as you on our team, Margaret.'

'Not really. I'd expect my counterparts across the Queensland Police Service to take a similar broad interest in ballistics as well as pathology.'

'Or you could have done what I sometimes do,' interrupted Trevarthen. 'Taken a photo and Google searched the image.'

'Margaret, you didn't did you?' said Jack, one eyebrow raised in semi-mocking fashion.

'Not a chance,' she protested, shaking her head. 'I'd never resort to such cheap tricks. It's also common knowledge that the 9x19 parabellum is about the most popular handgun cartridge around, so odds are that's what we have here. Nailing down the weapon used to fire them is going to be difficult, though, if not impossible.' She turned to Trevarthen. 'Could you please place that shell on the fold-out table with the others?'

'Sure.' Trevarthen complied with the request, exchanged a word with Littlejohn, who was busy cataloguing the evidence, and returned to the confab.

'We'll send them off to the Ballistics Unit in any case,' said Batista, watching the sun ascend higher into the sky as afternoon superseded morning. We'll be waiting at least a month for a report, dammit. Now, Margaret, the victim... can we?'

Proctor led the officers to the spot where Paul Keenan lay. She knelt on the turf and pealed back the white sheet. She pointed at the two entry points in the middle of his forehead, 3 cm apart. 'The bullets ripped through his brain, killing him instantly, and exited out the rear, making a right mess of the back of his skull. Want to see?'

Batista held his hand up. 'No thanks. Perhaps back at the mortuary.'

'I'm good.' Trevarthen screwed up his face.

'And I thought DC Taylor was the most squeamish amongst us,' said Jack with a slight tut-tut.

'Aden's quite right to decline,' said Proctor. 'I don't want this crime scene tainted by anyone's vomit.'

'You're kidding, aren't you? He's spent the better part of the morning trying to stop a man bleeding to death. Look at the state of him? Covered in blood like Jack the bleedin' Ripper after a night out on the town.'

'Free flowing blood is one thing,' said Proctor, covering the dead man's face again. She stood, brushed grass from her knees. 'Bone slivers and gooey brain tissue, quite another. It's time to bundle the chap up and take him back to the lab. It's getting hotter by the hour, there'll be flies about soon, not a great place for a corpse to be festering. Clara and I will keep searching for another sixty minutes or so, but I reckon we've got all we could possibly use from a scene like this.'

'How far away was the drone when the shots were fired, d'ya reckon?' said Jack.

'Ah ha. Now that *will* be a question for the Ballistics Unit. I'd say, at a guess, point blank range, not more than two metres away and probably no closer than one. But I could be wrong. There's a myriad of mathematical calculations to be done, angles to be worked out. The experts may want to take a trip out here and take some of their own measurements.'

Batista scratched his head. 'Oh boy. I'd better give them a call and see if they can get their specialists up from Brisbane. I'm not going to be making any new friends today.'

Jack sensed where the Inspector was going with this. 'You're gonna shut the course down until further notice, ain't you?'

A deep sigh. 'Yes.' He turned back to Proctor, who appeared impatient, her foot tapping almost imperceptibly. 'Margaret.'

'What now? Like I said before, we need to get the victim transported ASAP. I'll need ten minutes to prep him as best I can in terms of patching up the back of his noggin. The meat wagon should be here shortly.'

'Yes, sorry. One more thing before I let you go. What about the second victim? He received a number of bullet wounds, too.'

'Ah, good point. Clara's taken plenty of photographs and collected blood samples from where the second victim lay on the grass. Not that we'll learn the slightest thing from that, we need evidence left by perpetrators, but here there's none! It's like...a drive-by shooting with no one driving the car.'

'Perfect summation, Margaret.' Jack nodded in appreciation.

'However, the formalities of evidence gathering need to be observed. Ask the surgeons at the hospital to make sure they retain any bullets retrieved from the man. Any word on his condition, by the way?'

Jack checked his mobile phone. 'I've asked for updates. Lemme see. Nope. Nothing since the last one twenty minutes ago that said he was in a critical condition, but they were expecting him to survive after a blood transfusion.' He pocketed his phone. 'Alright, Aden. Looks like you and me can finally go and get cleaned up.' He inclined his head in the direction of the tee block. The meat wagon was trundling along the fairway to pick up its cargo.

Chapter Nine

CONSTABLES KYLIE SMITH and Noah Semmens sat quietly in the Ford Territory, the only sound inside the vehicle their shallow breathing, the soft crackle of the radio and Smith's fingernails rapping on the dashboard. Outside, the tops of palm trees standing like sentries up and down the deserted street swayed silently in a light breeze. The officers exchanged a momentary look of apprehension. Smith hadn't been the messenger of death in a murder case before, although Semmens had. Once. And it was at least five years ago.

'I guess we'd better get this over with,' Smith said, unbuckling her seatbelt. She checked her cumbersome body kit, stepped out into a sunny cul-de-sac, the warm air like an encouraging embrace. She clunked the door shut and looked up. The bright sky and softly chattering birdlife created a stark contrast with the grim news, about to be home delivered like a pizza nobody had ordered. Well-manicured kikuyu lawns – the same grass that carpeted the fairways at the Country Club – stretched around the curve of the street, each front yard landscaped with neat tropical gardens. Smith glanced over her left shoulder, admired the view of rolling gentle hills to the west. This was one of Yorkville's nicer neighbourhoods.

Semmens marched in lockstep beside Smith towards the front gate. 'You wanna speak first?'

'No thanks.' Her tone was decisive. 'You're the one with the most experience in these matters.'

'C'mon, Kyles. You were the one who broke the news to that poor Aboriginal mum on the mission, remember? You got this.'

'Yes, well…That case just about saw me quit the force.' She blinked hard, pictures of the anguished mother creeping into her memory. Grief on a level she'd never imagined possible.

'You managed, though, didn't you? Did a great job, in fact. Wilson told me you took control of that one, left him standing there like the ugly stepsister.'

'Geez, Noah! Why did you have to bring this up?' The woman's three children had perished in a horrific car crash late last year. The stolen utility the teens were joyriding in ploughed head-on into a gum tree and burst into flames. Only dental records could identify the victims. A week before Christmas.

'Because you've got more guts than you give yourself credit for.'

'No way. This is premeditated murder, not a freak accident. Totally different scenario, brother.'

'Bullshit. If anything, this is easier. She was estranged from Keenan and…'

'That doesn't mean she hated him. Lots of separated couples have amicable relationships, friendships even. She could be devastated after we tell her.' Smith was searching in the bottom of the suitcase for excuses now. 'Besides, you could do the gentlemanly thing and–'

'Stop right there.' Semmens held up both hands and shook his head vigorously. He appeared to be suppressing the urge to laugh. 'You're always banging on about equality, Kyles. Step up to the plate and practice what you preach. Or are you only interested in equality when it suits you?'

He had an excellent point, one that was hard to argue against and even harder to admit. She *did* harp on about equal rights, the wage gap, all kinds of "social justice" issues. When she got on a roll with her rants in the lunchroom, her colleagues scattered. 'Right,' she said through tightly drawn lips. 'I'll do it then.' She chided herself for the petulance, but, on reflection, this *would* be easier than telling a mother her kids had died. Far easier.

They followed a slate tile pathway through lush rainforest ferns and bright tangerine and violet bird-of-paradise flowers, reached the sprawling wrap-around front porch. The panelled white double doors stood well over two metres high. Smith removed her hat, tucked it under her wing, smoothed down her close-cropped dirty-blonde hair. Semmens followed suit. The pair looked like Jehovah's witnesses in rented police costumes out looking for converts. She reached for the brass knocker in the shape of a snarling lion, pulled back the ring gripped between the beast's teeth. She was about to pound it against the metal plate, when the door opened with a sharp tug. It was then Smith glanced up and saw the security camera. 'Yes?' said a wide-eyed woman impatiently. She held the door so that only her head was poking through the gap, like she had something incriminating behind her she didn't want the cops to see.

Smith opened her mouth to speak, but Semmens beat

her to the punch. He spat out the words. 'Are you Sabrina Keenan?'

He couldn't suppress the urge to take charge, Smith thought. And after everything he said about Smith stepping up. Typical.

'Yes, that's my name,' the tousle-haired woman replied in a clipped tone. Her eyebrows dived into a steep V as her shaky right hand flounced a generous crop of curly brunette locks that looked damp, perhaps from a recent shower. 'What do you want?'

'We have some serious news. May we come in?'

'Is it about my kids? Are the girls all right?'

'Why wouldn't they be?' said Smith. 'Aren't they here with you?'

'They're supposed to be at my mum's for the weekend while I have…um…a break.'

'We have no news about your children,' said Semmens. 'This is another matter altogether.'

Mrs Keenan showed no inclination to grant the officers access to the house. If anything, she closed the door even closer against her body, leaving only enough room for her head to poke through. She blinked large, dilated eyes hard a couple of times, the muscles in the rest of her face seemed to be moving in all directions. Smith read the signs – cocaine. She checked her watch. 13:30. A bit early in the day to be snorting lines.

'What then?' Mrs Keenan spat, like a challenge. Her pupils were so dilated there was only the thinnest circle of green iris showing.

'It's…ah…' stammered Smith. 'It's…ah…'

'For fuck's sake, can you stop jabbering?' Mrs Keenan's head dropped a couple of inches, her unseen feet were slipping behind the door. She gripped the doorframe harder to prevent herself falling further.

'Look.' Semmens fumbled his hat in his hands. 'It'd be best for all concerned if we came in.'

'No! I've got a...guest...inside and he...I mean they... won't be too happy about the cops rocking up. On a Saturday afternoon without prior warning, if you please. Fucken embarrassing!' She boldly stepped out onto the porch and Smith caught her breath at the sight of the almost naked woman. Semmens reflexively looked at his shoes. 'Now, what's the bloody problem?' Mrs Keenan placed her hands on her bony hips, tilting one of those hips up and to the side like a poorly executed Beyonce dance move.

Smith wrinkled her nose as she was hit with the blended scent of stale booze and cigarettes. But the visuals had the greatest impact. The scanty apparel clinging to Sabrina Keenan's body had less material than a handkerchief. The ensemble comprised a tiny black G-string and a flimsy pink bra. And a lick of coral pink lipstick to match the bra. Smith's eyes were drawn to the woman's belly button, which sported a glinting multi-faceted piercing, possibly a diamond. Mrs Keenan's facial and bodily contortions continued as she waited for an explanation.

'Can't we go inside? And perhaps you'd like to put on a dressing gown or something.' Semmens raised his eyes a fraction, then abandoned meekness and locked eyes with the occupier of 28 Lang Street. Or he would have done, had hers not darted all over the place like a monkey jumping from branch to branch.

'No. I don't want you in my house, OK? Start talking or the pair of you can piss off and leave me alone.'

'Your husband's dead,' said Smith. *Enough mucking around with this obnoxious woman.* 'He passed away this morning on the golf course. Now, can we come in?'

Chapter Ten

SABRINA KEENAN POURED a shot of pink gin from a two-thirds empty bottle, loudly clanked her tumbler down hard on the marble-topped breakfast bar. Smith juddered in her seat, Semmens winced. 'Tell me again, so I can raise my glass and toast his untimely demise.'

'I think you've grasped perfectly well the meaning of what you've been told.' Smith couldn't decide to be angry with the woman or feel sorry for her. She chose neutrality. 'I gotta say, though, I didn't anticipate your joyous reaction to the news.' Smith held her hands in her lap as she gazed at the woman. At least she'd had the decency to put on a satin dressing gown after finally allowing the officers into her domain. The spacious lounge room they traversed to reach the kitchen was clean in a clinical sense, but messy as a teenager's bedroom with clothes, blankets, pillows and magazines strewn over the floor. Leather furniture spoke of expensive taste and the television that clung to the wall was of a size more suited to a sports pub. Relics of Mr Keenan's presence, perhaps. A framed picture on the wall contained a photograph of the Keenans' wedding. Or rather, a ragged partial photograph – the print had been torn in half, no groom and only the beaming bride on display. At least five kilograms heavier than she was now.

'How'd you expect me to react, huh? Did you think I'd break down and cry? The arsehole dumped me, a 46-year-old female past her use-by date, for a younger and prettier model. A bloody Irish banshee! We've been married for twelve years and produced two beautiful children, but what does that matter to him? Bugger all! I say, good riddance to bad rubbish, don't you agree?' She tilted her head back and tossed the contents of her crystal tumbler down her throat.

'Who's the man upstairs?' said Semmens, not desiring to enter into the debate about Paul Keenan's moral qualities or comment on the callousness of the woman's words. The officers had heard a short muffled conversation coming from a room on the top floor while they waited for Mrs Keenan to cover up. The male's voice was a deep baritone that echoed down the stairway. 'Is he someone who didn't like your husband?'

Smith cast a sideways glance at Semmens. It was a little early to be questioning the woman about possible motives. Then again, as DS Lisbon says, strike while the iron's hot.

Mrs Keenan rocked on her stool and cackled like a hen laying a larger-than-usual egg. 'You wanna know who he is?' She didn't wait for a reply. 'He's my toy boy, that's who. A frickin' gigolo I pay for afternoon sex while the kids are at grandma's! If Paul can have a 25-year-old girlfriend, I can indulge my whims, too. Chip, he calls himself. Which I find hilarious, since it's a kind of a golf shot, right?' She poured another nip, spilling some of the gin down the side of her glass, and more as she took a sip. The officers observed her antics with eyes agog. 'And Paul being a mad golfer! Poetic justice, I say. As far as I'm concerned, Paul can go fuck himself...ha ha ha!' Her body leaned forward, she instinctively made a pillow out of her forearms and rested the side of her head against one of them.

Smith bent down to check on the woman's welfare. Was she unconscious? Her words hadn't been slurred, and she didn't appear to be intoxicated despite the boozy breath. Smith had no doubt Mrs Keenan would test positive for cocaine; perhaps they'd have a quick search before they left if she didn't wake up. No time to ponder that thought any longer, though. No sooner had Smith's hand touched Mrs Keenan's shoulder than the woman sat up with a jerk, like she was waking from a bad dream. 'What's going on? You're wearing uniforms. Hey, you're the police! Why the hell are you in my house?'

'Mrs Keenan, it's all right,' said Smith in a soothing tone. 'We came to tell you your husband died, don't you remember?'

'What? Paul's dead? Nooooo!!!!' The transformation in her demeanour made Smith take a step back. Her partner shook his head slowly.

'Yes, he's dead,' said Semmens testily, shifting his weight from one foot to the other. Smith noticed him sneakily press a button to activate his body camera. She thought this a good idea and did the same. This bizarre situation could spin in any direction. 'We've told you already. Why are you playing these games? My gut tells me you've got something to hide.'

'Noah!' said Smith, wrapping her arm around Mrs Keenan's trembling shoulder. 'Let's give her a moment.' She locked eyes with the woman. 'Would you like us to take you to a doctor?'

'No, no.' Translucent eyelids fluttered. 'I just need to...

oh, Paul!' Her body heaved as tears cascaded down her cheeks. She dashed them away with the back of her veiny hand, new tears appeared to replace them. Her slender body rocked back and forth, sharp breaths racked her puny chest. The coral-pink lips silently formed her husband's name, over and over, for about a minute. Finally, her breathing normalised. Her gaze switched rapidly from Semmens to Smith as if pleading for understanding.

'I've had about enough of this bullshit,' Semmens whispered to Smith. 'She's playing us for fools.' He placed his hat back on his head, addressed Mrs Keenan. 'Would you be so kind as to put some clothes on and accompany us to the mortuary.'

'Sorry?' confusion knitted her brows. 'What for?'

'You are technically still the next of kin. Therefore it's appropriate you come with us and officially identify the body.'

Smith shook her head. There was no need for this. Having distraught relatives identify bodies was the stuff of TV cop shows, not reality. 'There's no need to traumatize Mrs Keenan further, Noah. Geez. Dervla Morris has already…'

Smith ducked her head as the crystal liquor glass missed her right ear by millimetres and smashed into hundreds of pieces against a wall of green subway tiles.

'Do NOT mention that Irish slut's name in my house! Do you hear me?' The woman roared, jabbing an index finger at Semmens. She was up on her feet, lithe as a jaguar, top lip curled up in front of her top teeth. 'Unless you want to arrest me for something, get the hell out of my house!'

'Not a problem,' said Semmens. 'Our detectives will be along later to try and get some sense out of you.'

'You all right down there, sweetheart?' called out the

alpha sex worker from upstairs. The word "sweetheart" was an incongruous term of affection in the booming deep voice.

Sabrina Keenan tilted her head back, put her hand to her mouth. 'They're just leaving!' She glared at Semmens, gave him a dismissive flick of the wrist. 'As for identifying my husband, that bitch can do it.'

Semmens wasn't beyond doing his own finger pointing. 'You've raised massive suspicions with your behaviour, which I'll pass on to the CIB. And perhaps a search warrant to scour this place for narcotics. It's clear to me you're off your face.'

'Wrong officer.' She stood, wiggled her backside, took off her bra and circled it around her head like a lasso. 'I'm off my tits!'

'Fine.' Smith pursed her lips, any desire she had to ensure the woman's welfare had gone. 'I've had enough of this charade. C'mon, Noah. Let's leave the lady in peace to enjoy the rest of her afternoon with her rented lover boy.'

About to get in the police vehicle, movement at an upper floor window caught her eye. A tall and well-muscled man with shiny olive skin, wearing only fluorescent green-and-red candy-striped boxer shorts, was staring intently at the officers. Realising her body camera was still running, she turned front on – hopefully the device was good enough to pick up his image from this distance, about 60 metres. Perhaps sensing her intent, he quickly closed the curtain.

FIVE MINUTES later the two officers had driven a couple of kays through sparse traffic. They'd offered up scenarios explaining Sabrina Keenan's behaviour: the drugs were affecting her; the shock of the news was affecting her; she was acting and nothing was affecting her. Smith pulled up at a set of lights three blocks from Yorkville Police Station, humming along to an infectious new Adele song on FM radio. Semmens scrolled through his iPhone, checking sports betting odds for the upcoming rounds of rugby league and soccer matches. He stopped scrolling and looked up. 'Hey, Kyles.'

'What? Found a game to throw your money away on?'

'No. It's Sabrina Keenan.'

'Christ,' she huffed, stepping on the accelerator as the lights turned green. 'I'm trying not to think about her. Wait till the detectives get a load of the footage from our BWCs. DS Lisbon's gonna have fun questioning that one. I still can't believe the way she—'

'Kyles.'

'Yes?'

'Shut up for a sec, will you! Didn't you notice something odd about the whole situation back there?'

'Yeah, are you kidding me? There was plenty odd.'

Semmens gave a shallow laugh. 'That's true. But I just realised something weird. We never actually got around to telling her how he died, and she never asked.'

'Holy shit, Noah. She didn't either!'

Chapter Eleven

THE HOSPITAL RECEPTION area hummed with activity. Automatic doors opened and closed constantly, like lungs breathing in and out. Doctors in white coats; nurses in blue scrubs with clipboards rushing here and there; mothers cuddling crying children too young to explain what was hurting; patients in pyjamas pushing mobile drips, out to the courtyard where they could assuage their insidious nicotine habits. Not as busy as it would get later tonight after the pubs closed, when drunks with broken limbs and busted noses, beaten wives and spaced-out junkies started flooding the emergency department. Nevertheless, the DS observed, trade was quite brisk for a Saturday afternoon.

Jack's phone buzzed in his pants pocket. A text message from Smith. He read it silently, nudged Taylor's shoulder with his shoulder, held the phone out so she could read it.

'Hmmm. I can't wait to see the BWC footage of that encounter.'

'Me either. Sabrina Keenan sounds like a wild one.' He grinned. 'I might let you handle her yourself.'

'Not a chance. I want you for backup. Psychotic women aren't exactly my forte.'

'You sayin' they're mine?'

'Oh, I don't know. What about that crazy woman you were dating, the Amazon, what's her name again?'

'Marietta.'

'That's right. Didn't she cause a scene in a restaurant when you said she was…?'

'Yes.' Jack decided one-word answers would be sufficient for any conversation about six-foot-one gym freak Marietta Szabo.

'Meaning,' she tapped his thigh. 'You've got experience with unorthodox females.'

'Right…' He rubbed his chin. He very much enjoyed her tapping his leg and in other circumstances he would… he truly had no idea what he would do…but it was time to change the subject. 'Get anything useful up at the clubhouse while me and Aden were elbows deep in blood at the crime scene?'

Taylor consulted a Spirax notepad. 'Nothing to crack the case open, I'm afraid. Let's see. Paul Keenan's nephew, Jasper, was there getting ready to play a round of eighteen holes with his mate, Darren Kovacs. The Keenans are a golf-mad clan, apparently. Anyway, the kid was so distraught at the news that he spewed his guts up all over the table. Sadly, he had no idea who might have it in for his uncle. He did identify a man called Hubert Johnson – he was with the party that was playing behind you and Aden. They left the car park in a hurry, the only ones to,' she made air quotes, '*escape the scene*. He and the other people in his group could be worth questioning, considering how eager they were to get away.'

'Nah. Probably just shit scared after they heard the shots and then I yelled at them.'

'But...'

'Yes, I know. Never rule anything out, especially early. I'll send Wilson over to have a chat with the bloke. Ruby can provide the names of the other golfers who were registered to play with this Johnson fella. Anything else?'

Taylor shook her head. 'A handful of witnesses who saw the drone. But their descriptions of it are vague, even contradictory. No one at the club took a video of the damn thing.'

'Don't worry. I could draw you a pretty accurate picture of it. Me and Aden got a proper close-up view. Man, we had no idea what was coming next.' He puffed out his cheeks. 'I might've tried to bring it down with a golf club or something.'

'How could you have known?' She turned sideways onto him in her plastic chair, gave him the "it's not your fault" look of empathy.

'The gun mounted on it, for starters. Looking back, it was as obvious as dogs' nuts.' He put his hands to the sides of his head, slowly pulled them back, rested them in his lap. 'Tell you what, though.'

'What?'

'This is gonna be the toughest murder case we've ever seen in Yorkville.'

'Didn't you say that about the last case? And the one before that?'

He grinned. 'Yeah. I did 'n all.'

Jack and Taylor stood as the head surgeon of Yorkville General Hospital, Dr. Pedro Pereira, approached with a no-nonsense gait. He had a look of earnestness about him that Jack didn't like.

The DS extended a right hand. 'Can we speak to him yet?'

Pereira ran a hand through his collar-length straight black hair. 'If you mean Lachlan Morris, then I'm afraid I'll have to say no.'

Jack's heart sank. 'Is he conscious at least?'

'Yes. Although he could be sleeping right now. You must understand, he's suffered three serious gunshot wounds.'

'You don't have to explain that to me,' Jack fought to control his tone. 'I was there, pal. I saw the damage that was done.'

The doctor looked at his watch. 'He had three bullets removed from his body and underwent a blood transfusion. Standard recovery period after that is 24 to 48 hours.'

Jack closed his eyes and rubbed his forehead. 'Are you effin' serious?'

'Very. The man needs rest, officer. You must realise…'

'Yes,' said Taylor. 'We're fully aware he needs rest. And he'll get plenty of it. But we'd like to talk to him while the incident is fresh in his mind. We're conducting a murder investigation that's offering up little in the way of clues.' She paused for a moment. 'And, attempted murder in the case of poor Mr Morris.'

'Exactly,' said Jack. 'Every moment lost decreases the chances of us catching the perpetrator.'

The doc folded his arms across his chest. 'The welfare of my patients comes first.'

'Listen.' Jack switched his tone to amicable. 'Judging by your name, we've got a shared heritage, you and me.'

'Sorry?'

'I happen to know Pereira is one of the most common Portuguese surnames there is. Common as Jones. My name, Lisbon, is the anglicized version of Lisboa, the capital of…'

'I'm fully aware of that piece of trivia. I came to Australia from Brazil, as it happens. What's that got to do with anything?'

'Well, since we're compadres, I thought…'

The doctor burst out laughing, asked a question in Portuguese Jack didn't understand, then made a gesture with open palms that said "come on, mate, I'm waiting." When Jack could only glare daggers, Pereira continued: 'I think the word you had in mind was compatriots not compadres, which isn't accurate in any case. And since you couldn't respond to words a person with even a smattering of Portuguese would know, I'm inclined to think you're… well…' He coughed into his fist. 'Manners prevent me from going any further.' Jack could imagine steam coming out of his own ears as the medico humiliated him. Pereira adjusted his black-rimmed glasses and said: 'I suggest you give us a call tomorrow to find out whether Mr Morris is in a fit state to answer questions.'

'What about Dervla Morris?' snapped Jack. 'She's here. I wanna talk to her.'

'She's in even less of a state to speak with you than her husband is. We've had a psychiatrist administer some pretty strong drugs and she's, how do you say, out of it.' The doctor offered a wan smile. 'So, you'll have to return tomorrow, provided the treating doctors give the all clear. Anyway, I have an urgent appointment to attend to. Good day.'

Back in the Kia Stinger and heading to the mortuary, where Proctor had prepared Keenan for a second viewing prior to autopsy, Jack confided to Taylor: 'Never in my whole life have I wanted to punch a doctor in the face. Until today.' He riffled around in the glovebox, tossing items onto the floor until he found the stress reliever – the treasured nicotine gum. He buckled up and turned to Taylor, who had insisted on driving while Jack worked off his stinking temper. 'Know what?'

'What?'

'Dervla Morris mentioned a voice coming out of the drone. Like a ghost, she said.'

'Any idea what she meant?'

'Nope. But we're going to talk to her tomorrow, and her old hubby, I don't care what Pereira says. I might dress up as an orderly like in one of those thriller movies.'

Taylor side-eyed him. 'Don't be ridiculous.'

'I'll get an effin' court order if I have to.'

'No you won't. It's the weekend.'

'Dammit.' Jack thumped his palms on the dashboard. The vibrations made his mobile slide off and land squarely and painfully in his crotch. 'Drive on, Claudia. And stop smiling!'

Chapter Twelve

THE BULL PEN WAS FULL, with all uniforms on stand-by to handle the expected Saturday night shenanigans. The Yorkville Scorpions basketball team was hosting the Sydney Kings tonight, so the constables were pumped, prepared for a little spice should the fans get rowdy. But that was a couple of hours away; right now they had a murder and attempted murder investigation to get on with. Inspector Batista called for quiet by tapping a ruler on a glass of water. Taylor smiled broadly, whispered to Jack: 'He pulled the same stunt at the Country Club. Like he's about to propose a toast to the bride.'

'From what Noah Semmens told me in the staffroom a minute ago, the bride...or should I say widow...would be joining in such a toast with gusto.'

'OK, everyone,' said Batista in a loud commanding voice. Amid murmured conversations, the repeated glass-tapping wasn't achieving the desired effect. 'Sorry to take up everyone's Saturday afternoon – and thanks to those officers who stepped up on their day off – but I want to get everything we know on the table without delay. I'd like to ask you all to make yourselves available tomorrow to help question witnesses and suspects. Any objections?'

Muttered assent among the team got the nod of approval from Jack. This was a far cry from his days in the London Met, where such a request – at least in his section – would have been met with groans of disappointment. He glanced around; all the uniforms were primed and eager to get into this case. It also helped that overtime rates were a healthy addition to a lowly copper's bank balance.

The chief spoke for five minutes, barely pausing for breath, outlining the basic facts and bullet-pointing them on a large rotating white board as he went. The victims, the method used, the time line, the amount and types of evidence recovered. He expanded: 'Now, unfortunately, there is zero DNA, fingerprint or any other type of physical evidence that could point to a perpetrator. The MO here is utterly ingenious. On a larger scale, you'd be thinking of terrorism.'

'Can we rule that out, sir, even on this scale?' said Constable Wilson. And a fair question, too, thought Jack.

'You're right, Ben,' said the DS. 'We can't exclude the possibility. Although usually a terrorist attack would be followed by some kooky outfit claiming responsibility. Which hasn't happened here.'

'The victim's got an Irish name, the girlfriend's Irish,' said Trevarthen. 'Maybe it's worth looking deeper into possible connections with the IRA, Sinn Fein, Loyalists, that kind of thing.'

Batista wrote on the whiteboard and underscored *Terrorism link?* He tapped on what he'd written with his marker pen. 'My instinct tells me this is a long shot, but let's chase it up anyway. Wilson, you've got an interest in international affairs. Get onto it.'

'Sir!' The station geek's eyes lit up. Wilson only had a minor role in the town's last big murder case, and he was clearly itching to play a bigger part in this one. Jack didn't have a lot of faith in the constable's street smarts, but this desk role suited him to the ground.

Jack hopped off the table, joined the Inspector in front of the whiteboard. 'If there's a link to terrorism, I'm sure young Ben will find it.' He nodded at Wilson, who responded with a prim smile. 'However, I think we're looking at a more mundane motive. One of the classics.' He counted off on his fingers. 'One: anger. Keenan's a banker and Morris had been accused of financial impropriety. They've put some noses out of joint and one's paid the ultimate price. Two: greed. Sabrina Keenan – or someone else – stands to gain by inheriting his estate. Three: jealousy. We're already looking at a bizarre love triangle, so I wouldn't be surprised if young Dervla was cheating on both of these blokes. She's got something mystical and alluring about her, possibly broke someone's heart and they never got over it.'

'What about revenge?' said Kylie Smith. 'Sabrina acted weird enough to...'

'Let me interrupt for a moment,' said the Inspector. 'Constable Wilson, could you play the body cam videos please?'

The footage from both Semmens's and Smith's BWCs left mouths agape. 'Blimey,' said Jack. 'Noah hinted she'd cracked up, but man, this is something else. The way she silently repeated the man's name, then the sheer hate. Towards him *and* Dervla. I gotta say, she's looming as the favourite based on that alone.'

Strips of neon lights in the ceiling flickered brighter in the station as fading day outside turned to dusk and then to night. The faint sound of a phone call being answered slipped through the glass of the operations room, rookie Constable Damien Wells's affable greeting. He'd wanted to be part of the discussion, but someone had to man the comms.

'Indeed,' said Batista. 'I'd like to get a behavioural psychologist to view this footage, see what they think. Is Sabrina Keenan piling on bullshit or are these extreme outbursts genuine? Smith and Semmens, you were there, what do you think?'

Smith cleared her throat. 'Even if you swallow that performance or you think she's legit, there's something else to consider. Noah made a great observation after we left her house. We didn't get a chance to explain the circumstances around her husband's death, and she didn't ask. Odd, huh?'

'Not if she knew the details beforehand,' ventured Semmens.

A silence fell over the group as the plausibility of Semmens's words struck home. The Inspector continued. 'I want everything dug up on this woman we can possibly find. DS Lisbon and DC Taylor.' He wrote SABRINA KEENAN on the whiteboard, two underlines. 'Make this your first priority.'

'Not tonight, surely?' said Jack. 'I'd love to get stuck into this one as much as anyone else, but it's what, nearly 7:00pm, sir. We're all exhausted.'

Batista took a deep breath. 'Yes. We've been through the ringer today. Especially you and Aden. I want to thrash out a couple more scenarios, then we can go home and regroup in the morning.'

'Thanks, sir. Much appreciated.' He resumed his seat on the table beside his partner.

'The press, sir,' said Taylor before Batista could proceed. 'You'll want to get our official statement out soon, won't you?'

The Inspector rubbed his equine chin, looked at Taylor. 'Can I call upon you to do that as soon as we're done here?'

She nodded slowly. 'Of course. Should I keep it vague, or give it to them with…ahem…both barrels?'

'Keep it to three paragraphs. The what, the who and the where. No hyperbole, play it straight and boring. Oh, and one more thing, the usual call for people to come forward if they have information, blah, blah, blah. Conclude with a press conference call for 10:00am tomorrow. Jack and I to front the vultures.'

'Got it.'

'Back to Sabrina Keenan. On Monday I'll ask the magistrate to authorise a production notice for Mrs Keenan's financials, phone calls, emails, the lot. And a warrant to search her house. Detectives Lisbon and Taylor to hold fire with Sabrina until we get that warrant. Then… POW! Old man Morris is going to be tougher, we can't go trawling his private information to find suspects. Once he's compos mentis again, we'll ask him to volunteer his personal data.' Batista glanced out the window as a semi-trailer sped past the station at least 10 clicks over the inner city limit and he didn't bat an eyelid. There were speed cameras at the end of the street; if the driver didn't slow down the robots would nail him. 'Now, speaking of revenge, let me tell you about the greenkeeper's daughter…'

Jack nudged Taylor and whispered, '*Sounds like the start of a bawdy joke*'. She kept looking at the chief as the aside fell flat.

'Did you want to say something, DS Lisbon?'

'No, sir.'

'Fine. As I was saying, Ruby Brownstone alluded to the fact the deceased victim had badmouthed her father at a public dinner. Keenan said the golf course was a disgrace and basically laid the blame at the feet of Mr Brownstone.' He paused for effect. Wrote the name REG BROWNSTONE on the board and an asterisk beside it.

'Why the asterisk?' asked Jack.

'Because.' Batista dragged out the word. 'I know for a fact they use drones to survey and photograph the golf course. Maybe Reg flies them? So we've got possible motive for Brownstone; he knows the course layout better than anyone. Ruby said he was at home, but we need to double check that. Proctor and Littlejohn had a poke around Brownstone's shed at the Country Club, found nothing incriminating.'

'Does he know anything about guns?'

'Good point. Let's look into the gun ownership registers. Although, as we know, guns used to commit crime are often off the radar.' Batista stepped in front of the whiteboard, hands on hips. 'That's a wrap for tonight. I'd like to see everyone on deck first thing in the morning.'

Semmens raised a hand. 'Kylie and I are on duty until midnight tonight, sir.'

Batista let out a puff of air. 'Then come in once you've had enough sleep. You two can help Wilson research potential suspects and the gun ownership database, see if you can find any clues there. The rest will be out in the field, banging on doors and asking questions.'

Jack wanted to get one more thing aired before they went their separate ways.

'The drone must have had a speaker attached. It could

have been that circular thing on the top of it. What do you reckon, Aden?'

'Could have been, sure.'

'Anyway,' Jack continued. 'Mrs Morris said the drone spoke to them "like a ghost". I'm not sure what that means, but I'm guessing the killer was either known to the victims and they suspected nothing, or they were lulled into a false sense of security in some other way. I'm itching to speak with her but we've got a bit of a roadblock in the form of Dr Pablo Pereira.'

'Perhaps he's got a point?' ventured Batista. 'We're talking about major physical and mental trauma. I wouldn't be surprised if neither of them are fit for questioning for some time yet.'

'I have to agree with the Inspector,' said Taylor, drawing a slight head shake from Jack.

'Whatever,' said Jack. 'But the Irish woman's the key to all of this, I can feel it.'

Five minutes later the officers were saying their goodnights and see-you-tomorrows in the car park, while DC Taylor sat alone in the open plan office, pecking out a press statement the likes of which she'd never written before.

Chapter Thirteen

AS SHE LAY IN BED, mesmerised by the lovelorn protagonist in Liane Moriarty's latest bestseller novel, her mobile chirped twice. Right when she was getting to the good bit. Thinking it must be Jack, the only person she knew rude enough to text her at 10:12pm, she ignored it. She fluffed her pillow, bashed it a few times with her fist to smooth out some lumps (*must buy new pillows*), and refocused on the plot. She ignored the phone when it beeped a second time, growled through gritted teeth. *Piss off!* Third time, not a message but a call. No ring tone, instead the insistent buzz of the vibrate setting. She slammed the book face-down on the sheet, reached across to her beside table, picked up the phone, swiped to answer. 'Seriously, mate? Ringing me at this time? Figured out who did it already, have you?'

'Ah, no.' It was a male voice. But not Jack's. She flipped the phone around to see if it was someone in her contacts. No. Brand new number, one she didn't recognise. Although the voice sounded strangely familiar. A bit of nervous breathing from the other end.

The pause accompanied by creepy breathing went on too long for Taylor's liking. 'OK, I give up. Who is it?'

'Gene Partridge. Hopefully you remember me from the Country Club.'

'Of course. But how did you get my private number?' There was no anger in her tone. He was rather a hunk after all, and he had come to the rescue like a white knight when Jasper Keenan lost his lunch. Hard to be mad at him. Even the late hour seemed a trivial matter, as did his stalker-like respiratory pattern. Perhaps he's an asthmatic, said her optimist inner voice.

'I rang the 24-hour line, told the cop I needed to speak with you about the murder.'

'I don't buy it. They'd tell you to come into the station if you had anything useful.'

'OK. You got me there.' An awkward laugh. 'You dropped a business card on the table you were sitting at.'

She smiled. It was no accidental drop. She'd hoped the man would find it when he cleaned up the table after them. Him ringing so soon was a surprise, though. 'Oh. How can I help you?'

'I actually do have some information that I think might be useful. About the incident on the golf course, I mean. I'd rather not speak over the phone. Can I meet you in person?' Her excitement rose. The urgency in his words suggested he was on the level. But it was late, and whatever he had to say could wait until tomorrow.

'Look, I'm going to be at the station from around 9:00 in the morning. Drop by then, OK? Inspector Batista and Detective Sergeant Lisbon will want to hear what you have to say, too.'

'That's not the optimal scenario.'

'Why's that? Are you in danger?'

He laughed. 'No. Nothing like that. I'm flying out of town tomorrow. Plus I got paid yesterday and I'd like to buy a nice lady a drink.'

Taylor was easing an arm into a dressing gown, heading for the bathroom to freshen up, the phone pressed tight to her ear. She had to hop to avoid tripping on a pile of clothes on the floor. *Careful, no accidents*. Going out at this hour wasn't the greatest idea ahead of a busy day tomorrow. But, no two ways about it, a date with a handsome real man trumped the vicarious excitement of the made-up hero in the novel. 'Pelican Pub?'

'Perfect,' he said with a slight wheeze. 'Meet you there at 11:00.' He disconnected the call.

HE SAT ALONE in a booth by the wall, tattooed snakes on display as he rested his thick arms on the tabletop. A silver vape stick sat next to his phone in front of him. A tight white t-shirt with the short sleeves unnecessarily rolled up high to reveal as much muscle as possible. Even in the semi-gloom she could make out two round nipple piercings under the material of his top. A cheeky smile played upon his lips. He beckoned with a flick of the finger. Taylor felt herself being reeled in like a fish on an invisible line. She smoothed her slacks, shook her straight, dark hair – out and on the loose for a change, no trademark scrunchy.

She slipped into the seat opposite him, stared into his green eyes. The dark lashes were set so close together they created a blackness, like the thinnest trace of eyeliner. She placed her handbag on the seat beside her. 'What information do you have for me?' she said, trying to sound uninterested in him as a man, despite her heart racing. 'I'm afraid I can't stay long. I've got to…'

In a flash his smooth-fingered hand was extended halfway across the table. He unclenched his fingers and dropped a folded-up piece of paper.

'What's that?' She narrowed her eyes.

'Cuppla names.'

This was *not* what she expected. Where were the promised drinks, the awkwardness of strangers making small talk? He's straight down to business. 'What names?' she said, hearing the fluster in her words.

'Names of people from the club I've heard saying bad shit about Keenan. Quite vindictive, too. Those toffee-nosed pricks think I'm too stupid to pay attention to their prattle. But I'm listening.' He pointed to his ear. 'All the time.' He leaned back, folded his arms across his chest and grinned with self-satisfaction.

The man's odd behaviour was quickly detracting from his physical appeal. She chided herself on being so superficial; *give the bloke a chance.* She picked up the paper and unfolded it. 'Michael Salesa, who is…' No, dammit. She wanted a drink. 'Hand me a twenty.'

'Huh?'

'You said on the phone you were going to buy me a drink. Give me the cash and I'll go and get them.'

His face fell. 'Oh, dear. Where are my manners tonight? I was so intent on giving you this,' he pointed at the piece of paper, 'that I completely forgot. Do forgive me.' He stood, practically bowed. 'What's your poison?'

Back from the bar with a dry white wine for her and a foaming pint of beer for himself, Gene Partridge again apologised. Tomorrow afternoon he was flying down to Brisbane to visit his unwell mother and he wanted to make sure his tip was received by the police in person.

'Hey, it's OK. Sick mums come first.' She reached across and touched him on the top of his hand. He smiled, placed a warm hand on hers. For a second Taylor thought they'd be playing a game of one potato, two potato. No danger of that, though, as he dragged his hands away.

Taylor got her wish – it was now starting to feel awkward. The guy had no gift for chatting up women; he sat there like a stunned mullet, looking at a point directly over Taylor's shoulder.

'Right,' she said. 'What can you tell me about this first name on the list.'

His eyes lit up. 'Mike Salesa. He was Keenan's right-hand man at the Trust Bank. Not sure of his official title, but a month or so ago, Keenan sacked him.' Gene raised his eyebrows and took a sip of his beer, which left a frothy moustache he seemed to be unaware of or didn't care about. 'They're both members of the golf club *and...*' his well-manicured fingernail tapped the tabletop, '...the Rotary Club old man Morris is president of. Lately, when Salesa pops into the bar for a drink after a round, he's been hopping about like an angry flea. Before that, he was one of the calmest blokes you could ever meet. Even when he'd had a bad round.'

'So you think he could have planned the attack?'

A shrug of broad shoulders. 'Dunno. But he didn't hold back to me with his opinions about Keenan. Said he'd make sure the arsehole paid for firing him.'

'What about Morris? Had he pissed of this Salesa chap?'

Another shrug. 'Not that he spoke about.'

Taylor read the second name. 'And this other person? Who's he?'

'She.'

'Glenn?'

'Yeah, like Glenn Close. Only this is Glenn Farr.'

'OK, who's *she*?'

'Businesswoman, self-made and proud of it. Plays off a pretty decent handicap, too, they say.' He spoke as if her skills equated to a virtuous quality in a person. 'She's eccentric, goes everywhere with this emotional support poodle.'

'What's her beef?'

'She got knocked back on a loan she needed to finish developing an apartment block. The project's about three-quarters finished, and now she looks like a chump unable to complete the job.' He leaned forward, dropped his voice unnecessarily in the near empty lounge area. 'Apparently, Keenan advised the lending department she was too much of a risk to fund the loan. No one else wants to help her out, and she's blaming it all on Keenan.'

Taylor scratched her cheek. 'You seem highly informed on the details.'

Shrug number three; he had an infinite supply of them. 'It's the nature of humans, especially in a clubby environment. Once people get a few drinks into them, they love to spread the gossip.'

'So you're saying all of this is gossip.'

A wink instead of a shrug, for variety. 'No smoke without fire, know what I'm saying? But trust me, these two are worth checking out.' He looked like he was about to expound on his theory of man as a social animal when they were interrupted by a slim man sliding into the booth seat next to Partridge. He wore an open-necked shimmery red shirt with a gold chain nestled on pale skin. Most striking was the blonde highlights in his spikey gelled hair. Taylor did a quick reassessment: most striking wasn't the hair, it was the loving kiss exchanged between the two men.

On the Uber ride home Taylor fought the urge to cry.

Chapter Fourteen

THE LATE NIGHT run around his new homestead turned out to be a bad idea. Upturned buckets marked off all the wombat holes he was able to find Friday afternoon, but the pesky antipodean moles would surely have dug fresh ones since then. Potential snapped tibias. He felt a piece of soft ground shift under his right foot. He gasped, then gave silent thanks it wasn't a burrow. With the murder and attempted-murder investigation set to hot up tomorrow, the last thing he needed was a broken ankle.

The strap-on headlamp lit up an area of a couple of square metres in front of him, enough to jog with some degree of confidence. The light flickered; Jack stopped running, swore under his breath, checked the battery. Loose contact, and the housing covering it was hard to close. He somehow wrangled it shut without cracking the plastic. The light glowed steady again. He pulled the strap tight, headed off into the semi-darkness with a careful tread.

Turning right at the far boundary of his property and almost stumbling into the barbed wire fence, Jack realized his mistake. He should have heeded the salesman at the sports store. After listening to Jack describe his requirements, the lad had argued for a headlamp that chucked out a super bright beam a distance of 170 metres. Over a thousand lumens, whatever the hell that meant. But no, Jack knew better. *$200? I'm not paying that*, he'd said, and settled for the cheapie. How he regretted that decision. A low-hanging half moon spread its cool whiteness across the sky, which helped Jack pick his way along the perimeter track. But then a bank of clouds covered the moon and again he had to rely entirely on the weak lamp.

What also didn't help was his new companion, Daisy, a black-and-white, panting, loping, tongue-lolling mixed breed. He picked her up – or rescued her, as he preferred to think – at the pound, a Christmas present to himself. She quickly developed an odd habit when running with Jack: she would dart off for a minute, then return to his side for a dozen strides or so, then run off again into the darkness. A stealthy canine ninja, every now and then she'd give Jack a surprise nudge at knee level, almost throwing him off balance. *This dog needs proper training if she's going to be my long-term running buddy*, Jack thought to himself.

Anxiety peaking, he slowed from a jog to a walk. He turned his head down and to the right to see the mutt staring up at him with a grin and loving, soft brown eyes. 'C'mon girl. It's too dark and too dangerous. Let's go back to the house. Time to hit the hay.'

Fifteen minutes later, after a warm shower and with Daisy curled and snoring quietly on her mat, Jack poured himself a camomile tea, settled on the couch. He pointed the remote at the TV in time to catch the late-night news. It was a pre-recorded stand-up piece by Channel 11 reporter Holly Maguire. She stood in front of the closed and padlocked wrought-iron gates of the Yorkville Country Club. She fixed her gaze directly at the camera, waved a couple of tiny insects away from her face, and began speaking in earnest.

'According to a statement we've just received from the police, a terrible tragedy occurred at the Yorkville Country Club this morning. Two men were shot on the golf course. One victim, 41-year-old bank manager Paul Keenan, died from his wounds. The other, 69-year-old Lachlan Morris, is in the hospital in a critical condition. His wife, Dervla Morris, was there with the two men but avoided physical injury. That's all the information we were given by the police, although a press conference has been called for tomorrow morning. We'll be sure to bring you updates as and when they happen.

Eyes drooping, Jack picked up the controller to switch off the TV, but Maguire wasn't done. *Despite the police being tight-lipped, we can't say the same for one witness.*

Jack's ears pricked up.

According to an anonymous call we received this evening, the attack was allegedly carried out by a drone. The nature of this crime is extremely concerning for the community at large. Our viewers can be assured we'll be questioning the police about their lack of transparency. Indeed, our source claims Inspector Joseph Batista asked witnesses not to divulge any information until the official statement was made. Well, it appears not all of those witnesses chose to comply with the Inspector's request. Now, back to the studio...'

Jack rubbed his forehead hard. Tomorrow's press conference had the potential to be a train wreck. He'd hold the chief's hand – figuratively of course – throughout the ordeal, take as much flak as he could. If he was going to be totally honest with himself, though, he rather enjoyed jousting with the media jackals.

A liver treat for Daisy, a pat on the head, and off to bed.

Ten minutes of tossing and turning later told Jack sleep

was going to come when *it* was ready, not when he was. Too many thoughts ran through his brain. The one that shoved all others to the side was THE DRONE.

How could he have missed the gun? Could he have somehow prevented the tragedy?

Probably not.

But the least he could do for the victims was learn as much as he could about the damn things, find evidence that could point to the pilot of the killing machine. One problem: research sucked and Jack hated it with a passion. Never mind, reading dry technical and legal texts online would either reveal answers or send him to sleep. Either result was a win.

Let's start with the bleedin' obvious. *Drones fly.* Meaning they may come under the umbrella of the government's Civil Aviation Safety Authority. CASA's website confirmed drones must be registered, but only for business purposes. That broad brush included selling photos or videos taken from a drone; checking on industrial equipment, building sites or public services; monitoring, inspection and safety operations; research and development. Wouldn't you know it? Nothing about murdering innocent people on a golf course. Guess that means the effin' thing wouldn't be on any government list.

Of course it wouldn't, you moron! Jack kneaded his eye sockets, feeling the painful frustration of ignorance.

Then, a light-blub moment. A quick check of the time zone difference. 3:15pm in London. Good to go. Jack threw on a terry towelling dressing gown, trotted downstairs, made a coffee and dialled his old friend and confidant Micky Knox.

'Micky. It's Jack Lisbon.'

'Jack! To what do I owe the unexpected pleasure?'

Micky's tone was upbeat, like he was genuinely chuffed to hear from his one-time boxing mentor. 'Your daughter's not been kidnapped again, has she?'

Jack's heart skipped a beat, recalling last year's frantic rescue mission to Scotland, the success of which was largely down to Micky's smarts. 'I'll call you back.'

'What the—'

A scroll through his contacts found the hairdressing salon where his ex touched up the purple do's of South London biddies. It rang for ages before the voice mail cut in. Must be a busy afternoon. He hung up and tried again. Success. A rapid and heated conversation with Sarah confirmed Skye was at school, presumably safe and sound. Reassured, he cut Sarah off as she launched into another personal attack on his character. He redialled Micky.

'Oi, you gonna finish this conversation, or what?'

'All good, sunshine. Had to make certain my kid was all right.'

'And is she?'

'Seems so.'

'What's the problem, then, guv? I've got a busy afternoon chasing up drop-shipping orders.' Down the line came the sound of gas escaping from a can of fizzy drink.

'I'm hoping I can leverage your vast store of technical knowledge.' Jack explained as quickly as he could the events of the preceding 15 hours. Gasps greeted each new detail.

'Wait a second.' There was a pause and some clicking sounds. 'Holy shit! There's already an online news story about it, syndicated through a London paper. Sassy headline. *Drone slays local businessman in broad daylight.* The cat jumped out of the bag fast.'

'Yeah,' Jack laughed sarcastically. 'Batista should have

known appealing to the general public for restraint would have the opposite effect.'

'So, what is it you want me to do?'

Jack struggled to verbalise the thoughts. 'Look into drones 'n that.'

Micky burst out laughing. 'Can you be a bit more specific?'

'Yeah, sorry.' Mental head slap. 'Lemme see. Can you find out the specs of a machine capable of carrying a semi-automatic pistol loaded with a 15-round clip and a megaphone about the size of a tennis ball? Maybe how far a drone like that can fly without losing signal from the operator. I've got a feeling the pilot would've liked to ensconce himself—'

'Or herself...'

'Don't interrupt, please, Micky. Or herself...as far away from the crime scene as possible.'

Micky slugged more of his drink before saying, 'I do know this about drones in general. You can only trace them in real time, and you need the right infrastructure to do it. Sensors in place, that kind of thing. Even if you've got that, Wi-Fi, bluetooth and other signals are gonna make your job real difficult.'

'Moot point, sunshine. The drone's done *its* job and disappeared. I reckon the pilot's either retrieved it, or, if this was a one-off job, destroyed it in a giant bonfire.'

'You're near the ocean, correct?'

'Yeah. Right on the Pacific coast.'

'I'd lay odds the killer has ditched the drone out at sea.'

'I've had that thought too.'

Jack heard the echo of someone knocking on a door. 'Listen, I've gotta go. Give me a day or two to do some digging around. I'm not hopeful, but you never know. I'll be following the story with interest from over here.'

Jack profusely thanked his mate, who had gone above and beyond the call of duty a couple of times before. Not least when he helped cover up a murder and conceal the evidence of a very large theft, the proceeds of which helped pay for the rundown farmstead Jack had recently purchased and now lived in. But Jack never lost a wink of sleep over that. The man he killed in the South London gym had deserved to die.

One last glance at his Samsung mobile. Bad news and good news.

Bad news – it was already past two in the morning.

Good news – a text from Taylor. Got a couple of surprising leads. All will be revealed tomorrow.

What on earth could those leads be? The temptation to ring her was strong, but Taylor was probably asleep. The text had come through just after midnight.

As exhaustion struck and Jack finally drifted off, an image came into his mind. That awkward moment at the height of last year's big case, the murder of local tennis star Roderick McAdam. With the case drowning in quicksand, Taylor did something clever that was integral to solving the crime. In his excitement, Jack had grabbed her face in his hands and planted a quick kiss on her lips.

He really regretted that moment. The kiss was too quick.

Do it properly next time, Lisbon.

Chapter Fifteen

IT WAS a hellish night of pulsating nightmares, no pause between them. First, not one drone, but a squadron of them. As big as buses and armed with submachine guns, they fired at screaming civilians, ripping holes in bodies, severing limbs and heads. Streets awash with blood. Next up, Doctor Pereira, carrying out medical experiments on live people. He cackled like an evil scientist in a B-grade movie, yellow teeth bared, scalpel raised and then descending towards the dotted line drawn on Jack's bare stomach. Last, Taylor in chains, on her knees and sobbing hysterically, held hostage by a faceless lunatic in a dungeon. The kidnapper had sent MMS images of her, cut and bruised and bleeding, but Jack couldn't figure out where the hell she was. Jack jolted awake at 03:15 bathed in a sheen of sweat, heart pounding. He gulped down half a litre of water from the bottle he kept beside the bed, waited for his pulse rate to settle, and crashed back to sleep within minutes.

The deepest REM sleep closer to dawn produced even more realistic scenes. The last dream, so extraordinarily vivid that Jack would later wonder if he'd had an out-of-body experience, again featured Taylor. It was that kiss; a kiss then spontaneous and innocent, now impassioned, lustful. Her tongue, my God, he could never have imagined this. He struggled to breathe, almost asphyxiating, a pressure in his skull threatened to break the bone. *Open your eyes!* It was a trap, he had to push her off.

Awake now. The dog was sitting on his chest, licking him like its life depended on it. Slobber coated Jack's lips, cheeks, nose. 'Geddorf me, will ya!' He pushed Daisy's 25 kilo bulk away like he was bench-pressing at the gym. She gave a soft bark, leapt off the bed and, tail wagging, trotted off down the stairs, satisfied with her improvised wake-up-call.

Phone check. 07:35. Time was a'wasting. If not for Daisy he'd have slept through and missed the morning brief. He'd buy her extra treats at the supermarket tonight.

Dog fed, coffee machine on, shower complete, coffee drunk.

Keys, car, highway.

———

HE'D BEEN the last to arrive this morning, but not by much. Constable Noah Semmens's bulky, swaying behind disappeared through the front door as Jack ripped the handbrake of his Hilux. He would have been breathing down his colleague's neck if not for the incoming call. Micky Knox.

'Micky.' Jack pressed hands free, checked his hair in the rear vision mirror. Not that much could go wrong with his short style, but one could never be too sure. 'Found anything?'

'Yeah. Dunno if your techies have found it yet, but I'm about to send you a link.'

'What is it?'

'Video of a home-made drone shooting a pistol. It was taken down from the Internet five years ago. Maybe the US government didn't want a tutorial like this floating around online.'

'How did you get hold of it if it was deleted?'

'There's a thing called the Wayback Machine. An archive of stuff off the 'Net. Whatever you put on the Web will leave a trace forever.'

'I've never heard of it.'

'Many haven't. Anyway, link's on its way. It might help you, might not. I'll contact you if I find anything else, but this'll at least give you an idea of a possible configuration the killer may have used.'

The DS thanked his friend and hustled to the morning briefing. He'd share the link with the crew inside the station; they could all get educated at the same time. To Jack, the other cops looked chipper and ready for action. Nothing like the reflection of his own tired face that greeted him in the bathroom mirror this morning. Taylor sat a metre away, also with droopy eyes. Geez...he could barely look at her after that last dream. His skin prickled under his shirt. He sensed his Adam's apple rising and falling, thought he could even hear it clicking inside his throat. That was one of the "guilty" tells that had lost him a few hundred quid at poker back in his corrupt British copper days. But what did he have to feel guilty about this time? Apart from being unable to rescue her and later ravishing her in his sleep. Weird, but even though those events were not real, his feeling of guilt, that he let her down, was.

Inspector Batista clapped his preying-mantis hands

together, the sound like echoey thunder in the sparsely furnished incident room. 'Nice of DS Lisbon to finally join us this morning.'

'I've got a valid excuse, and a note from my mum.' His tone was deadpan. Everyone laughed. Except Batista. 'Why so glum, sir?'

The Inspector narrowed his eyes, accentuating the crow's feet that stretched almost to his temples. 'Unfortunately, a member of the country club chose to ignore my instruction not to blab to the media.'

'Nothing you can do about that,' said Jack matter-of-factly. 'I saw Maguire getting all high and mighty on the telly. Don't worry, sir. Let me handle her at the press conference.'

'I'm tempted not to have one. I mean, we only do these things out of courtesy.'

'I beg to differ,' said Jack. 'It's been common practice for…I dunno…but it's what the public want when tragedy strikes. The cops giving reassurance.' He paused for a second to rub an errant crumb of sleep dust from his eyes. 'The press will annihilate you if you cancel. Any deviation from what they expect will be grist to their scandal mill, innit.'

The Inspector sighed. 'I guess you're right. But what are we going to tell them?'

'We're going to show them.' What that looked like, Jack had no idea. He was going with blind trust when it came to Micky's link.

'What?' said the Inspector, optimism bringing some colour to his high-boned cheeks.

Instead of explaining – except for stating the fact it was a video of immense interest – Jack forwarded the link via the station's general email address to Constable Wilson, who set up the large monitor that sat on a portable metal shelf.

'Your sense of drama isn't appreciated by everyone,' Taylor whispered in Jack's ear as the chief exchanged a word with Wilson. 'Look at the face Batista's pulling.'

'Yeah,' Jack replied behind his hand. He wondered if she could sense the combination of emotions her mere presence created in him. He pushed the thoughts out of his mind. 'He's probably thinking I've found the killer on CCTV. Not that exciting, I'm afraid.'

The video elicited a reaction in the Inspector contrary to Jack's expectations. 'This is extraordinary.'

It is? thought Jack, who found the footage rather underwhelming. A grainy 35 seconds of a drone firing single shots in a forest somewhere. Then, interviews with American police and locals condemning the fact the machine had been built at all. Calling for *laws against this kind of thing*. 'Glad you think so, boss' said Jack. 'To be honest, I was hoping Micky would come up with something better than this. Some specs, numbers, a manufacturer. I've changed my mind about showing it at the press conference.'

'Agreed,' said Batista. 'But it at least gives me an idea of what's happened out on the golf course.'

Constable Trevarthen chimed in: 'That one in the video is about three times bigger than the one we saw yesterday. It also looks, I dunno, clumsy by comparison. I reckon that clip's at least 10 years old. Technology has moved on since then.' He pulled out his phone held it up demonstratively. 'I've done a bit of research myself.' He walked over to the keyboard in front of the monitor and tapped something in, a video ready to play appeared on screen. Then he pressed enter, took a step back.

The crew stared open-mouthed as a man in camouflage

gear, speaking in a sing-song foreign language peppered with throat-choking diphthongs, used black gaffer tape to secure a Glock G18C to a quadcopter drone. The man launched the device by hand like he was setting a dove free; the point of view quickly switched to that of the drone's camera, cross hairs clearly visible. The machine flew around rugged bushland, in and out of derelict brick buildings, and back to the operator. The man caught the drone by the low-hanging extended ammunition clip. He said something to whomever was filming him, then relaunched. Back to the drone's POV. From his tucked-away position, the man piloted the machine with great skill, getting as close as a couple of inches from tree branches and other obstacles, and then shooting a line of beer bottles to smithereens from a distance of about 10 metres.

'Where did you find this?' said Jack. 'Dammit, this looks very similar to the drone we saw.'

'It comes from a Hungarian war games forum.'

'A what?' Jack's eyebrows hoisted up his forehead. 'What the hell do you know about war games? Or Hungarian for that matter?'

'Got a good mate, Laszlo. Everyone calls him Les. Anyway, we were in the army reserve together. Last night I remembered how his dad's real technically minded, loves building gadgets from scratch, so I gave Les a call. His dad, who's from Budapest originally, had a hunt around the Hungarian Internet and found this hiding in plain sight.' Trevarthen pulled a piece of paper from his pocket. 'Here's a transcript in English of what the dude was saying.'

The Inspector held up a finger. 'Brilliant, Aden. Let's get this link and that text sent down to Brisbane, see if the specialists down there can dig up anything about makes and models of these machines. Find out where they're sold.

Wilson, get onto it after this meeting.' Batista slugged a glass of water, his tone and body language indicating he was happier now that at least some progress was being made. 'Anyone else make any startling discoveries? If not, let's move onto questioning...'

'I did.' Taylor cleared her throat.

'Did what?'

'Not much,' she replied with a smidgen of false modesty. 'Just found a couple of leads that's all.'

'Excellent. And we haven't even started in earnest,' said Batista. 'Please, go on DC Taylor.'

Jack walked to the watercooler, filled a paper cup. No need to be breathing down her neck as she adds her two cents worth to the growing yet disjointed streams of information.

She related her conversation with Gene Partridge, the barman from the Country Club, how he'd made the late night call and demanded to meet her in person. She kept her voice neutral and measured; Jack got the feeling she was holding something back about the encounter. The old green-eyed monster loomed in his brain, and he couldn't help reacting to its presence. 'Interesting he chose to call you in the middle of the night rather than wait until the morning and simply drop by the station.'

Taylor shrugged. 'I left my business card on the table at the Country Club. We'd exchanged a few words, so I guess he felt a connection had been established. Probably easier than speaking to an unknown person via the hotline.'

She had a valid point. Not that she had to explain herself to him. 'So,' he said, patting his pockets to make sure his keys were there. 'What are we waiting her for? Let's go chat to these people, Salesa and Farr.'

'Not so fast, DS Lisbon,' said Batista, holding up a

hand. 'The press conference is scheduled for 10:00, just over an hour away. I'm going to need you for this one.'

He stared at the chief open-mouthed. 'I thought it was planned for midday.'

'You should check your phone every morning like I do,' suggested Kylie Smith, who'd remained quiet during the briefing. 'Notifications like that should automatically land in your work calendar. It's linked to the email program that—'

'Yes, yes, I know that.' Jack waved dismissively. He never checked his work calendar on his mobile phone and wasn't about to start. He glanced at the chief. 'Are we finished here, sir? I've gotta do some mental preparation before we face the press. Maybe a cryptic crossword or a spot of meditative yoga on the floor.'

'Commendable, DS Lisbon.' The Inspector shook his head before consulting a notepad. 'But first I want to make sure we're all on the same page.' He proceeded to allocate persons of interest to be approached for questioning as a matter of priority. Lisbon and Taylor — Morris and his wife, also Sabrina Keenan, and the new potential suspects named by the barman, Michael Salesa and Glenn Farr.'

The detectives nodded.

'Uniforms are to squeeze these jobs in between any call outs. Wilson.'

'Sir?'

'As I already said, liaise with Brisbane HQ on the drone. Check for possible terrorism links with Irish organisations, which will include the victims' online footprints. And those of their immediate and extended family members.'

'Roger that.'

'Constable Smith, hit up Reg Brownstone and his daughter. Ruby was expecting to speak to DC Taylor, and

Claudia may well follow up later, but I want to cover as much ground as we can as quickly as we can.'

'Understood, sir.'

'Constable Trevarthen, I'd like you to chase up Keenan's brother, Rohan. We've already spoken to his son, the victim's nephew. The lad was hurting badly at the news, so go easy on him. However if he is keen to talk, great.'

'Paul Keenan's parents,' said Trevarthen. 'Are they local, anyone know?'

'I've already found Keenan's Facebook page,' said Wilson, holding up his mobile. 'Mother and father recently deceased. He's got a portrait of them as a pinned post.'

'A blessing in some ways that they're already dead,' observed Batista. 'Nothing worse than parents outliving their children.'

A murmur of general agreement.

'Finally, Noah Semmens. See if you can find out anything from the old fellow Bert Johnson.'

'Remind me who he is, sir?' said Semmens, drawing a chuckle from the other officers.

'He was with the party playing behind Jack when the drone attack happened.'

'Gottcha.'

'Is that it?' said Jack, his head swimming with the task ahead of them. No doubt uniforms would be called out to all manner of incidents, as they always were, meaning the burden of interviewing the names Batista listed would fall squarely on him and Taylor. Like a curse coming true in real time, Constable Damien Wells stuck his frowning face around the door.

'Sorry to interrupt, but there's trouble on the waterfront.'

'What sort of trouble?' said Batista with a fatalistic note.

'A shop owner's reported a wild brawl at one of the cafés down there. Terrified, she is. Men punching the crap out of each other, tossing outdoor furniture into the dock.'

'How many?'

'Six or so.'

Batista looked down at his notepad, then back to the uniforms, each wearing an expression of apprehension mixed with curiosity. 'Ok. I'm sending two of you to deal. Who wants it?'

Silence and shuffling feet.

'No volunteers, huh? In that case, you're all going.'

A chorus of sighs.

'And be careful. Negotiation as a first step. Truncheons before tasers. If it's too overwhelming for the five of you, call for backup. Jack used to be a boxer, you know.'

'Then why isn't he going?' said Wilson.

'Cos I'm a bleedin' detective, innit!' said Jack.

The blue shirts hustled out the door, Jack on their tail.

'Where do you think you're going, DS Lisbon?' Batista said reproachfully. 'Jack...?'

The door closed behind Jack as he made his way to the car park. A murder case was a big deal, but a chance to knock a few hooligans' heads together with the constables was a spot of fun he'd hate to miss.

Chapter Sixteen

A DAB of Taylor's tan foundation helped hide the blooming bruise on his cheek. It wasn't caused by a thug's punch, but the result of friendly fire. As the cops sprinted to the melee, they were funnelled through a narrow walkway between the street where they parked and the promenade by the dock. The officers soon found themselves jammed up tight in a running scrum. As they burst through the narrow gap and into the open plaza, Constable Trevarthen's swinging pointy elbow connected hard with Jack's cheekbone. 'That really got me fired up, Claudia. I was ready to take the lot of them on by myself.'

'Really, Jack. You're too much.'

'Yeah, but my enthusiasm for the fight faded pretty quick. No sooner did we appear on the scene, the uniforms with their truncheons drawn, than the participants ended hostilities. A couple of 'em even shook hands, can you believe it?'

She shook her head slowly, lips pressed firmly together. 'Amazing,' she said flatly.

'I tell you, Claudia, I was tempted to charge the bleedin' lot of them with wasting police time.' He checked his face in Taylor's makeup mirror, smiled and gave her a thumb's up. Handing the compact back to her he added, 'On the positive side, the café owner's gonna press charges against one of the idiots for destruction of property.' He chuckled softly. 'Can you believe it, the instigator was one of the MAMILs!'

'The what?'

'MAMILS. Middle-aged Men in Lycra. You know, those fat wankers on racing bicycles who hog the roads and then take up all the tables at coffee shops. The sight of their flabby bodies in those tight clothes is enough to turn your stomach. Anyway, one of these geezers said something sexist to a waitress and a young bloke jumped to her defense and then it was on!'

'Server.'

'What?'

'FYI, the word "waitress" is sexist nowadays. You're as bad as the man who started the fight.'

'Bleedin' heck, Claudia. You can't be serious.'

She refused to be drawn any further into the argument, instead stashed her compact back in her bag. 'Whatever,' she said with a wry grin. 'But I can't believe you risked missing the press conference to satisfy your primitive bloodlust. Batista's relying on you to keep Maguire and company in check.'

He quirked an eyebrow at her, which made him wince, 'Bloodlust? You kidding me? After the rivers of blood yesterday?'

'You know what I mean. That urge to get involved in violence.'

'Anyway, I'm here, innit. No harm done.'

THE INSPECTOR TAPPED THE MICROPHONE, introduced himself and DS Lisbon. Jack looked straight ahead at the journalists, eyes unblinking. The numbers told the story. The murder hadn't generated the worldwide interest of the last case, but it was a bigger ensemble than usual. In addition to the regular locals, Jack clocked a couple of nationally syndicated reporters, Liisa Scheer and Robert Ivins. They must've flown up from Sydney to cover the sensational story.

Batista wiped a bead of sweat from his brow. 'All questions are to be directed to Detective Sergeant Lisbon, who is heading up the investigation as per usual.'

A weird silence hung in the air for a moment, then the hands shot up like kids in class busting for the bathroom. Jack pointed at the heavily made-up Holly Maguire. Her sprayed hair had set like a hard watermelon skin around her narrow head, reminding Jack of cartoon character Baby Stewie. *Let's get her out of the way*, he thought to himself. But he'd make sure to get the first word in, set the rules of engagement. 'I saw your hit piece on the Inspector last night, Holly. I expected much better from you.'

'What I said was merely a statement of fact. Someone leaked information Inspector Batista didn't want the public to know about.'

Jack leaned forward. 'Let me set you straight on one thing. Nothing is being held back. We are now revealing everything we know about the murder of Paul Keenan and the attempted murder of Lachlan Morris.' He saw the extended arm of the reporter from Channel 3. Jack nodded in his direction.

'Why the delay, though?' said Jonno Peroni, a handsome

former professional footballer and now popular TV personality. 'The public have a right to know about serious crimes of this nature as soon as possible.'

'Obviously, crimes like this don't happen every day,' said Batista, a gritty edge to his voice. 'We didn't want to send the town into a panic unnecessarily.'

Jack's muscles stiffened under his starched shirt. Time to take the reigns back before the boss says something he regrets. 'What the Inspector means is that we wanted to make sure we had analysed all the information to hand before making a considered statement about the tragedy. Which is what I'm going to do now, with your indulgence.' He coughed twice before reading from a one-page document prepared by Taylor a short while ago. It contained only facts relating to the crime itself and the status of the victims, no theories or speculation about suspects. As he spoke, cameras flashed and reporters gasped. At the end of the statement, Constable Ben Wilson played the clip made by the Hungarian war games enthusiasts. Jack commented as the video came to an end, 'This drone closely resembles the machine witnessed by myself and Constable Aden Trevarthen at the Yorkville Country Club yesterday. At this point I'd like to appeal to the public.' He looked earnestly into the bank of cameras. 'If you have footage of a drone like this flying within a 10 km radius of the Country Club at any time yesterday, we want to see it. If you know someone who's been carrying out unusual activity with a drone, we want to hear about that too. Pronto.' He took a deep breath. 'Any questions?'

He pointed at the visiting crime reporter from the *Sydney Morning Herald*. 'Liisa.'

'With the use of an armed drone to commit this crime, are the police looking at links to extremist organisations?'

'That's not been a priority.' Not a direct yes or no. 'Additionally, no group has claimed responsibility for the atrocity.' Jack clenched his jaw, experienced a flash of pain from the blow he'd received earlier. The hits you weren't prepared for always hurt the most. 'Our belief is that this was a targeted attack and no other members of the public are at risk. Most likely the killer is local, however, given the victims were both influential figures, that's not a hundred percent certain.'

'What about motive?' said Maguire without being called upon. 'Who would want to hurt these men? You've just said they were,' she made air quotes, '*influential*, but from what I've been able to learn they weren't exactly celebrities.'

The tone of her voice verged on rude, but Jack held his nerve. 'Don't worry, Ms Maguire. We're investigating all possibilities, taking particular interest in business and personal associates of the victims.'

'How are the victims' families holding up?' asked a frail, grey-haired woman from an aisle seat. 'They must be devastated.'

Jack smiled inwardly. Veteran scribe Fiona Wagstaff from the *Yorkville Times* offered respite, focussing on the human interest angle. 'Very good question, Fiona. The families are understandably shaken to the core by these events, and we would ask you to respect their privacy. Any complaints made by them about invasive behaviour from the press or anyone else will be treated with the utmost seriousness. Any more questions?' Three eager reporters had their hands up. Jack raised his eyebrows like he was searching for someone in a crowd, then dropped them. 'No? Well, that about wraps it up.' Groans of annoyance rose from the gallery. 'Thanks for your time everyone.'

Batista stood, shuffled blank pieces of paper, leaned into

the microphone. 'We'll let you know of any major breakthroughs as and when they happen.' The relief in his voice was clear. He ignored the shouts of displeasure from the assembled throng as he and Jack exited the press room and headed for the back landing and fresh air.

Batista plucked a cigarette from a packet, offered one to Jack.

'I haven't smoked for years, sir. You know that.'

A couple of wide-eyed blinks from the chief were followed by a mumbled apology. 'Oh dear. Maybe I'm losing my marbles.'

'Not at all sir.' The certainty in Jack's words failed to match his thoughts. The Inspector *had* been acting a little doddery lately. 'But I'll happily stand next to you and get a free hit of the second-hand variety.' He smiled as his boss applied the lighter to the tip of his Marlboro. The man was approaching retirement age; perhaps that time would be sooner rather than later.

'Right.' Batista sucked in a lungful of smoke before launching a pair of perfect rings into the still morning air. 'Let's get a hustle on with the questioning.' He restated the officers' program for the day precisely as he'd outlined at the briefing. Jack grinned. The old boy hadn't lost it completely.

Chapter Seventeen

'I'M afraid Mrs Morris has been discharged.'

'I beg your pardon?' said Jack, edging closer to Pereira. 'Yesterday you said she was under the care of a bleedin' psychiatrist. Today she's out and about? Who came to collect her?'

The doctor's eyebrows knitted together. 'No one. I believe she left of her own volition in a taxi.'

'But surely she wasn't in a fit state to leave,' Taylor protested. 'After what happened she'd be a mess!'

'The psychiatrist said she was good to go.' Pereira tapped a pen against a clipboard. 'Ever heard of triaging, officers? This hospital has a limited number of beds. If there were two crimes of varying gravity, you'd prioritise the allocation of resources to one of them, wouldn't you? That's exactly what we do. We needed to free up the bed Dervla Morris was occupying for a drug overdose patient we suspect was an attempted suicide. On objective merit, the drug addict was more deserving.'

Jack let out a groan of exasperation. 'What about her

husband? I assume he's still here, what with being shot in the stomach and all.' He couldn't hold back his disdain for the surgeon.

'He's still here and will be for a number of days yet.'

'Are we able to speak with him?'

Pereira smiled. 'Of course.'

The sudden change in attitude caught the detectives on the hop. Taylor voiced her surprise: 'You're suddenly very co-operative. How come?'

The faint lines around Pereira's full-lipped mouth softened as he broke into a congenial smile. 'I'm always co-operative. However the welfare of patients under the roof of this hospital must always come first. Mr Morris is out of danger. He's conscious and on a pain control regime. He may be a little woozy due to his meds, but if you want to catch the killer – and we all want that, don't we? – then I'd suggest you head up to his ward and talk to him. Come on, let me take you there.' He gestured towards a bank of gleaming elevators.

Pereira ushered the detectives inside, something in his pocket bleeped and he hurried off to the next emergency. A nurse was replacing the bag on a drip as Jack and Taylor entered the stark-white single-bed ward. There weren't many private spaces like this in the hospital, Jack knew from experience. He spent two sweaty, shivery, shitty nights here last November. He'd caught a nasty virus after swimming in a mosquito-infested creek despite Trevarthen warning him against it. With fevers racking his body and his digestive system on the blink, he'd had to share a curtained-off area with three other patients. Some of them were even sicker than Jack, keeping him up all night with their horrible noises. It occurred to him to upgrade his health insurance policy at the earliest opportunity.

The nurse finished with the drip bag, jotted something on a clipboard at the end of the bed, apologised when there was no need, and exited the room on soft feet.

Jack and Taylor approached the patient slowly.

'Who is it?' Lachlan Morris said in a weak croaky voice. His shaking fingers gripped the edge of the blanket. 'Dervla? Is it you, dear? Are you all right?'

Jack pulled up a plastic visitor chair for Taylor, one for himself. Then he realised Morris wouldn't be able to see them from his position. Standing it would have to be. He motioned for Taylor to stay door-side of the bed, he walked around to the window.

Jack showed his ID, introduced himself and Taylor, gently asked if it was OK to put a few questions to him.

'I...think so. I don't remember much.'

'That's all right.' Taylor's voice was soothing, reminded Jack of his favourite teacher. He'd had a crush on that woman, too, even though he was only seven at the time. 'We won't take up too much of your time.'

The tendons in Morris's neck stuck out as he tried to lift his head. 'I can't see you properly. Can you raise this contraption for me?'

Taylor adjusted the pillows behind the man's head, found the button on the electric cord that elevated the back half of the bed. 'That far enough?'

Wide eyed, Morris gave a slow nod of confirmation. He blinked in the harsh light beaming down from the ceiling. *Why do hospitals have to have such bright lighting?* Jack wondered. Can't be good for the recuperating patients. Then again, maybe it was. Wiser heads had designed all this crap, after all. 'That's perfect.' Morris's eyes darted back and forth, searching for something. 'Where's Dervla? Didn't you bring her with you?'

'Ah...didn't she come to see you before she was discharged?' said Taylor.

A quiet melancholy seemed to exacerbate the dark circles around his soft grey eyes. 'No. What do you mean, discharged?'

'She stayed here overnight after the...incident,' said Jack. 'She was in shock but physically unharmed.' Surely he knew that.

'Oh, so she was in the hospital too.' It was a statement but almost sounded like a question. He grimaced slightly, baring stained, yellowish teeth and lots of gum. Long in the tooth, as the saying goes. A machine hummed and droplets ran along the tube from the drip bag into the catheter embedded in Morris's liver-spotted forearm. Morphine, Jack surmised.

'Perhaps you were asleep when she dropped by to check on you,' suggested Taylor. 'I'm sure that's it. But don't worry, she's managed to get herself home in a taxi.'

'Hmmm, I guess I must've been sleeping, like you say.' He didn't sound convinced. 'She'll come and visit me when she's feeling better. Or maybe they'll let me out soon. Do you think they will?'

Jack shrugged. 'No idea. Let's hope so.' He offered a wan smile.

'The doctor told me I was...shot in the stomach and the arm and they've removed bullets. That can't be true, can it? Doesn't feel like I've been shot.'

'I'm afraid it is. The morphine's masking the pain.' Jack leaned closer. 'Can't you remember what happened at the Country Club yesterday?'

'Yes. Some of it. We played the first hole. I got a birdie.' A trace of a smile crept across his lips. 'I hardly every birdie that one. Dervla scored a par, and Paul...ah...also a par, I think. I'd have to check the score card. And then...no...we didn't get to finish the round.' A flash of recollection as one eyebrow rose a fraction. 'Something strange...a drone. It hovered near us, and then a voice. It said...it said...'

'What did it say?' Jack barked, then reproved himself for his impatience with a wounded old man.

'I couldn't hear it very well.' He coughed a couple of times, winced as his stomach muscles contracted. 'It was speaking to Paul.' His hands darted to his face, covered it like he was hiding from the officers. Then a protracted primal howl. 'Nooo!'

'He's remembered it now, all right,' said Jack as the volume of the wailing crescendoed, levelled off to steady crying, then subsided to soft sobs.

Morris slowly drew his hands from his face, tucked them back under the blanket. 'Is Paul...OK?' He glanced first at Taylor, then at Jack, who pursed his lips and gave the tiniest of head shakes. Morris swallowed hard, switched his gaze to the ceiling like he was checking it for cracks. His eyes closed slowly, tears ran past his temples and formed little damp patches on the sheet next to his ears. The grim truth had hit home. Paul Keenan was dead.

Once the tears subsided, Lachlan Morris looked pleadingly at Jack and then Taylor. The DS took his partner by the crook of the arm and led her out of the ward. Lachlan Morris wasn't fit for any more questioning today.

Chapter Eighteen

DERVLA, dressed sombrely in navy blue slacks and long-sleeved black blouse, opened the door to the house she shared with Lachlan Morris, and at least one Burmese cat. The sleek chocolate feline gazed up at the visitors, raised its tail in welcome. Dervla held the door knob with one hand and waved the officers inside with the other. Her spider-veined eyes glistened. 'Let's get this over with.' The purring cat padded its way to the front of the trio and escorted them down a dimly lit hallway into an open-plan living area.

'Are you sure this is a good time?' said Jack when they reached the end of the corridor.

'There won't ever be a good time.' She slumped into a kitchen chair, grabbed at a box of tissues. A crumpled wad of them lay in the middle of the table. A kettle whistled, she turned her head towards the sound. 'I was just making meself a pot of tea. Care to join me?'

Jack was glad the woman hadn't sought solace in alcohol, like the recently bereaved are wont to do. 'I'd definitely love a cuppa. Claudia?'

Taylor accepted, herself offering to assist the woman in the kitchen. Left alone, Jack took in his surroundings. Morrison may well be the local Rotary President, a member of an exclusive country club and a retired civil engineer with a stellar career behind him, but the interior of the family home was modest. Simple grey slate tiles covered every inch of flooring apart from a black-and-white rug in the middle of the lounge. No flashy furniture, electronic gadgetry or expensive art works adorning the walls. A plain, middle-class home. The only hint at a healthy bank balance was the expensive BMW iX3 electric SUV parked in the driveway. Jack checked the price online. A cool $120,000. No doubt a browse of the garage would reveal top-of-the-range golf clubs and accessories. Musings about Lachlan Morris's financial situation were cut short by the return of Taylor toting a tray and Dervla carrying what looked like the weight of the world on her slender shoulders.

'Please.' Dervla waved a hand at the kitchen table. 'No, on second thoughts, let's go to the garden instead. I need some fresh air.'

Walking along a white pebble path flanked by red and pink hibiscus hedges, Jack admired the neatness of the outdoor space: the golden cane palms typical of northern Queensland, rockeries full of succulents, a couple of water features. The landscaped gardens drew a smile of appreciation from Taylor, stepping carefully on mossy pavers on the way to an ornate gazebo. Brightly coloured butterflies flitted between the branches of overhanging trees, dancing in the dappled sunlight. On any other occasion, Jack would be asking all kinds of questions about the garden; he was keen to establish something more welcoming in his own bare front yard. But today was not such an occasion.

They sat in silence for a moment while Taylor played

mother and poured the tea. 'Is there no one who can be with you at this time?' she said. 'I'm not sure being on your own is a good idea.'

Dervla waved away the concern. 'It's OK. I've had a long conversation with my mother in Cork. She's the only person I want to share my grief with.' She grabbed a tissue, wiped a tear away. 'I've not managed to make too many friends since I moved to Australia. Not close ones, at any rate.'

'What did the voice from the drone say, Dervla?' said Jack. 'Your husband can't remember too much.'

'Jack!' Taylor interjected, spilling tea on the wooden table, glaring daggers at him. 'You can't just…' She shook her head in seeming bewilderment. 'Geez…'

'No,' said Dervla, rubbing her puffy eyes. 'I understand Detective Lisbon's desire to get to the point. We Irish are like that. No fookin' about.' She stared at Jack. 'It was a man's voice I heard, not one I recognised. He said he was taking pictures for the Country Club album.' Her eyes were like little bird baths, overfilled after heavy rain, water dripping from the bottom lids. Her voice, though, was white hot with anger. 'A damn dirty trick! Whoever did this is the scum of the Earth!' Her chest heaved. 'The last words he said before…before the shooting started, were…*Say cheese*. Can you fookin' believe it!'

Jack never took his eyes off Dervla while Taylor scribbled notes; there was something riveting about the woman, mesmerising. Not in a physical-attraction kind of way, although Jack had to concede she was stunning by most standards. It was something else he couldn't put his finger on. 'Incredible,' said Jack.

'Fiendish,' echoed Taylor. She rested her notepad on the wooden picnic table. 'I'm going to ask the most obvious question first. Who do you think could have been behind this atrocity?'

Dervla ran fingers through her hair, reached for her mug of tea, then retracted her hand. 'I have a couple of theories.'

'Your husband?'

'What? Heavens no! You think he'd arrange to be shot in the fookin' stomach? He almost died! Anyway, Lachie knew about me and Paul. In fact, we had his blessing.'

'Excuse me?' said Jack, leaning back and folding his arms. 'I find that hard to believe. Back at the hospital he was most distressed you hadn't come to visit him. He didn't let on, but I could see the sadness in his eyes. If that pissed him off, being cuckolded would…'

'For heaven's sake, Detective. Don't read too much into that! Yes, Lachie loves me, and I him, in my way. But I'm more what you'd call a trophy wife.'

'Who else knew about your intimate relationship with Paul Keenan?'

'Oh, no one officially. But I'm sure many had their suspicions. We didn't flaunt our love for each other, but sometimes, you know, you can't help yourself with a touch in public. Standing too close to each other. Maybe a sneaky kiss in a car park someone may have witnessed. We were *very* careful, though. On the record, it was only Lachie who knew for definite.'

'Why are you lying, Dervla?' said Jack. 'His ex-wife knows.'

'Sabrina? That bitch might suspect, but she wouldn't have any proof. Like I said, we were careful as could be to keep everything quiet. For Lachie's sake.'

Jack scratched his head. 'Now, don't get me wrong, but as a warm-blooded heterosexual male, I know how jealous some men can get when they find out their women have been playing around. We've all seen what violent things they can do. The courts are flat out keeping up with domestic violence problems. And very often infidelity is a factor.'

'It wasn't playing around! Didn't you hear what I said? He knew about it!' Her tone then dropped from almost hysterical to conversational. 'It's not nice to say this, but Lachie had… problems in the bedroom department.'

'From the start of your relationship with Mr Morris?'

'No. It came on a while after we met.'

'And how *did* you meet?' said Taylor.

'Four years ago Lachie came to Ireland on a golfing holiday with his eldest son, Mitchell. A lovely man, he is. Just like his dad. Anyway, Lachie had recently been widowed, lost his wife Tessa to breast cancer. To get his mind off things he took a golfing holiday to the UK and Ireland.' Dervla painted a story of an innocent acquaintance that blossomed into something more. A friendship that deepened, culminating in Morris popping the question the day before returning to Australia. She'd not given an immediate answer, said yes after a two-month wait for the old boy, who dropped everything to fly back to Ireland and marry Dervla in a hastily arranged ceremony.

'Very romantic,' said Jack dryly. 'But let's circle back to your husband's sexual issues. It must have been frustrating for a young and vital woman like yourself.' Jack could almost hear Taylor's eyes rolling in their sockets as he pursued this line of questioning.

Dervla, though, felt no embarrassment about the topic. 'All was good for the first two years. I was mighty impressed at how a man his age could…you know. And even though there was the big age gap, it never bothered me. I found him a rather attractive man. Still do. But then something happened, it was like a switch got turned off. His mojo was gone. He tried pills, even painful injections for a while, the poor love. But in the end he gave up.'

Jack wasn't sure if he imagined it, but her fleeting half-smile said to him And despite what I said about him being attractive, I'm bloody glad he gave up trying.

'And that's when he introduced me to Paul.'

'I'm sorry?'

'He introduced us. They've been friends for years, both members of Rotary and the Country Club.'

'So, what,' said Jack. 'The old boy suggested his mate take you for a lover?'

'Not in so many words. It was kind of…implied…that Lachie wouldn't mind if Jack looked after my…needs.'

Jack stood, paced back and forth. 'No. I think you're rationalising this in your own mind. Making excuses for your infidelity.' He could feel Taylor's eyes directing a laser stare at him, but it didn't matter. She was lying and he needed to expose it, grief and shock notwithstanding. 'I saw the expression on your husband's face when he understood you hadn't been to check on him, instead you got the hell out of the hospital and…' He heard a crashing sound, the clatter of a chair on the terracotta tiles.

'Jack!'

He spun around. Taylor was supporting the woman by the back of the neck as she convulsed on the floor, her body jerking like she'd been electrocuted. Dribble leaked from the corners of Dervla's lips. He was right about Taylor's eyes. They were burning a hole through his head. 'Call an ambulance, for fuck's sake!'

JACK STORMED into Pereira's office on the ground floor. 'Nice work on the triaging, pal!'

The doctored carefully put down a sheet of paper, peered over the top of his glasses. 'I beg your pardon?'

'Dervla Morris is back at *your* hospital. She threw some kind of fit, rolling all over the floor she was, foaming at the mouth like she had rabies. She's in the ED as we speak, hooked up to all manner of monitors. My colleague is sitting in a corridor waiting to hear what's going on.' He jabbed a finger in the air. 'Letting her go home was a mistake, sunshine. You should have known she had epilepsy. Don't you check your patients' effin' health records?'

'I'm sure the treating staff would have asked her the standard questions. Let me see what's going on.' Pereira made a phone call while Jack stood, hands on hips. The office was as pristine as Jack's desk was chaotic. Hardback medical tomes crammed onto shelves. The top row had little skulls either end to stop the books from falling over. It wouldn't have surprised the DS to learn they were the shrunken heads of Pereira's enemies.

'Well?' Jack said at the end of the phone conversation.

'Dervla Morris was asked on admission if she had any conditions, she said no. We have to take her word on it.'

'She barely knew what her own name was at the time. What about looking up her details? It's all on a thumping great database, innit.'

Pereira removed his glasses, wiped them on a cloth, slowly placed them back on his head. The DS's intimidatory behaviour wasn't washing with the doctor. 'It's not our business to pry unnecessarily. She came in suffering severe shock following a traumatic incident. No fits were observed then, so nothing was suspected. The nurse I spoke to told me Dervla's not been admitted to any hospital since moving to

Australia. Her record basically comprises a compulsory medical she underwent in Ireland before she applied for her permanent residency visa. The woman is healthy as an ox with no underlying problems.'

'Then what's the deal with this fit she's just had?'

'Most likely a trauma-induced non-epileptic seizure. But I'm not the examining physician, so that's speculation.'

'Meaning it's the waiting game for us again, right?'

'Not necessarily,' Pereira tilted his head slightly and grinned.

'Come again?'

'You could always go and question some other witnesses while Ms Morris recovers. Give me a call tomorrow and I'll give you the latest. Here.' He handed Jack a business card. 'Ring me directly on my mobile.'

Jack let out a sigh. The smug git was offering career advice without being asked. The worst part, he was also correct. The DS thanked the doctor for his time, gathered Taylor from the corridor where she was chatting to a girlfriend on a messenger app, and headed out to speak with Michael Jay Salesa, erstwhile close colleague of the deceased.

Chapter Nineteen

THE SUN SPARKLED off the water at the Yorkville marina, little beads of reflected light twinkled at the detectives as they strode along the boardwalk. Here and there leaked engine oil formed multi-coloured blotches on the surface, like Rorschach patterns. Yachts, motorboats and other craft of various shapes and sizes rocked gently back and forth on their moorings. The cawing of seagulls, the soft whistle of the breeze through ropes and wires, the occasional flapping of ensigns gave the location an idyllic feel.

The detectives ducked down a concrete pier that branched off from the main one, counted off the boats until they reached *Hammerhead*. They weren't a hundred percent sure the man they wanted to speak with would be here, but it was worth a try.

'Geez, it's much bigger than I expected,' said Taylor.

Jack choked off an inappropriate retort and said, 'It's is 'n all.'

The luxury catamaran was not only big, it reeked of money. At around 50 feet in length and shiny as a diamond, the twin-hulled fibreglass vessel must have cost a pretty penny, Jack thought to himself. On the stern deck sat the man they were looking for, in the company of another man and a woman. All three were sitting on wraparound benches on the spacious deck, imbibing something from champagne flutes.

'Hello,' Jack called from the pier. 'We're looking for Michael Salesa. Would one of you be him?' He already knew the answer after a quick Google search turned up many photos of the man. Quite the social butterfly.

'That'd be me.' Salesa grinned amiably as he looked up at the visitors. 'And I'm guessing you're a pair of cops, right?'

'Nice guess,' said Taylor, extending her ID as Jack did likewise. 'Mind if we come aboard for a chat?'

'It's not me you need to ask.' He took a long draft from the champagne glass, placed it back on a highly polished table affixed to the deck, where it joined a bucket of peeled prawns, a wicker basket of sliced baguettes, crackers and several plates of tropical fruit.

'It's fine, Mike,' said an obese man in a broad-brimmed straw hat, his hairy paunch straining at the buttons of a gaudy Hawaiian shirt. 'Lulu and I can make ourselves scarce for a while. She's keen to do a spot of shopping at the mall.' The man led the woman, angular features and severely tied-back blonde hair, off the boat and down the pier towards the exit to the town centre.

Once on board, Jack decided to go for the jugular. 'You think it's appropriate to be indulging like this,' Jack gestured towards the abundance of goodies on the table 'when a man you used to work with has only just died? What about some decorum?'

Salesa shrugged his slim shoulders. He sported a thick

crop of brown hair, standing up like a wall thanks to generous amounts of product. His ears protruded slightly, giving the impression of car doors slightly ajar. His eyes were hidden behind a large pair of designer sunglasses. 'This get-together was planned ages ago. Think I should be shedding crocodile tears for a man who despised me?'

'Perhaps not,' said Jack, helping himself to a plump strawberry from a silver platter. He chewed it thoughtfully and not without appreciation. The berry was juicy and bursting with flavour. After wiping his face with a paper napkin he resumed the interview. 'Still, this could almost be regarded as celebrating his death. What do you think, Claudia?'

Taylor took a seat on the bench opposite Salesa, pulled out her notebook. 'A casual observer could interpret it that way.' She paused, scribbled something in her book. 'But if Mr Salesa says he has a reason, then let's give him the benefit of the doubt.' She tapped a pen on the edge of the table. 'It's rather warm out. Any chance we could have a glass of water?' She gestured towards a full crystal carafe with slices of lemon floating in it.

'Of course!' Salesa leaned across the table, poured a glass for each of the detectives. His hands were steady, his overall manner confident. Clearly not worried about the presence of the police on the yacht, nor of their questions.

'So,' Jack continued. 'We've been given information that you harboured a serious grudge against Paul Keenan after he fired you.'

'I did, I'm not going to lie. Since he's dead now, I guess you could say that grudge is buried with him.' A hint of a smile curled his mouth. He raised his glass, 'To Paul!'

Jack shook his head. 'What's with the theatrics,

sunshine? Apparently you had a very good reason to kill Keenan. Left jobless in a volatile labour market.'

Salesa tilted his head back and laughed. 'Look, I'm doing fine. How much do you think this pretty little yacht costs, huh?'

'What's that got to do with anything?' said Jack. 'You aren't the owner. That other guy is.' He pointed in the direction the man had headed with his female companion.

'Correct. Quite the detective, aren't you. But I'm in the process of buying it from him. A bargain at a snick under $450,000, wouldn't you say?'

'Where'd you get that kind of money?' Jack screwed up an eye.

'Do I have to tell you?'

'No. But if you don't I'll drag you down to the station where you'll be subjected to a full-on formal interview. Or I could skip that part and get a search warrant from the magistrate. Right now, you're shaping as our number one suspect. We have a credible witness, reckons you said you'd *make the arsehole pay* for firing you.'

Salesa swallowed hard. 'Yeah, I may have said that, but it was just words, you know.'

'Really?' said Taylor.

'You wanna know where I got the money? All right, I'll tell you. I inherited a pile when my grandmother died. At the time Keenan sacked me, the will was being contested by my bitch of a cousin. She thought she deserved the lot. For a while things were looking uncertain, so losing the job kinda rocked me. Maybe I said things in anger about Keenan I shouldn't have. But,' he raised his glass, 'the decision went in my favour and I got the bulk of the estate. Enough to pay out my mortgage thirty years early and...

indulge in a little whimsy.' He broke into a broad, self-satisfied grin that Jack wanted to wipe away with a left hook.

'Why exactly did Keenan fire you?' said Taylor. 'Incompetence?'

'No way!' The word had pricked Salesa's pride. 'I was bringing in extra business to the bank. New loans, corporate accounts, you name it.'

'Then why?' said Jack. 'Anything to do with his dalliance with…'

'Dervla Morris? Nah, I'm not the blackmailing type.'

Jack folded his arms across his chest. 'She reckons no one knew about the affair.'

'Ha! She's delusional.' Salesa shook his head slightly. 'It's the worst kept secret in Yorkville.'

'I'll ask again,' said Taylor. 'Why did Paul Keenan fire you?'

Salesa weighed his response for a moment. 'It was one of those personality things.'

'Meaning?' said Jack.

'He didn't like me as a person. To tell you the truth, his behaviour verged on bullying.'

'I don't believe you.' Jack took a sip of water. 'You could have sued him if he sacked you without a valid reason.'

'Oh, don't worry. I was sharpening those legal knives, so to speak. If I'd lost the contest over grandma's will, I was gonna set the lawyers onto Keenan so fast he wouldn't have known what hit him…oh, that's probably a bit off right now, but you get my drift.'

Before Jack could comment, a small drone flew across the rubble-mound breakwater at the entrance to the marina. It maintained a steady height of around 50 metres before it disappeared behind a line of trees at the edge of a small headland. 'Know anything about those things?'

'Bugger all. Never flown one in my life.'
'Know anyone who does?'
'Yes, as it happens.'
'Who?'
'Paul Keenan.'

Jack sat back in his seat. 'You suggesting he committed suicide in such a contrived fashion?'

'No. You asked me a straightforward question and I gave you an answer.' Salesa poured himself another drink of sparkling wine, offered the cops one, they declined. 'I don't think Keenan killed himself. His interest in drones dropped off over time. He used to go flying every weekend and post the videos online. If you look at his old Instagram posts you'll see all these cheesy nature videos set to music. I don't reckon he'd been doing it for at least a year, though. Much more interested in playing golf. Especially with the Morrises. No prizes for guessing why.'

'Where were you yesterday between 8:00am and midday?' said Taylor.

'That's easy.' Salesa placed two tiger prawns on a plate, squeezed the juice from a wedge of lemon over the top. 'Here on *Hammerhead* negotiating the final terms of the purchase. The owner and his partner Lulu will confirm we spent the entire day together. We sailed up the coast to Cairns and back. Beautiful day it was!'

'Right,' said Jack. 'We'll be looking further into your affairs, talking to your co-workers from the bank to get their angle on your bullying accusations.'

'Hey.' Salesa held his arms out, palms up. 'Talk to whoever you want. I'm an open book. And if you feel the need to question me formally, no worries. As much as I hated Keenan for firing me without cause, I'd never want to see anyone murdered. Now, as a sign of my good faith, can

I offer the two of you a little trip out to sea? We could sail across to Crocodile Island and be back in under two hours. I'll ring the owner and let him know.' He already had his phone out, ready to make the call.

'How much have you had to drink?' said Taylor, tucking her notepad into her handbag.

'Oh, yeah.' Salesa offered a guilty smile, pocketed the mobile. 'Maybe some other time?'

Jack jangled his car keys in his pocket. It was time to move on. His instincts told him Salesa was on the level. But, like always, every claim would be double and triple checked. And if he came up clean, maybe the bloke could take him and Skye on a fishing charter when she came for a holiday next Christmas. If he passed a breathalyser test, that was. Jack led Taylor onto the gangway, then turned to offer some parting words to Salesa. As the man poured himself yet another glass of champagne, Jack said: 'If I get word this vessel has left Far North Queensland waters before the murder enquiry is completed, I'll be coming after you.'

'Understood.' Salesa tipped Jack a friendly finger-to-the-forehead salute and, with a slightly unsteady gait, clambered down a short flight of stairs into the cabin of the vessel. Jack had taken five strides when Salesa's voice rang out. 'Hey, Detective!'

Jack turned on his heel. 'What?'

The man was wobbly after the amount of booze he'd tucked away, his words beginning to slur. 'How d'ya know where to find me?'

The DS tapped the side of his nose, said, 'Trade secret', and began to walk away.

'Come on, how?' The man spoke through hands cupped like a megaphone.

The cops pulled up again, this time Taylor turned to

face Salesa. 'You posted a couple of photos of *Hammerhead* on Instagram with the tagline, "New addition to the family. Watch this space". Ring a bell?'

'Oh yeah,' he said with a tipsy chuckle. 'I'd forgotten about that.'

'Policing's so much easier with people like you assisting us without even trying.' She gave the man a wink.

As the detectives strode back to their vehicle, Jack smiled to himself, savouring Taylor's sweet parting rebuke.

Chapter Twenty

CONSTABLE KYLIE SMITH tapped on the door of the double-storey cedar A-frame home. A dog barked from the backyard, setting off a chorus of mutts in the street. She glanced around at the front yard and marvelled, and not in a good way. The shambolic mess made her double check she'd got the right address. Surely a golf course superintendent would maintain his front lawn in better condition that this? Bare patches, clumps of flowering weeds, piles of broken bricks. She had no more time to think about this paradox when Ruby Brownstone answered the door.

'Yes?' Ruby's dark brown eyes gave Smith the once over. When men ogled her body, Smith usually wanted to punch them in the face. When Ruby did it, a tingle ran along her spine. A hair flick and a lick of the lips from Ruby, who wore shredded jeans and a loose-fitting white tank top. A swallow tattoo adorned one arm, an eagle with wings outstretched the other.

'Ah…hi there,' Smith stammered, then introduced herself.

'The Inspector told me a Detective Taylor would be dropping by.'

'She's busy chasing up an important lead with Detective Sergeant Lisbon. Any chance I could come in and ask a few questions?'

Consternation furrowed Ruby's brow. 'Sure. Is it me you want to speak to or my dad?'

You, Smith thought to herself, definitely you. She said, 'Both of you, if that's OK. We're trying to get a handle on what happened out on the golf course yesterday.'

'What a tragedy. Me and dad are still coming to terms with it. If they didn't rely on him so much to keep the course in good order, he'd be taking leave.' She waved a hand down the corridor. 'Follow me. Dad's out in his shed tinkering around with something.' She flashed an amicable smile, revealing even white teeth, although slightly prominent incisors gave her a mildly vampiric look. The name Ruby itself hinted at red blood. *You can bite my neck, Ruby.* 'Mind your step, officer. I've been meaning to pick up the toys, but haven't got around to it.'

A toddler's cheeky face peaked at Smith from behind a kitchen chair. The child, clad only in a disposable nappy, squealed before running away on bandy legs into an adjoining room. 'That's Jessica. She's a handful, but I love her to bits.'

Smith scratched the fantasy of Ruby from her mind. Such a young kid in the house, most likely means there is or was a male partner somewhere. Wrong orientation, but also a blessing in disguise. Chatting up witnesses wasn't considered appropriate police behaviour.

Ruby led Smith down a small set of stairs, along an overgrown garden path to a large free-standing shed. 'Dad, the cops are here!' Her voice was nonchalant, almost jokey, as if the visitor were of no more concern than a girl guide selling cookies. 'Excuse me while I put the little one to bed.' Ruby disappeared inside the house as Smith turned to see her father's shadowy form moving about inside the Colorbond steel shed.

Reg Brownstone emerged from the building, almost as big as the house, wiping his hands on a dirty rag, a grey-muzzled fox terrier by his side. A wiry, sinewy man with dark leathery skin, Brownstone wore tattered dungarees, a pair of well-worn Blundstone work boots and a suspicious smile. 'Yeah?' The single syllable dragged out slowly in the North Queensland country fashion.

'Is there somewhere we can sit down for a bit?' said Smith. 'I've got a few questions I'd like to ask you, Mr Brownstone.'

He nodded understandingly, repeated the "yeah", but even longer this time. 'I knew youse'd be wanting a word.'

'You did?'

'Mmm. You prob'ly reckon I had it in for Keenan after what he said about me at that dinner.' He placed his hands on his hips, not quite defiance but heading that way.

'Did you?'

'No way. C'mon, let's go inside.' He commanded the dog to lie on a raised canvas bed by the back door; it obediently scampered off and curled itself into a ball, eyelids twitching.

Brownstone excused himself, went to the bathroom to wash the grime of engine oil from his hands, returned in a fresh shirt, shorts and flip flops. 'Right, let's get this nonsense over with.' He scraped a wooden chair towards himself, spun it around and sat on in backwards. Smith grinned, remembering how DS Lisbon often did the same thing, and took a seat opposite the man. Brownstone's gnarled fingers tapped the table. 'Before you arks where I was yesterday, I'll tell ya. Here at home from dawn till dusk, nowhere near the golf course. It was my day off and I had jobs to do around the place.'

'Can anyone substantiate that claim?' said Smith, gratefully accepting a glass of cold orange juice from Ruby, who then poured one for herself and her father. Probably homemade – the constable couldn't help noticing a tree beside the shed laden with ripe oranges. Ruby leaned her back against the kitchen sink, arms crossed. Smith glanced at the woman to gauge her attitude – impassive.

'Yep,' said Brownstone. 'And it ain't a claim, it's a fact. My neighbour Alan Lundgren was here giving me a hand patching up a cuppla holes in the perimeter fence. We've been having trouble with wallabies getting in and eating me veggies. I'm dead-set against shootin' the buggers, even if I lose some of me crops. But enough's enough, hey? Go talk to Alan, he'll back me up.'

Smith nodded. Was he emphasising his humane side to deflect guilt? 'I'll certainly do that.' She paused, glanced at Ruby again to see her staring straight back with unblinking eyes. Smith took a sip of the juice: not strained perfectly, rather pulpy compared to the supermarket stuff. Still, it tasted like heaven in a glass. What sort of taste would her next question leave in Reg Brownstone's mouth? Only one way to find out. 'You know how to fly drones, don't you? In fact–'

'I'll just stop you there.'

'Why?'

'I gave it away after I had a couple of minor crashes, and then a real bad one when a drone smashed into a tree. Totally destroyed. Luckily, the club's insurance covered the cost of replacement.' He took a deep breath. 'I heard a rumour some prick on the board wanted to dock me fucken pay…oh, sorry, pardon my French.'

'It's OK. I've heard a lot worse than that, believe me. Does the club still use drones?'

'Yep. They were going to outsource the work, but one of the young fellas on my staff turned out to be an expert pilot. He does it when we have to get some photos or video.'

'The man's name?'

'Errol Sibley.'

'Would Errol have any reason to want to kill Paul Keenan?'

A strong headshake. 'Not a chance. The lad's basically a labourer who helps out with heavy lifting, mowing, all the menial jobs. We haven't put a drone up for over a month, not since the new works were approved.'

'Not even to check progress?'

'Nope. Maybe when we get to the halfway stage, depends what management wants to do.'

'And where is the drone kept? At the golf club?'

'Nah. I keep it locked up in the shed. Wanna have a look?'

Brownstone led the Constable outside with Ruby tagging along behind; dad's minder, Smith thought. She could sense a real bond between the two, something she missed out on in her own dysfunctional family. She hadn't been close to either parent. Never mind, *play the hand you're dealt* had been her lifelong motto. Reg's flip flops kicked up dust on the dirt floor of his tin shed; they passed wooden saw horses straddled by pieces of four-by-two timber, a lathe on a bench together with a drop saw and some hand tools. In a far corner, a mower and brush cutter. The placed smelled wonderful to Smith; scents of wood shavings, grass clippings, turpentine, petrol. Strangely, there was a greater sense of order in this cramped space than there was in the garden.

At the very back of the shed, Reg stopped in front of a solid steel cabinet. He punched a code into a panel, opened the door and reached inside. Over his shoulder Smith could see two rifles set in a rack, with space for more weapons if necessary.

'I thought you said you didn't like shooting animals,' said Smith.

'I don't.' His back still turned to Smith, Brownstone pulled out a drone from a shelf at the top of the safe – much smaller than the armoured one Trevarthen had found on the Internet. He turned to face Smith. 'Ruby and I do a bit of clay pigeon shooting now and again. By law we have to keep the rifles in a gun safe. Ain't that right, love?'

Smith glanced at Ruby, who smiled, showing those little vampire teeth again. 'Yep. Wanna try it out with me one day, officer?'

The constable's heart fluttered. 'I only saw two rifles in the safe. Does your husband participate in the sport, or is it just you and your dad?'

Father and daughter burst out laughing. 'My little girl's not interested in the fellas,' said Reg. 'A real tom-boy, she is. That's why she's so handy about the property, and on the golf course.'

Ruby blushed. 'Come off it, dad.'

'It's true. I'd struggle without you.'

'But the baby?' said Smith.

'She's my sister's child. Abby and her bloke took a trip to Fiji, left the little tyke with me.'

Smith's heart raced. *Concentrate on the case.* 'Let's get back to the drone. It looks more like a toy than a professional device.'

'Don't be fooled by its size,' said Reg. 'The Phantom 4 Pro does the job it's designed to do.'

'May I?' Smith held out her hand. She hefted the device. Unlike the killer drone, which was black, this one was white. She guessed it weighed no more than 1.5 kilograms and was about 30 cm across the diagonal. Unlikely you could modify this one to carry a heavy semi-automatic pistol.

'Careful how you handle it,' said Brownstone. 'That baby costs about $3,000 out of the box.'

Smith quickly handed the craft back to Reg like it was a red-belly black snake. She wasn't sure the QPS would cover the cost if she damaged the machine. Reg turned to put it back in the cabinet when Smith thought grabbing a couple of photos couldn't hurt. Unlikely to have any bearing on the case, but she could at least show the Inspector she was using her initiative. Reg obligingly placed the drone on a bench, Smith snapped away on her mobile from a couple of angles.

With the machine back in the safe, Smith pressed on. 'OK, let's assume you were able to wear the…criticism… levelled at you by Keenan and you had nothing to do with the attack.'

'Assume nuthin. That's the way it is!' said Reg. Another check on Ruby – nodding support for her dad.

'Fair enough. Do you have any theories yourself?'

'None. The bloke was a pain in the arse, but he never done anything that deserved being shot for. Same goes for Lachlan Morris. To be honest with you, most of the gossip that goes on between the members doesn't make its way down to us shit-kickers. I've got zero interest in their personal lives.'

Smith contemplatively ran her top teeth over her bottom lip. Brownstone was a working-class man to the core; she couldn't imagine him mixing with the Country Club members apart from a friendly wave and some golf-related chit chat on the course. Nevertheless, she'd check in with neighbour Alan Lunegren to confirm the man's alibi. And pay Errol Sibley a visit.

Ruby accompanied Smith to the front gate, closed it behind the constable as she ambled across the street to the police vehicle. 'Hey,' she called from the gate. 'I wasn't kidding about going clay pigeon shooting.'

Her heart in her mouth Smith replied, 'Not sure it's my thing, but I'd be willing to give it a go.'

'Nice one.' Ruby winked, turned and walked back up the untidy garden path.

Chapter Twenty-One

THE CALL CAME over the radio as Constable Aden Trevarthen was pulling into the driveway of the ramshackle government Housing Commission home.

'Yes, Damien? This better be good. I took too long to get here as it is. Now the woman—'

'She's changed her mind.'

'What?'

'The woman rang back to say she didn't want to proceed with the complaint. Her husband didn't hit her, she reckons she made it all up.'

'Let's see about that!'

Five minutes later Trevarthen was back in the vehicle, fuming. With real domestic violence cases through the roof, fake call outs leached resources away from where they were most needed. If not for the squalid mess inside the house and the fact the woman was clearly drug-addled and hopeless, he would have charged her with wasting police time.

But there were bigger fish to fry. He buckled up, switched on the engine, engaged reverse and gunned the car out of the driveway, narrowly missing a child's upturned tricycle. An opportunity had opened to assist with the murder enquiry. Detectives Lisbon and Taylor were busy at the marina and Jack had sent a text asking Trevarthen to check up on Rohan Keenan. He flicked the indicator, turned left onto an arterial road, popped on the blues and twos just for fun. Zipping past well-behaved motorists who politely gave way, he made the call, confirmed the man was at home, and made for the residence of the deceased's brother.

ROHAN KEENAN SHOOK Constable Trevarthen's hand like the cop was an old friend he hadn't clapped eyes on for years. Keenan's face was long and sagging, dark eyes a chasm of confusion. 'Please, come in. You want to speak to my son, I gather?'

'Actually, it's you I'm interested in talking to first.'

'It won't take long, will it? Only…'

'I hope not. However we're conducting a murder investigation, so it'll take as long as necessary.' Trevarthen had learned a thing or two from Jack about being direct.

'Yes, yes. I understand. We're all in deep shock. I'm trying to get my head around what to do next.' He wrung and shook out his hands like he'd washed them in cold water. 'It's Jasper I'm worried about. He's taken it very hard. Let's talk inside, hey?'

In a sunken loungeroom with a 1970s feel – velour sofas and armchairs, beanbags and lava lamps – Rohan Keenan touched on the grief his family of three had endured over the last 36 hours or so. Rohan sat in the middle of the sofa, Trevarthen took a seat opposite in a plush recliner. There was a lever on the right-hand side that would have tilted the seat to a lovely relaxing position, but the officer overcame the temptation to get too comfy. Not a professional look. He sat up straighter than a schoolboy trying to avoid detention.

'Has there been an autopsy?' said Rohan. 'No one's contacted me about identifying the body. Can you tell me who did that? Was it Sabrina?'

'Yes, an autopsy *has* been carried out, but since the cause of death was clear it was a standard one. Under the circumstances, a formal ID was deemed unnecessary. There was no doubt who the victim was.'

'Oh, boy.' Rohan expelled a sharp breath. 'What next then?'

'Someone will have to arrange for a burial or cremation. Will that be you or…?'

'Excuse me?' He shook his head slowly. 'Wow. I hadn't thought about it.'

'Two officers have spoken with Sabrina. She's refusing to help out in this regard.'

'Yeah, I don't doubt it. Paul's split with her was hardly amicable.' He stared at the ceiling for a moment. 'Geez, when I think of the state of this family I guess *I'll* have to take responsibility for the funeral. Shit, I don't even know where to start.'

'I'll forward you some information on funeral homes. Hopefully the coroner will release the body quickly and you can get on with things.'

'Not too soon, I hope. It hasn't even sunk in properly.'

'I'd like to ask you about your son. You said he's taking the death of his uncle badly.'

Rohan explained that since Jasper's mate delivered him home yesterday afternoon, the lad had shut himself away in the downstairs rumpus room, playing computer games for hours on end. A social worker had turned up soon thereafter, thanks to Inspector Batista's intervention, but Jasper told her to piss off. 'Since then he won't speak, refuses to eat, only offers grunts and tears when spoken to. He'd rather hold that damned Nintendo controller for comfort than talk to me.' Keenan gazed out an open window, fine lace curtain flapping in a slight breeze, then looked back at Trevarthen. 'It'll take some time for him to get over it, I suppose.'

'Years.' Trevarthen almost barked the word, then softened his tone. 'Would you like me to look into some grief counselling for him?'

The man's eyes brightened for a second. 'Can you do that?'

Trevarthen gave a little nod. 'I'll make a phone call after we're done, see what I can arrange. Hopefully he'll be more inclined to accept professional help in a couple of days.'

'Thank you.'

'And your wife? How's she holding up?'

'Not great. She took a couple of tranquilisers last night, been snoozing all day.'

'Were she and Paul close?' Trevarthen thought it odd a relative by marriage – a sister-in-law – would be so rattled that she needed medication. Had the murdered banker been spreading his affections further afield than Dervla Morris?

Rohan gestured dismissively in the direction of a hallway, at the end of which presumably lay the bedroom Penny was hiding in. 'She's an emotional person. When our dog was euthanised she didn't emerge from under the doona for a week.' He shook his head. 'Even a soppy film will have her mourning dead fictional characters for days.'

'And you?'

Rohan sniffed back a tear. A dry one, Trevarthen observed. 'My head's a mess, I admit.'

'Would you also like to see a counsellor?'

He waved the offer away. 'I'll manage.' Rohan explained how he hadn't been close to his brother in recent years. The opposite, in fact. They began a feud several years ago that they never got around to ending. 'I'm angry with myself for being so bloody stubborn.' He thumped a fist into an open palm. A tad melodramatic, Trevarthen thought. 'Now he's gone and it's too late.' He rubbed his eyes with the heels of his palms.

'What was the disagreement about?'

Rohan's mouth twisted into a distorted ellipse, like he was about to suffer a mini-stroke. 'Huh...what?'

'The feud. Are you OK?'

'Yeah, sorry. Dunno what came over me there.' The weird spasming of the guy's mouth was over as quickly as it began.

'Sorry,' said Trevarthen. 'I thought you...anyway, let's get back to this fight you had with your brother'.

A sign of hesitation, perhaps regret he'd brought the matter up. 'Is it actually relevant?'

'Could be.'

'I'm rather embarrassed by it, to be honest.'

Trevarthen gave a soft chuckle of reassurance. 'I've heard pretty much everything in this line of work. The best policy is to get it all out in the open straight up. If our detectives later think you've been hiding something...well... it might look odd.'

'Right, understood.' He took a measured breath. 'We were at a family gathering for some cousin or other's engagement. I caught Paul making a pass at my wife but he flat out denied it, used the old "it's not what it looks like" line you hear in all the movies. I knew he was lying. Paul was practically massaging her thigh underneath a table. He was still with Sabrina at the time.'

'I can see how you would've got the hump over that. And that incident led to a heated argument?'

'I won't go into all the details, but we almost came to blows over it across the dinner table. But with the passage of time, and now this tragedy, I'm thinking maybe there was nothing in it after all.' The expression on Rohan Keenan's face looked like true remorse. He stared through the window again. 'I don't know. To this day my wife denies they were up to anything, but I guess I'll never know the truth.'

Trevarthen took out a notepad, jotted details of the filial spat. 'Your son Jasper was pretty close to him.'

Keenan nodded. Although they lived in the same town, separated by a few blocks, Paul hadn't set foot in his brother's house for over three years. 'But I couldn't deny Jasper having contact with his uncle. They got on like a house on fire.'

'How did your son take to the possibility that very same uncle touched up his mum?'

'He reckons I blew the whole thing out of proportion. And,' he shrugged, 'maybe I did. I just don't know anymore.' He paused for a moment, picked up a wrapped sweet from a bowl on a coffee table, placed it gently in front of himself and promptly ignored it. 'It was a shared interest in golf that forged their friendship, so to speak. For me it's the most boring pastime imaginable. Who was it that said golf was a good walk spoiled?'

Trevarthen shrugged. Trivia was not his strong point.

'Mark Twain,' said Keenan after a short, thoughtful

pause. 'Or was it Winston Churchill? Never mind, whoever said it was spot on. Boring as bat shit.'

Trevarthen decided to push on with the theme of infidelity. 'You know, I can't blame you for suspecting your wife was playing around with your brother. Especially since he later took up with Dervla Morris.'

'Hmmm. I've heard those rumours.'

'No, sir. Fact. She admitted it. Told DS Lisbon that Paul was, and I quote, *the man I love*. His ex-wife knows all about it, too. So, it seems your brother had a bit of form. Perhaps your instinct about him and…Penny was it?…was correct after all.'

'What can I say?' He turned his palms upward. 'I don't want to speculate any further on these matters.' Rohan blinked hard, twice, like a light bulb went off in his head. 'You know, I'm feeling rather drained. If you need to ask me any more questions, let's do it another time.'

'I was hoping to—'

'No, I'd like you to leave now.'

'What about Jasper? Can I have a word with him?'

'Sorry, no. But if you could arrange that counsellor, I'd be most grateful. Get them to give me a call and we can set up a time.' A forced smile ruffled the man's brushy moustache.

'Your wife. Can I—'

'Like I said, some other time.' Rohan stood abruptly and hurried Trevarthen to the front door. 'It's Sunday evening, and I have to get ready for work.'

'What do you do?'

'What's that got to do with anything?' He didn't wait for a reply. 'If you really need to know, I'm a shift worker. I was made redundant from my previous position as an insurance broker and now I'm reduced to stacking goods on supermarket shelves.' His eyes welled up with moisture.

Trevarthen ignored his play for sympathy. 'Please let me speak with your wife and son. In your presence if you like. I promise to be quick and out of your hair as quick as I can.'

'Nope.' He shook his head. 'I don't consent to any more of this. Please leave.'

Back in the car, Trevarthen texted Jack a summary of what had gone down. He emphasised that Rohan pretended to cry when speaking of his brother's death but the real tears came when speaking of his own problems. It might mean nothing, but still worth a mention. As he reflected on the hasty way the victim's brother had hurried him out the door, Trevarthen could only scratch his head. He waited patiently at a busy T-junction for a south-bound road train to pass, nosed the vehicle out into the late-afternoon traffic then barrelled down the highway, eager to write up the details of the strange interview into a report while everything was fresh in his mind.

A buzz in his pocket was a reply from DS Lisbon. It contained the address of a Hubert Johnson and a request to talk to him before ending his shift. Constable Semmens had been tasked with this job, but he'd witnessed a serious road rage incident and had to intervene. Trevarthen sighed. The report on Rohan Keenan would have to wait.

Chapter Twenty-Two

'I DIDN'T EXPECT to see you so soon.' Hubert "Bert" Johnson beamed a welcoming smile with such enthusiasm Trevarthen wondered if the man's clacking false teeth would leap out of his mouth. 'The detective who called me said you'd be around later.'

Trevarthen glanced at his watch. Almost 6:00pm. Grateful for the Sunday overtime rate, he was nevertheless keen for the day to end so he could hit the gym. He'd agreed to a bout of sparring with DS Lisbon at the Iron Horse fitness centre. If this interview went quickly, he could still make it by 7:30pm. Lisbon had the measure of Trevarthen last time, and the time before that, although Trevarthen was improving with every session. But the reality was, the canny detective had years of fighting experience under his belt that could never be overhauled.

'Well, I'm here now. Mind if I fire off a cuppla questions?'

'Not at all. Glad to assist the police any way I can.' The man sat opposite Trevarthen behind a green Formica table with a riveted metal border that might have been as old as the weatherboard house. Johnson's blue-rinse-haired wife hovered around, fussing with cake and a pot of tea complete with knitted cosy.

'Why did you and your party flee from the golf course yesterday?'

'Simple.' The man's posture stiffened. 'I didn't want to die. Instinct kicked in. The sounds I heard yesterday, the crackle of gunfire, it was like I was back in Long Tan.'

'I beg your pardon? Where?'

'Vietnam, sonny. I knew the education system in this country was rubbish, but I didn't think it was that bad. Everyone should know about the Battle of Long Tan.'

Trevarthen thought Long Tan sounded like a type of beauty cream, and inwardly he was ashamed of his ignorance. 'I guess they should.'

'Damn right. Anyway, when I heard the bangs I knew it was gunfire. When the cop confirmed it, well, all the memories of the battlefield came flooding back. I told my friends there was some bad shit going on and we were best out of there!' Johnson's slightly rheumy eyes were wide as he recalled the events.

'Right.' Trevarthen took a bite of lamington, spilling desiccated coconut on his shirt. As he chewed, he took in his surroundings. Along with numerous shiny golf trophies and medals in a glass cabinet, faded portraits of Johnson in army fatigues adorned the walls. The man would have brought back a suitcase full of mental scars from Vietnam. His explanation for running away from the scene was definitely plausible.

The interview wasn't throwing up any solid leads. Trevarthen sensed it was time to pull the pin, get back to the station and write up the details of Rohan Keenan's performance. As he got up to leave, Johnson stayed him with a touch on the forearm.

'Don't go yet.'

'Is there something else you want to tell me?'

'There sure is. What happened on our beautiful golf course yesterday is nothing short of an atrocity. It needs to be cleared up and it needs to be cleared up fast.'

'No arguments from me,' said Trevarthen.

'I've got some theories, wanna hear 'em?'

Now we're getting somewhere. The Constable nodded.

'Start looking at the top.'

'Of what?'

'The guys who run the golf club, of course. Absolute pair of dickheads, oh, sorry, I mean rogues.' His cheeks reddened, the sinews in his neck tensed.

Trevarthen smiled at the man's embarrassment over a word Australian cops hear all day long on the street, often directed at them. 'Why would you suggest we look there?'

He folded chunky hairy arms across his chest and leaned back in his seat. 'A fish always rots from the head down, don't it!' He pouted as if he'd made a profound point.

Trevarthen rubbed his pen behind his ear. 'And what would their motives be, do you think?' *This is where the old boy's theories are going to unravel.*

'That's your job.' Johnson stabbed a finger in the direction of Trevarthen's badge as his wife, muttering something incomprehensible under her breath, poured a stream of brown tea into her husband's mug.

'If you're suggesting…what are their names again?'

'Jeff Bloomberg, he's the president, and Wayne Fletcher, the managing director. Both think their shit don't stink. I've never liked either of them. We need new blood at the club.'

'Why should we investigate these men? Have they had run-ins with Paul Keenan or Lachlan Morris? Made threats?'

Johnson slurped his tea, wiped a couple of droplets from his chin with a napkin. 'There's rumours going around the club that Keenan was fooling around with Fletcher's missus. She's a bit of all right if you ask me.'

His wife, silent until now, decided to chip in. 'No one asked you, Bert.' She glared at her husband then switched her attention to Trevarthen. 'Please forgive my sexist dinosaur of a spouse.'

'Doris, please...'

Time to intervene. 'And what about the club president?'

'I can't think of a motive for him, but he's a pompous bastard who looks down on everyone else.' Johnson paused for a second. 'Actually, he might have been jealous of Morris. Having that lovely Irish lass Dervla hanging off his arm while he's stuck with his own bitch of a...'

'Bert!'

'Sorry, love, but Bloomberg's missus *is* a nasty dragon.'

Doris had run out of words. She shook her head and disappeared into the kitchen, muttering again.

'Enough to try and kill Morris with a drone? And why kill Keenan?'

A shrug. 'Like I said, these are purely theories. Perhaps they're innocent as lambs, but worth checking out, huh?'

It was pure vexatiousness, Trevarthen knew that. An old bloke looking to stir up trouble. However, judging by what he'd learned so far, Keenan certainly had a penchant for targeting other men's women, so maybe the angle with Fletcher and his wife was worth a look.

'What about the superintendent, Reg Brownstone?'

'What about him?'

'Surely you're aware Paul Keenan attacked the man over the state of the golf course.'

'Ha! Most people knew Keenan was talking out of his arse because he'd played the worst round of his life and blamed it on a few piles of rubble. Besides, Reg isn't the type to bear a grudge over that.'

'The statement was made at a public event. People have been known to kill over lesser slights.'

Another noisy swig of tea. 'I've known Reg for years. He's a good man, heart of gold. No way he's mixed up in this sort of thing. If he had an issue with Keenan, he would've sought him out and given him a piece of his mind. At worst, a black eye.'

Trevarthen flicked over a page of his notebook. 'Do the names Michael Salesa and Glenn Farr mean anything to you?'

A sluggish nod. 'The names are vaguely familiar. I think they might be members of the country club.' He screwed up his eyes, trying to recall, then shook his head in defeat. 'Nope. I don't know them.'

Trevarthen thanked Johnson for his time, Doris for the hospitality, gathered his things and headed for the door.

'You'll thank me later for putting you onto Bloomberg and Fletcher,' Johnson called from the front porch.

'I'm sure,' Trevarthen called back with as much sincerity as he could muster, which wasn't much. This had been a wasted effort, not counting the cake. The sun had set some time ago and the air had cooled off nicely. The car dash said it was a pleasant 22°C outside, humidity low. No time to waste, he broke every traffic rule in the book en route to the station while keeping an eagle-eye out for speed cameras. He logged onto his computer, wrote an account of the day's activities and printed it off for tomorrow's briefing.

A quick check of his emails – no reports from Proctor or the Brisbane techies, which wasn't surprising so early in the investigation. He grabbed his sports gear from the locker and cruised over to the Iron Horse, his earlier crazy driving giving him a surplus fifteen minutes to get there without rushing. Tonight he was determined to hand Jack his own arse in a pair of boxing gloves.

Chapter Twenty-Three

'LEAVE the nice police lady alone, Emily.' The woman flicked a hand towel over her shoulder and bent low. She shook a finger at the curly-mopped toddler who was gleefully tugging on DC Taylor's trouser leg. The child had something sticky and red on her face and hands. She gurgled and gave another sharp tug.

'It's fine,' said Taylor. 'Dry cleaning's tax deductible in my line of work.'

Jack chose to glare at the other, equally grubby, child who stood on bowed legs a couple of metres away. Unfortunately, Jack only had one set of clean clothes for work, the clothes he was currently wearing. The door of his washing machine was almost bursting from the pressure of the dirty laundry inside. The kid locking eyes with the DS blinked first, spat out her dummy and ran up the hallway, bawling and windmilling her chubby arms. Sabrina Keenan's mother, Karen Moore, excused herself with an apologetic frown, hared off after the runaway toddler while the first one clung tight to Taylor's leg.

'Your think this is a bad time?' said Jack. 'I ain't too comfortable around unruly children.'

'How on Earth did you cope with one of your own?'

'I didn't. I was a terrible father. I—'

Before he could confess to the sins of his previous life in the United Kingdom, Moore had returned, puffing hard, face pink. 'I think she'll calm down now. I switched the TV on in the spare room. The Wiggles. It's like hypnosis.' At mention of the word "Wiggles", the child harassing Taylor released her grasp and quickly followed in her sister's footsteps.

'Please, let's talk in the sunroom.' Moore escorted the detectives towards a small sitting area in an enclosed patio. Wicker chairs with white cushions and a glass-topped rattan coffee table. The woman's gait was unsteady, Jack noted, a minor limp favouring the right side. Self-medication, or maybe the effects of aging. In contrast to the gloomy atmosphere, bright sunlight beamed in through large windows. On the sills sat neatly arranged succulents and flowering cacti.

'You sure the kids'll be all right on their own?' said Taylor.

Moore tugged on a heavy hoop earring. 'The girls will be glued to the screen for an hour. If they start squabbling I'll nip it in the bud.' She laughed uneasily. 'Can I get you something to drink?'

'No thanks,' said Taylor.

'Coffee would be great.' Jack picked up a magazine from the cane chair he was about to sit in, placed it on the table which was already covered in celebrity gossip magazines.

'We've not long stopped at a café. My colleague will be

fine.' Taylor side-eyed Jack, who met her reproving look with one that said *What? She offered*.

'You're doing a fine job with the wee tikes at a very difficult time,' said Jack as he popped a nicotine gum into his mouth. 'Very admirable. Something tells me you'll be looking after them longer than this weekend. Am I right?'

Karen Moore cradled her head in her hands and wept, tears leaking through the gaps in her fingers. Taylor went to the woman, rested an arm across her heaving shoulders, offered a couple of soothing "it's-all-rights" and "there-theres". Jack observed the scene keenly, and not without empathy. The woman had her hands full minding two girls with boundless energy; that alone would be enough to test anyone's mettle. Throw into the mix the murder of your daughter's ex-husband and that same daughter being completely unhinged, and it was no wonder the woman was a wreck.

It took about three minutes before she composed herself. 'Oh, my. I'm so sorry. You must think I'm a fool.'

'Not at all,' said Taylor. 'This is what everyone undergoing a traumatic event has to deal with.'

Moore wiped her face with the hand towel she'd been clutching, leaving on her cheeks a red streak. 'You've got a spot of…' Taylor pointed at Moore's face.

'Oh, it's just jam.' She smiled awkwardly. 'I can't even manage…' Another river of tears.

Jack glanced at his phone. A text from Trevarthen. *Finished with today's interviews. Report written and on your desk. Catch you at the gym.* The DS shook his head. The rate this crying-interrupted conversation was going, he wouldn't make the sparring session with his mate. Too bad. Moore might have some valuable insights to offer regarding the love triangle between her daughter's ex, Dervla and old man Morris. Salesa said it was the worst-kept secret in town. If so, Karen Moore must be in the loop.

After the woman recovered her breath a second time, it was time to start digging.

'Ms Moore,' said Jack. 'Do you think your daughter could have hated Paul Keenan enough to have him killed?'

'No way! What on Earth are you suggesting? Look, I know Sabrina's got some issues. She struggles with the girls. I look after them so often they call me mummy by mistake sometimes.'

'Crikey,' said Jack, slipping in one of his favourite Australian words. 'Very confusing for the kids.'

'Uh huh. Lately her mood is…well…I'm sure you've spoken to her and seen how unstable she is.'

Taylor offered Moore a half-smile. 'Yesterday two of our officers informed Sabrina of Paul's death. They were confronted with a difficult…situation. DS Lisbon and I intend to speak with your daughter as soon as we can. After hearing about her, let's call it erratic, behaviour, we felt some time was needed.'

'Of course,' Moore sighed. 'Very thoughtful of you. She needs to process this…tragedy.'

'Indeed,' said Jack, leaning forward and resting his forearms on his knees. 'My idea of "some time" is vastly different to DC Taylor's. We'll be chatting with her tomorrow. To be honest, the guy I originally had in the frame for the murder, and the attempted murder let's not forget, has a clear-cut alibi. I hate to say it, but Sabrina's shaping as the top suspect right now.'

Karen Moore's ashen face dropped into her hands again, muffled sobs filling the small sun room. Taylor disappeared for thirty seconds, returned with a glass of cold water. Jack squinted as if to say *where's mine?* Moore gripped the glass with two shaky hands and half emptied it with a noisy glug. Her eyes shifted from one cop to the other before she said, 'I liked Paul. A lovely man, the ideal son-in-law.' Tears dropped into her lap. 'I thought he was the perfect match for my daughter. They were happy until...'

'Until he started up with Dervla.' Jack crossed one leg over the other. 'I completely—'

'No! It was Sabrina.'

'Sorry?' said Taylor, tilting her head to one side.

'She started seeing these strange men she met off the Internet. Sex workers. She's still doing it!' Jack fought the urge to tell her Sabrina was discovered indulging herself as recently as yesterday. 'It's some kind of addiction,' Moore continued. 'Anyway, one day Paul comes home early from work and finds her in bed with a young escort. Paul was furious. She begged for forgiveness, but he wouldn't have a bar of it. That was the end of their marriage.'

'So, you're saying. What are you saying?' said Jack, uncrossing his legs and planting both feet firmly on the ground.

'I'm saying if Sabrina's claiming she was jealous of Dervla Morris it's bullshit. Paul hooked up with her *after* he left Sabrina.'

'It's not unknown for exes to be jealous of people who come on the scene late,' said Jack. 'And for their hatred to be directed back at someone they once loved. I've seen a lot of cases like that.' He stopped for a second to pick at a loose thread on the cuff of his shirt. 'Sabrina could still have despised Paul for his relationship with Dervla, even if that emotion was irrational. Most emotions are irrational, at the end of the day.'

'Nope.' Moore shook her head emphatically. 'I know she adored him deep in her heart. She'll be grieving for months, if not years. She's got nothing to do with murdering Paul, I'd stake my own life on it.'

'What about his will?' said Taylor. 'She could have–'

'Nope. Once Paul learned of Sabrina's dalliances he got the will changed. He left everything to the girls, to be held in trust until they come of age. Sabrina's happy with that.' She took another sip of water.

'I'm curious,' said Jack, scratching his chin. 'Where does Sabrina get her income from?'

'She's on a government benefit for supporting parents. Plus what child-maintenance money she got from Paul for the girls.'

'So in your opinion, there's no way she can benefit financially from Paul's death?' said Taylor.

'I don't think so. The house she lives in is rented, as is Paul's. I'm pretty sure all his money was tied up in shares. For some reason he shied away from the property market.'

'Thanks for your co-operation.' Jack stood, pulled down the cuffs of his jacket. 'Let's go, Claudia.'

On the drive back to the station, New Order's classic 80's synth-dance number "Bizarre Love Triangle" played on repeat in Jack's head.

Chapter Twenty-Four

TREVARTHEN JOGGED up to the ring, dodging gym patrons on their way to weight benches and work-out machines. Sports bag swinging from his shoulder, he had to excuse himself a couple of times as he bumped into customers. The Iron Horse, the town's most notorious fitness venue and linked to Jack's first homicide case, was getting very crowded these days. The owner had confided to Jack the notoriety hadn't done his business any harm.

'In the nick of time, young man,' said Jack, slapping his red boxing gloves together. 'I was starting to think you were gonna stand me up.'

'The interviews took longer than I thought they would.'

'Which means you did your job properly.'

A shrug. 'Not sure any of it's going to point to the killer, but I heard some fascinating stuff.'

'I'm all ears.'

'I never got to speak with the victim's nephew Jasper, or his mum. Only the brother Rohan. He reckons he and Paul had a long-standing feud. He suspected the guy of trying to seduce his wife, maybe even having a clandestine affair with her. Then, just when I thought I had his trust, Rohan Keenan decided he'd said enough and sent me packing.'

'Interesting.' Jack twisted his lips into a half smile. 'Sabrina's mum reckoned it was *her daughter* who was the promiscuous one. Hiring gigolos. Well, we know that part is true. Smith and Semmens witnessed it. This saga gets crazier by the minute.' Jack took a drink from a plastic bottle. 'What about the old golfer, Bert Johnson?'

'Waste of time, I reckon. Although he suggested Paul Keenan might have been getting it on with the operations manager's wife.'

Jack burst out laughing. 'So,' he counted off on his fingers. 'Keenan's been shagging Dervla, his sister-in-law AND Wayne Fletcher's missus. All while running a bank. I find that hard to believe.'

'I've left a summary of the interviews on your desk for tomorrow. Also emailed it in case you wanna read it tonight.'

'No chance. Let's put thoughts of the case to one side for an hour and have some fun.' He gestured towards the ring, both men clambered under the ropes and headed for opposite corners.

'Hey, you're probably too young to remember the song "Bizarre Love Triangle" ain't ya?' Jack called out. 'Could be the theme tune to this case when they make it into a movie.'

'I actually know that one.' Trevarthen bounced his back against the ropes as he prepared to take on DS Lisbon, rehearsing moves and combos in his mind. 'My old man played it to death back in the 90s. I ended up hating the song.' He stopped bouncing, slowly walked to centre ring and started winding protective tape around his wrists. 'The woman who sang it had an annoying voice.'

'What?' Jack shuffled towards the centre of the ring, rolling his shoulders as he went. 'There *was* a woman in New Order, as it happens, but she didn't sing that one, sunshine. You're confused. Stay focused.' Jack quickly shoved in his mouthguard before flicking out a gentle jab that struck his unsuspecting opponent a glancing blow to the chin.

'Hey, not fair!' yelped Trevarthen, dancing about to avoid another tap from Jack. He shook his head, the loose headgear strap flapped against his neck. 'I'm not bloody ready. Hang on a sec.' He finished wrapping the tape, did up the headgear strap, donned the Everlast 16-ounce gloves. 'OK, come at me, Sarge!' He shaped up and waited to defend the next punch.

Despite mustering his best evasive manoeuvres, Trevarthen failed to parry many of Jack's stinging shots. Ribs and stomach muscles began to ache, his temples throbbed. Six three-minute rounds in, Trevarthen had lost plenty of sweat, taken dozens of hits and landed few of his own, his energy levels were depleting. After Jack delivered yet another jab-cross-hook combination, a primal instinct switched on inside Trevarthen's brain. *Damn technique to hell. Just let him have it.* As he ducked under a powerful swing aimed at the middle of his nose, Trevarthen kept his head down for half a second, then exploded upwards from the knees. Eyes shut tight, he launched a haymaker uppercut in the general direction of where he expected Jack's ugly chin to be hanging.

Instead of the punch continuing upwards through fresh air as expected, his fist came to an abrupt halt as it impacted with Jack's...what? Neck? Jaw? Trevarthen opened his eyes, then made a massive mistake. He dropped his hands. Before he could get his dukes up again, Jack's right glove came flying towards Trevarthen's face. He felt his knees buckle as all remaining strength seeped from his body, which slid to the canvas like jelly poured from a jug.

As he lay on his back, staring up at Jack's grinning face, he managed to stick out a hand. Jack heaved, got his mate to a standing position. Like in the Roadrunner cartoons, little stars swam before Trevarthen's eyes.

'Geez, you can take a punch, sunshine,' said Jack, patting his friend on the back. 'That's a big plus for any boxer.'

Trevarthen spat out his drool-covered mouthguard. 'I really...thought...I got you that time.'

'Ha ha! You did. Flush on the shoulder. A solid punch and it's gonna bruise like a rainbow, but I reckon you'll remember to keep your hands up next time.'

Trevarthen felt his right jaw, that side of his face already puffing up. 'Not sure there's gonna be a next time.'

Walking out to their cars, the evening air cooled the sweat on the men's faces. As Jack inserted the key into the door of his Hilux he felt a tap on the shoulder. 'Ow!' He gave the spot a rub with exaggerated care. 'No need to attack an injured man.'

'Listen to this, mate. That song we were talking about earlier. Band's called Frente.' Trevarthen held his mobile up; a wistful tune played on YouTube to the accompaniment of a simply choreographed video. The melody was instantly recognisable, but the arrangement was stupefying. Jack stood rooted to the spot until the short tune was over.

'Her voice ain't annoying, it's bleedin' angelic. That version's a cracker. Even better than the original.' He gently ran a finger down Trevarthen's swollen jawline. 'Unlike you, sunshine.'

Chapter Twenty-Five

MONDAY MORNING, 08:34, two days after the murder. Back in the incident room again. Batista would scale the meetings down, with uniforms rendering assistance if and when required in between day-to-day police work. The bulk of the investigative tasks were down to Jack and Taylor. Hard evidence was in short supply, the main players in the saga behaving like B-grade actors in a tawdry soap opera. On balance, it was shaping up as one of the weirdest cases in Jack's career. And he couldn't wait to get stuck in.

Jack tipped the paper cup to his lips, took a sip of the hot, strong double espresso purchased from the Good Bean café around the corner. He kicked his legs back and forth under the modular table he sat on next to Taylor, the outside of his calf occasionally brushing her leg. She stared straight ahead, watching Batista closely. She made no move to edge away as their legs touched for those brief moments. Jack swallowed hard. When would he summon the courage to tell her how he really felt? Not today...

'Let's hear from Constable Wilson first,' said Inspector

Batista, thick black marker pen poised in front of the whiteboard. 'What have your searches turned up?'

The station's resident geek stood beside the Inspector. Not a great off-the-cuff speaker, Wilson began by reading from a sheet of paper. In terms of the attack drone, a couple of potential models had been identified by QPS technical services; the one most closely fitting the descriptions given by Jack and Trevarthen was the Autel Robotics EVO II. Wilson looked up from his notes. 'I was lucky there were a couple of officers working over the weekend. The case fascinated one of them and he was keen to get on board. He emailed me a photo and description of this machine, which I've forwarded to everyone. Size-wise, it's a match, and its long range of 9 km and flight time of 40 minutes make it a likely candidate. The base model costs about two and a half grand to buy new. The top of the range model with all the bells and whistles – upward of ten thousand.'

Batista wrote the name of the model on the white board. 'Good work, Ben. If someone paid ten grand for a drone to kill Keenan, they must have been highly motivated. I'd like Taylor to try and track the sales of this particular model. Go back in time as far as you can. We've got no idea when the killer acquired the drone.'

'This one was released January 2020, if that's any help,' said Wilson. 'You can buy them in electronic and camera stores, online, from overseas manufacturers direct. To be honest, sir, it's needle in a haystack stuff.' He held the piece of paper by his side, pessimism etched into his deeply freckled face. 'And it might not even be this model.'

'Still worth a try. Claudia, check hobby clubs and online forums in North Queensland, that kind of thing.'

'Will do,' said Taylor

'Did you speak to ballistics?' Batista asked Wilson.

'I did. I got a bollocking for my troubles when I rang them. They've got a huge backlog of work.'

'Typical,' Jack huffed. 'Under-resourced where it matters.'

'They might have an excuse this time,' Wilson ventured. 'Remember they're dealing with the fallout from that biker gang shoot-out on the Gold Coast last week.'

Jack nodded. 'Fair call. Four gang members dead, civilians wounded in cross fire if I recall the details correctly.'

'You do, sir,' Wilson replied. 'Untold rounds were fired. Dawn raids led to the confiscation of a ton of weapons. Long story short, they'll be processing the material for weeks if not months.'

'Listen, we can't control that stuff, so let's not stress about it,' said Jack. He flipped a pellet of nicotine gum into his mouth, savoured the peppery flavour on his taste buds. A dull ache made him wince – Trevarthen had snuck through a few blows to Jack's head; they must've been harder hits than Jack registered at the time. He mentally acknowledged his mate's efforts. *Well done, Aden.* Then back to business. 'Proctor was iffy about relying on ballistics for a lead. The casings we found at the crime scene are so common as to be almost generic. As for the gun, that could be almost anything, innit. It'll be a miracle if the ballistics report – when it finally turns up – points to a perpetrator. And I don't believe in miracles, only hard graft.' Jack took another swig of coffee, rolled the wad of gum around with his tongue.

Batista flipped the board over, tapped the words *Terrorism link?* 'Anything in regards to this, Ben?'

An unsteady laugh. 'This is where it gets interesting. But whether there are real links to this crime, I couldn't say.' He grabbed an iPad from under a trolley, brought up an electronic document on a large monitor linked to the tablet via bluetooth. 'A couple of key figures in the IRA had the surname Keenan. Brian and Sean. The first one died in 2008 in prison. He was a real hard nut. Made bombs that killed innocent people. The other Keenan died in 1994, not as influential in the movement. As far as I can tell, our man Paul Keenan was no relation to either of those men. I also couldn't find any connections between Dervla Morris and either the IRA or Unionist movements. But,' he looked up at the gathered officers, 'that's very superficial research.'

'This is a big area,' said Batista, nodding sagely. 'A lot of complex history and politics involved. I'll pass on what Constable Wilson found to the Federal Police. They've got better resources for this kind of thing. That said, my intuition tells me this case revolves around more personal matters.'

'Agreed,' said Trevarthen. He swapped places with Wilson, gave a rundown of his findings. Yawns and limb stretches greeted some of his words – not because the team were bored. Just dog tired and a tad unmotivated. They'd gone hard early but so far failed to find solid clues.

When Trevarthen concluded his summary Jack said, 'The brother's behaviour was certainly weird, Aden. But compared to the ex-wife's carry-on, he's the picture of sanity. Still, I'd like to book him in for a grilling here at the station.'

'You got a good reason to drag him in?' said Batista.

'Yeah. I don't like the way he hustled Aden out of his house. Gets my Spidey senses tingling.'

'Mine too,' said Trevarthen. 'It could be down to the shock, but Rohan Keenan went from friendly and cooperative to hostile and uncooperative in the blink of any eye.'

Jack turned towards the Inspector. 'I'd like your permission to present some search warrant requests to the magistrate. I've got a feeling the feud between the brothers might at least get that one over the line.'

'I agree, it's the best chance. Who else?'

'At this stage, I'd focus on seeking warrants for the ex, Sabrina and old man Morris.'

Batista shook his head. 'DS Lisbon. You've got the greatest instincts of any detective I've worked with. However, are you seriously entertaining the idea Morris took a potentially lethal bullet to the stomach to avenge an affair? An affair that may have had his blessing in the first place?'

'I don't believe the Irish woman, boss, despite her assertions. Besides, we're all familiar with the concept of murder-suicides. Jilted males seeking revenge and then ending their own pain by going out in a blaze of glory.'

'Possible, but I'm not buying it.' Batista shook his head slowly.

'Look,' Jack persisted. 'Morris might even be pissed off he's still alive. If it turns out he did orchestrate this stunt, he'll be sorry he didn't die once he's tucked away with the scum in Copperhead Jail.'

Batista stroked his chin. 'Make the application as convincing as you can. You've failed to sell it to me, so getting the magistrate to believe it won't be easy. Taylor, help him out on that.'

'Sir,' she replied with an oblique tilt of the head.

To round off the session, an upbeat Smith confirmed that Reg Brownstone's alibis checked out. The labourer Errol Sibley swore Reg was a great greenkeeper but a lousy drone pilot and that the Country Club's machine hadn't been in the sky for months. The neighbour Alan Lundgren showed Smith a hand covered in blisters and a pair of scratched wrists in evidence of his fence-repairing session with Brownstone.

'How about his demeanour?' said Batista.

'He seemed on the level to me.' Smith smiled. 'His daughter offered to take me clay pigeon shooting, so that'll give me a chance to press for more details.'

'Is that all you'll be pressing for?' said Jack. He felt Taylor's eyes drilling into him. It was inappropriate, but he couldn't help himself. He had nothing to base it on, but he felt Ruby was the type of woman that would appeal to someone like Smith.

'I'm sure I don't know what you mean.' Smith's averted gaze, twisting fingers and flushed face told everyone she knew precisely what DS Lisbon meant.

'Very well.' Batista clapped his hands to break up the awkwardness. 'Let's get on with it!'

Chapter Twenty-Six

A ROW of four stumpy poles blocked car access to the Yorkville Pedestrian Mall. Exceptions were made for delivery trucks, emergency vehicles, and anyone smart enough to hack into the remote-controlled pop-up bollard system.

Jack approached slowly from the Oliphant Street end, pressed the button on the blipper and waited for the steel cylinders to briefly retreat into their burrows. He gently nosed into the mall, a couple of pedestrians with shopping bags parted like water before him. He parked the Ford Territory under a shady tree outside the Yorkville branch of the Trust Bank of Australia. No Taylor to accompany him this morning, the DC was busy drafting appeals to the common sense of the on-duty magistrate. The consensus view among law enforcement folk in this town – she was harder to crack than a fossilised macadamia nut. Jack had his fingers crossed Taylor could work her word-magic, but his hopes weren't high. The grounds for the applications were objectively weaker than last week's coffee dregs.

Jack acknowledged nods and smiles from passers-by: it wasn't hard to be a celebrity in a town this size. Big fish, small pond. Being at the forefront of a number of infamous criminal cases didn't harm the recognition factor either. The younger generation, those who didn't watch the news or read the papers, were less aware of the identity of DS Jack Lisbon. The bank's meet-and-greeter, a greasy-haired man in his early 20's with the name Radu affixed to his chest, fell squarely into that category. Jack headed for him, mustering his *don't-muck-me-around* expression.

'Good morning, sir.' Radu kept his hands behind his back and smiled nervously. The lad reminded Jack of a cinema usher. 'How can I help you today?'

'To be honest, I'm surprised you're even open after what happened to the manager.'

Radu said in a whisper, 'I know, right? I was surprised, too. We were notified by text last night we wouldn't be closing.' He shrugged like he was trying to dislodge something from his shoulders. 'Head office reckons the customers need the bank to be open, life must go on, that kind of thing... Anyway, what is it you need? A credit card, home loan or...'

'I'm a police officer, sonny, and I'd like to speak to whoever's in charge today.' Jack held out his ID like a matador dangling his cape.

'That would be the head accountant, Mr Kam Fong. Please follow me.' Radu escorted Jack to a pair of polished oak doors with a manager plaque bearing the name of the deceased. 'We're leaving it up as a sign of respect until...'

'Yeah, thanks.' Jack didn't wait to hear the rest of what the lad had to say. Then, second thoughts. 'You been here long, sunshine?'

'Two years. I started straight out of school.' Pride in his

modest achievement made Jack grin. Two years was long enough to get a handle on all the gossip.

'When I'm done with Mr Fong, I'd like a word with you, if you don't mind.'

Radu frowned. 'We've only got a skeleton staff. Apparently some of the workers ignored the order from HQ.'

'Is it mainly the female employees off?'

'Yeah, how'd you guess.'

'They're more empathetic than us blokes, or so I'm led to believe. So, up for a chat when I'm done in there?'

Radu did a half body turn towards the entrance. 'I've got to man the door all day.'

'Don't you get a lunch break with this outfit?' If the lad progressed far up the ladder in the banking world it would be a miracle, Jack mused.

'Oh yeah, of course.' Radu grinned awkwardly. 'Around midday. I guess someone will relieve me on the door.'

Jack pressed his lips together, curbing the urge to make a smart comment on the double entendre. Radu shuffled past Jack, tapped on the door, announced the arrival of the law and resumed his post.

'I guess you want to ask some questions about poor Paul, may God rest his soul,' said Mr Fong. He was a portly gentleman with a flat-top haircut favoured by the US Marines and a pair of thick-lensed glasses. He rose to his feet, extended a chubby-fingered hand across the desk.

'Yeah, I would 'n all,' said Jack, squeezing perhaps a fraction too hard as he pumped the man's paw.

Fong winced before saying in an apologetic tone, 'We've had a few call in sick today. Perhaps…'

'I'm happy to start with you and catch up with the rest of the employees later.' Jack pulled up a seat, cracked his knuckles in his lap. The audible pop made the accountant raise his pencil-thin eyebrows. 'How come you've moved into the manager's office already?'

'Excuse me?' The man's jowls juddered.

'He's barely had time to go cold, and here you are lording it up in his domain.'

'This is where all the files are that I need to access. Things like that.'

'Bollocks.'

'What?' Fong reached into his pocket, dabbed his gleaming forehead with a handkerchief.

'It's all electronic these days, innit. You could be sitting in your old office, the one I saw with your name on the door, and be doing exactly the same job. Lemme guess, the chair in here's more comfortable, is that it?'

'Look, I'll be back in there,' Fong pointed a fat forefinger at the wall dividing the two offices, 'as soon as a new franchisee takes over.'

'Will you be applying to buy the franchise yourself?'

A hesitation from Fong, and then a slow nod. 'Yes, I will, but it's not like…'

'Not like what?'

'Not like I organised the murder so I could take over. Geez, are you kidding or what?'

'You tell me,' said Jack, fishing around for his mobile which had just vibrated an alert. He glanced at the screen. A text from Taylor. He'd read it later, this was too enjoyable to interrupt. Fong was wriggling like a worm, exactly how the DS liked it.

'It works like a tendering process. I'll be going up against a number of competitors. How many? I couldn't guess. But this branch has the runs on the board, so it'll attract a lot of interest. Sixty percent of Trust offices are franchised, and this one is in the top five performers in the state. Say what you like about Keenan, but he took this branch from nowhere and made it a ripping success.'

Jack leaned back in his chair. 'So the new owner would be inheriting a gold mine, yeah?'

'I wouldn't put it quite like that. A profitable business with plenty of room for growth, certainly.'

Jack ran his finger along the top of the desk, blew away imaginary dust. Fong was sweating more freely now. *Perfect.* 'Did anyone in the business stand to gain materially from Keenan's death?' Jack pointed a finger at Fong, flashed a sly grin accompanied by a slow wink. 'Apart from you, I mean.'

'Please! I won't have you accusing me of…of murder. Paul was someone I liked and admired a great deal.' Droplets formed in Fong's eyes. His handkerchief took on tear-wiping duty. After a couple of dabs he said, 'To be honest, I'm rather nervous about taking on the responsibility. Paul was an all-round banker, old school, real good with the customers. I'm more a numbers guy.'

'Then you'll be long odds to score the franchise. Customer relations is what it's all about these days, right?'

Fong set his jaw. 'I'm going to give it my best shot.'

'Not the most appropriate choice of words under the circumstances, Mr Fong.'

The accountant's mouth formed a perfect circle, his head shook. 'Oh…no…please…I didn't mean.'

Jack's instinct told him Fong wasn't faking it. Most "numbers men" weren't that talented in the acting department. 'Forgive me. I'm putting out thought bubbles. Don't take what I say personally. What can you tell me about Michael Salesa?'

'Mike?'

'Yeah. I understand he was 2IC and then one day Keenan fired him.'

Fong sighed. 'Yes, a very unfortunate thing that was.'

'Salesa claims he was bullied by Keenan and that he was sacked due to a personality clash.'

Confusion wrinkled Fong's brow, until then so smooth Jack thought it might have been Botoxed.

'No, no, no.' Fong waved his hands about. 'It was something a lot more sordid than that.'

'What?'

'I can't say.'

'Can't or won't?'

'Can't. I've signed a non-disclosure agreement. All I can tell you is an incident occurred and Mike was asked to leave.'

'Nothing to do with his performance at work?'

'Mike was one of the best lending officers in Queensland. In fact, Paul fought tooth and nail to keep him, but head office was adamant. Mike had to go.'

The cogs started spinning in Jack's brain. Sexual harassment leapt to the top of the pile of possible reasons. Taylor had already dug a little into Salesa's background. No prior criminal convictions, not even a parking violation. Surprising for a man who had, in an intoxicated state, offered the detectives a joy ride on a yacht. A single man with no relationship histories of note. 'Who did he touch up?' Jack blurted.

Fong blinked three times fast. That was it! Salesa had acted inappropriately towards a colleague and he'd been shown the door. And the victim had chosen to keep it in house, too, Jack imagined. There had been no complaints made to Yorkville police by any Trust Bank employees. Perhaps the victim had been paid off, too. To protect the bank's reputation.

'I'm waiting for an answer, Mr Fong.'

'You'll be waiting a long time, I'm afraid.' He wiped his brow again. 'If I breach the agreement, the penalties are severe. And then I can definitely kiss the franchise goodbye.' The phone rang on his desk, his hand darted to grab the receiver. No doubt he relished the chance of a reprieve from DS Lisbon's uncomfortable questions. Fong told the caller he was busy but would ring back as soon as he could. He hung up, gave Jack a blank look. 'I'm happy to cooperate with your investigation as much as I can. We all loved Paul.'

Jack took another tack, asked about Lachlan Morris. Fong wouldn't confirm he knew the man or if he had an account at the bank. The accountant also refused to comment on businesswoman Glenn Farr, named by the Country Club barman as having a motive to off Keenan. With a grudging admiration for Fong's dedication to clients' privacy, the DS returned to questions about the dead bank manager.

'What about his affair with Dervla Morris.'

Fong did the triple-blink thing again, then inhaled deeply. 'I'm sorry.'

'Surely that's not covered by a bleedin' confidentiality clause!' Jack couldn't help raising his voice. Fong's head sunk slightly into his shoulders, the yellow-and-blue butterfly- motif tie at his throat rose and fell.

'It's not, but I'm not comfortable talking about Paul's personal life. Not that I know much about what he did in his spare time. My relationship with Mr Keenan was purely on a business level.'

'My friend, the man's effin' dead. Do you want us to catch the killer or not?'

'If there's anything else, I'd be happy to talk to you later at the station, but right now, as you can probably imagine, I've got lots of other matters to attend to.'

Jack understood the non-disclosure agreement was a wall Fong could hide behind. No doubt all the bank's employees had signed one. The only way to get it out in the open would be through the courts, if he could persuade the magistrate there was merit in bringing the incident into the public domain. He absently patted his pants pocket, felt the reassuring lump of his bundle of keys. He knew deep down there'd be no convincing the magistrate on this one. He nodded at Fong, shook his hand across the desk, thanked him for his time and headed for the exit.

'Still up for that chat at lunch?' said Radu, a hopeful gleam in his eye. He stepped aside to let a blue-rinsed elderly woman with a Zimmer frame inch her way to the lone teller.

Jack checked his phone. The message from Taylor was about the warrant applications. 'I'm short on time, pal. Unless you can spare me ten minutes now it'll have to wait.' A shadow of disappointment crossed the young man's acne-scarred face. 'There's one thing you can do though,' said Jack. 'Answer a quick question.'

'Sure.'

'Who did Mike Salesa harass?'

'Pardon?' The kid looked about furtively, perhaps hoping no one would overhear the conversation.

'Who was it?'

'That's one thing I'm definitely not allowed to talk about.'

'OK.' Jack shrugged dismissively. 'If it's critical to the investigation, it'll come out eventually. We'll have to waste time mucking around with court orders and the like, but...'

'It wasn't really sexual harassment.'

Progress. 'What? It either is or it isn't.'

'It's not as simple as that.' The kid started scratching the inside of his elbow.

'Stop beating around the bush,' Jack said quietly through gritted teeth. 'Tell me what happened. Off the record, OK?'

Those unenforceable words, much loved by journalists, did the trick. 'Mike had a few too many red wines at a business lunch one day. When he staggered in Mr Keenan had a few words to him and Mike went into his own office, we all thought to sleep it off until closing time. In the afternoon Debbie...oh shit...sorry.' He rolled his lips together, then burst out contritely: 'I've gone too far.'

Jack grabbed the lad by the shoulder, edged him into an alcove of ATMs. 'C'mon son. You may as well be hung for a sheep as a lamb.'

'All right, but you promise this is off the record? I'm trusting your word. I'll be fired if anyone finds out.'

Jack grunted in a vague way he hoped would be interpreted as a yes.

'Right.' Radu smoothed his trousers; Jack could have sworn the kid's knees were knocking. 'It involves Debbie Markham...but I'm not telling you her last name.'

The lad really wasn't very sharp. Jack gave him a two-handed *go-on-then* gesture.

'Right,' Radu continued. 'She walked into his office to get a signature on a document, when she saw Mike doing something in there that he shouldn't have.'

'Was he...um...pleasuring himself?' The DS was shaking his head in anticipation of the disgusting details.

'No. He was pissing into a wastepaper basket, but not aiming too well. Deb's yelled out in surprise, he's turned around with his whatsit still in his hand, and he's hit her with a stream of pee. I think she ended up getting a nice little compensation payout for the shock she suffered. Post dramatic stress—'

'Traumatic.'

'Yeah, that. And then it was decided Mr Salesa simply had to go.'

'Who decided? Paul Keenan?'

'No way! Mr Keenan nearly cried the day Mike packed his stuff into the cardboard box and left for good. Mike drinks too much, but he also helped Mr Keenan make the branch successful.'

'Do you reckon Mr Salesa liked Mr Keenan as a person?'

A nod.

'That's odd, because Salesa told me Keenan bullied him and that he was preparing to sue for unfair dismissal.'

Radu touched a finger to the side of his nose. 'I'd say that was Mike trying to throw you off the scent. He'd be embarrassed if anyone found out the real reason, hey? And you do promise not to tell on me, right?'

'Of course not. Your secret's safe with me, sunshine.'

Radu gave a sigh, his shoulders relaxed. 'Awesome.'

Jack quickly pondered the details of Salesa's behaviour. Disgusting, all right, but totally unrelated to the enquiry. Especially with Radu confirming the accountant had no axe to grind with Keenan. One more angle to try. 'Do the names Lachlan or Dervla Morris mean anything to you?'

'Never heard of them,' came the confident reply. Then, the screwed-up eye indicating a sudden realisation. 'Actually, wasn't that the guy shot on the golf course who survived?'

'Yes. Is something coming back to you?'

'Nope. I've remembered it from the news on the telly.'

'Thanks for your help,' Jack said curtly, brushing past

the public-spirited bank employee. There was nothing more to be gained here today. He wouldn't divulge the information he'd received from Radu. He'd given his word after all. It would be prudent to pencil in a chat with Fong down at the station, lawyer for company if the man so desired. The franchise magically opening up with the death of Keenan needed exploring further. Fong was a champion stonewaller, but the stark white decor of Interview Room 1 might loosen his tongue.

He called Taylor, quickly filled her in on what he'd learned from Fong. The old Jack would have regaled Taylor and his other colleagues with the real Salesa story, lapped up the laughter as he downed pint after pint of lager at the pub before waking up with a pounding hangover. The new Jack, despite cutting the odd corner or occasionally roughing up thugs to elicit information, would never break his word to a witness. 'What was it you wanted to tell me about the warrant applications?'

'Nothing, I'd just like you to run your eye over them before I send off the email.'

'I'll be back at the station in twenty minutes to pick you up.'

'Where are we going?'

'Sabrina Keenan's. I need to see this woman for myself.'

Chapter Twenty-Seven

'HER MOTHER'S answers didn't convince you yesterday?' said Taylor, pushing the button to close the window as Jack parked the Ford Territory in the driveway of Sabrina Keenan's house.

'Convince me of what?' Jack killed the engine.

'That her daughter was incapable of killing Paul Keenan.'

'Ha! As if a mother's going to blame her own kid for a murder.'

'Why not? She was straight up in admitting Sabrina was the adulterer in the relationship.'

'It's not an unheard of tactic. Admit to one thing to deflect attention away from another, more serious crime.'

Taylor readjusted her scrunchie. 'Adultery's not on the books as a crime as far as I'm aware.'

'You know what I mean. She wasn't up front about everything.' He jabbed a finger at the windscreen in the direction of the front door. 'Karen Moore said Sabrina was on welfare and got some money from Paul for the girls.

That place is way too expensive for her to afford on that amount of money.'

'You're making one big assumption.'

'Yeah, and what's that?'

'That her mother knows the full story.'

Jack nodded. 'You'll make inspector before me at this rate.'

Taylor blushed. 'Get away with you.'

Jack bashed on the door with the heel of his fist. They waited thirty seconds, watching ants crawling along mortar between bricks, but there was no sign of human life. Jack repeated the knock-and-wait sequence three more times. Taylor rang Sabrina's mobile number, retrieved, along with others belonging to persons of interest, from the list of contacts in the deceased's phone. She placed her Samsung on loudspeaker. The call rang out, no voice mail prompt. The car registered to Sabrina, a white 2002 Toyota Corolla Conquest, sat parked under a galvanised iron carport.

'Maybe she's gone for a walk,' said Taylor.

'Perhaps,' said Jack tersely. 'Or she could be indulging her carnal desires again. Wait here a second in case she comes to the door.' He marched down a side pathway, leapt on a green wheelie bin and launched himself over a timber fence. He landed in a well-mulched garden bed. The back yard was beautifully manicured and maintained. The faint scent of menthol cigarette smoke guided him around a lush oleander bush, where an entertaining area opened up. Brick barbecue, spacious wooden deck and an above-ground swimming pool. Sabrina Keenan, sporting a black one-piece bathing costume and octagonal-framed sunglasses, lay on her back, floating on a rainbow-coloured lilo. She puffed away on a cigarette, flicked a collar of ash into an ashtray on a floating table. Also on the table – a bottle of

Tanqueray Gin, a crystal glass filled with, presumably, some of the contents of the bottle, and a mini ice bucket. From ten metres away Jack barked, 'Mrs Keenan!'

The woman's thin body jerked in surprise, teetered as her balance shifted. Ripples radiated to the edge of the pool as she fought to stay on the inflatable lounge. 'Who the hell are you? Get out of here before I call the police!'

'I am the police.' Jack advanced to the edge of the pool, the top coming up to his waist.

Sabrina raised her sunnies, squinted and said, 'Wait a minute. I recognise you. The famous Detective Jack Lisbon. I suppose you've found the evidence and you've come to arrest me, have you?' She let out a cackle a witch would be proud of.

'That remains to be seen.' Jack folded his arms across his chest.

'Jack!' Taylor's faint voice sounded a mile away.

The DS returned to the fence he'd jumped over, asked Taylor to wait on the other side, then marched back to the pool. 'I'd like my colleague to be with me when I ask you my questions. Is there another way around the…'

'I'm here, Jack,' said Taylor at his right shoulder. 'I'm quite capable of a bit of parkour myself.' She brushed dirt from her knees, then turned her attention to Mrs Keenan. 'If you don't mind getting dressed, we can get down to the business of you helping us with our investigation.'

'Ask your damned questions here. I've only just gotten into the pool and I'm rather comfortable. I'm not moving unless you're arresting me.'

'Fair enough,' said Jack 'Our colleagues told us you put on quite a turn yesterday.'

'Did they?'

'Yes,' said Taylor. 'They reported that you acted very

strangely upon hearing news of your ex-husband's death. One minute you were angry, the next stricken with grief and wailing.'

Sabrina sighed. 'Must have been the coke.'

'Are you a regular user?' said Jack.

'No. Strictly recreational and very rarely. Any more questions?'

'You bet. How do you afford all of this?' Jack waved his hand around.

'None of your business, that's how.' She flipped the sunglasses back down over her eyes, took a sip of the gin and let out an *aahh* of appreciation and smacked her lips in an exaggerated fashion. 'Now piss off.'

'No need to be rude,' said Jack. 'By the way, I've made an application for a production order to be served on your bank and phone company and any other entity that's got data on you. There's no way on God's green earth you can pay for this joint on a government handout and the drips of pocket money for the kids that Paul gave you. And we already know it's peanuts because we've checked into his accounts.'

'How can you do that? It's a breach of privacy, even if he's dead.'

'You don't need to ask permission from murder victims.'

Sabrina shrugged. 'Whatever.'

Jack continued. 'You received a weekly payment of $250. The rent for this joint alone must be $500 a week. Plus you've got that nasty cocaine habit.'

'It's not a habit, I already told you.'

'One thing we know *is* a habit,' said Taylor, 'is the gigolos you engage for sexual services. You admitted as much to Constable Semmens and Smith.'

Sabrina reached out, grabbed her glass and drained it. 'For detectives, you guys are pretty dumb.'

'Sorry?' said Jack. 'We're repeating back what you said to our officers.'

'I was totally bullshitting.' Her tone was deadpan.

'Your mother told us you were using male sex workers. So your own mum is lying, is she?'

'No. She thinks she knows the story, but it's the version I led her to believe was true.' She paused, chewed on a fingernail for a second then said bitterly, 'She shouldn't be telling tales about me anyway. I ought to stop her from seeing the girls.'

'Look, you can either tell us the truth now, or I'll make damned sure you spill your guts at the station,' said Jack. He felt a throbbing in his temple, the beginnings of a migraine were stirring. He craved caffeine.

'I don't pay men for sex.' She fanned her fingers towards her body, jiggled about on the lilo. 'I mean, why would I?' A quick puff on her cigarette and a skyward expulsion of smoke. 'It's the other way around.'

'Pardon?' said Taylor, eyes slowly contracting.

'Exactly what I said. The bloke Paul caught me in bed with, he was my first ever client.'

'Unlucky,' said Jack, wondering if this saga could get any weirder.

'A rookie mistake on my part. I should have gone to his place or booked a hotel, but I guess I needed to feel safe in my own space. Paul forgot his phone or something, came back to get it and…ta dah!'

'In flagrante delicto,' said Taylor.

'Anyway, I told my husband *I'd* hired the guy because the idea of me paying for sex seemed…I dunno…less demeaning than being paid for it. Nothing worse for a woman than to be considered a whore, is there?' She lit a cigarette, took a deep drag. 'And Paul believed me because the man happened to be rather attractive. Very stupid of me, and it killed the marriage on the spot.' She poured herself another gin, pointed the neck of the bottle at the detectives and asked if they'd like to join her. They declined. She sipped daintily, inhaled a lungful, and continued speaking with alacrity. 'You know, I actually got over it pretty quickly, him leaving I mean, which surprised me. I thought I loved him, but I guess not.' She crinkled a nostril, gave a sniff. Jack wondered if she was itching for another line of powder. 'But believe it or not, his death saddens me deeply. He's the father of my children and we did have some happy years together.'

'And the guy Constable Smith saw at your window?'

'Another punter. A regular. He's also the one who treats me with coke from time to time. That explains my behaviour yesterday. I'm a bit ashamed...no, let me rephrase that...embarrassed about exposing myself. I usually charge for that privilege.'

'You spoke in very disparaging terms about Dervla Morris yesterday,' said Jack, not wanting to discuss Sabrina's impromptu striptease performance. 'In fact you called her a slut. That doesn't tally with what you've just said about getting over your marriage breakup quickly.'

'No, but it does tally with what I said about the blow affecting my behaviour.' She laughed at her own observation. 'To be completely honest, I give zero fucks about her and, before you ask, I've got nothing useful to tell you about her sad old husband. Except the fact he played golf with Paul. Other than that, pfft.' Sabrina stubbed out the cigarette, flipped off the lilo and clambered out of the pool. She wrapped a beach towel around herself, relocated onto a foldout banana lounge. Without waiting for an invitation, Jack took up a standing position inches from her. His glowering was in vain; he could see her eyes shut behind the sunnies. Taylor kept a reasonable distance of about three metres. At Jack's request, made while Sabrina was getting out of the pool, Taylor had activated a sound-recorder app on her mobile.

'I'd like you to give us permission to take a look into your records,' said Jack. 'It'll save you the inconvenience of a formal interview and having to hand them over anyway when the court orders you to.' Jack knew without evidence there would be no chance of that happening. If she refused, he determined to make the drug raid a reality, which could turn up other incriminating evidence. 'If everything comes up kosher, I promise we'll leave you alone.'

'No more unannounced leaps over the fence?' Jack wasn't sure, but he thought a hint of flirtatiousness had crept into her demeanour.

'None.'

'Nice offer, but I'm going to decline.'

Jack shook his head. He had no idea how to deal with this difficult woman. He whispered in Taylor's ear, asked for advice, she too shook her head. Time to summon the old sneaky Jack. He took out his phone, pretended to dial a number. 'DS Lisbon speaking. Confirm drug raid on 28 Lang Street. The occupant has admitted on the record to the purchase and consumption of a Schedule 9 substance on the premises.' He placed a hand over the screen. 'Show her the app's running Claudia.' Taylor held up her phone, Sabrina's eyes bulged.

'Oi! I never paid for it. There was no sale. It was a gift!' Sabrina sat up straight, defiance on her face although her reedy torso quivered.

'Please don't interrupt me, Ms Keenan. We have all the evidence we require for the sweep to go ahead. I'm going to ask you to remain right here while I secure the front of the property. DC Taylor, cuff her if she tries to do a runner.'

'You must be fucking joking! This is nothing more than intimidation. You're judging me on my morals, that's it, isn't it!'

'Please calm down, Ms Keenan,' said Taylor.

'I'm no paragon of virtue myself, so I never judge other people's morals,' said Jack. 'But your behaviour makes me think you're hiding something from us about Paul. Therefore, I'm calling for an inspection of your property for drugs, and when we're looking for them, well, who knows what else we might find, hey?'

'Stop, stop, stop!'

'Yes?'

'I'll hand over my records.'

Jack smiled. 'See how easy it is when you co-operate?'

Taylor coughed into her fist, Jack glanced at her and she gestured towards the phone in the hand resting by his side. Jack brought the mobile up to his face, spoke to the imaginary cop on the other end and called off the raid. Sabrina Keenan wasn't the only one who could fool people with a bit of subterfuge.

Chapter Twenty-Eight

THE INSPECTOR GREETED Jack and Taylor at the door of Paul Keenan's sprawling mansion in leafy and wealthy Hagan Avenue, five minutes from the centre of town. Batista wore a pair of blue rubber gloves but no shoe covers. This wasn't a crime scene, full protective kit wasn't required. However police officers' fingerprints on items were to be avoided at all costs.

Batista directed the detectives to a small round table upon which sat a box of disposable gloves. As they walked, he said, 'How'd you two go with Sabrina? As much of a handful as she was yesterday?'

Snapping on gloves, Taylor briefed the Inspector on the interview; she was better at summarising events than Jack, and the DS was glad of it. The urge to waffle and embellish details sometimes got the better of him.

'Amazing how she fooled everyone,' Batista chuckled. 'Turning tricks from home while everyone thought *she* was the customer. I've been around the block a few times and I thought I'd heard it all. What do you say we remind her about her obligations to the Australian Tax Office?'

'Good idea in theory, only there's one problem,' said Jack.

'What?'

'People who do business exclusively for cash generally don't deal with the tax man.'

'True, but some people are more afraid of the ATO than they are of the police.'

'And for good reason,' said Jack. 'Those pricks are ruthless.'

The Inspector guided Jack and Taylor into a spacious kitchen, heavy on the gleaming chrome, with a broad island bench that was half the length of a cricket pitch. On it sat archive boxes full to bursting with documents and folders. Alongside them, a laptop computer, two mobile phones, old-fashioned floppy disks, CDs and DVDs, and a dusty off-white drone and its controller. 'We found the drone in the garage. There was no box to go with it, no instruction manual. Wilson took a photo of the device and made an Internet search,' said the Inspector. 'Apparently it's a DJI Mini 2.'

'Means bugger all to me,' said Jack. 'But it looks nothing like the one used to kill the owner of this one. I guess we can rule out suicide, yeah?'

'No need for the sarcasm, DS Lisbon.'

'My apologies.'

'Still, we'll send all this gear off to the tech lab in Brisbane and see what they can find.'

'Could be a waste of time and resources in terms of that toy drone.'

'Just following protocol,' said Batista. 'One never knows.'

Taylor pointed at the boxes of files. 'Find anything in that lot yet?'

Batista shook his head. 'No one's had a look, we're still at the collecting stage.'

'You mind?' Taylor inclined her head towards the boxes.

'If you could be bothered. Sure you don't want to wait until we've gathered everything, go over it back at the station?'

'Why waste time?'

Batista showed upturned palms. 'Go for your life. Jack, follow me to the study. Wilson's in there sorting through filing cabinets. Smith and Semmens are upstairs going from room to room, setting anything aside they think might bear on the case.'

'I'm suspecting not much.'

'I tend to agree.' They entered the study, lined with bookshelves loaded up with hardback editions in dust jackets. 'Find anything, Ben?'

'Plenty.' Wilson closed a drawer, turned to face the officers. 'But all of a boring business nature. What does surprise me is the extent of his library. There's plenty of high-brow literature among what you'd expect, books on financial matters, banking, that kind of thing. All arranged in alphabetical order.'

'Should we go through all these books, Jack?' said Batista. 'I read a detective novel recently where an incriminating letter was stashed between the pages of the killer's favourite Stephen King novel.'

Jack twisted his mouth as he pondered the size of Keenan's collection. He skirted the three walls that were covered by floor-to-ceiling shelves. There was barely any free space you could jam a new book into. 'It'd take many hours. I'd come back to it later if we can't solve...hang on a sec.' Jack stopped, plucked a book from a shelf at eye level. 'What have we got here? "Armed Struggle: The History of the IRA". The author's last name is English. Can you beat that for irony?'

'Any others like that?' said the Inspector with a glint in his hooded eyes.

'A couple more of that ilk.' Jack turned to Wilson. 'Have you heard back from that Fed you spoke to?'

'No, sir.'

'Get onto him today. Tell him about this find. Terrorism may be more than a tenuous link after all.'

'Or it could simply be a curious interest in history and world events,' said Batista. 'He's also got plenty of reading material on the world wars, the Russian Revolution, the American War of Independence. And that's just what I can see without even having a proper look.'

'Fair point, but his own Irish roots, Dervla, the violent MO, and…'

'Also fair points. Wilson, make sure to follow up like Jack suggested.'

'Sirs,' said Wilson. *Better than youse*, thought Jack with a smile.

Constables Semmens and Smith appeared in the library, the latter toting a plain cardboard box. Smith said, 'A few things we thought might be relevant to the case.'

'Namely?' said Batista.

'In a built-in drawer on the side of his bed we found an early model iPad, along with a collection of USB sticks. And another box with various…ah…'

'Sex toys,' said Semmens, apparently not in the least embarrassed by the discovery. 'Kylie wanted to leave them, but I insisted we grab 'em. I can't think of anything you'd get better DNA samples off.'

'Good thinking,' said Jack. 'Very proper to bag them up. We've had all kinds of allegations about Keenan fooling around with various women. This could be vital to establishing whether those allegations are true or not.'

'You're not suggesting we ask those...peripheral...individuals to submit DNA samples to compare with what we find on sex toys, are you?' said Smith.

'It may not come to that,' said Batista. 'However it's best we keep the items as potential evidence, just in case.'

Smith shook her head. 'I don't know.'

'Image the scenario,' said Jack. 'Some woman involved in the murder breaks in here after we've gone, gathers up the vibrators covered in her DNA, destroys them, and we've got no proof of the link.'

'Sounds like fantasy to me,' said Smith. 'And what if there's another bloke's DNA on them? Maybe he was bisexual.'

'Even more reason to analyse them! Statistics tell us the perp is more likely to be a male.' He turned to the Inspector, not willing to argue the point with Smith any longer. 'I'm keen to be off. Anything else Claudia and I can do before we go?'

'There's no need for you to hang about,' said the Inspector. 'I'm sure you'd rather be out on the road questioning suspects. Who's next?'

'Glenn Farr. We managed to catch her on the phone on the way over here. She came across as very willing to cooperate. Even offered to treat me and Claudia to lunch at Luigi's on the Esplanade. I'm a bit tired of my own boring sandwiches, to be honest.'

Batista shook his head. 'No taking gifts from the public, you know better than that. Especially from potential suspects.'

'But, sir, the entrees there cost a minimum of $40.'

'Tough. Keep the check and make an expense claim. You know the drill.'

'You're a pillar of virtue, sir. Thanks for keeping me on the straight and narrow. I'm a bit worried though.'

'Have you maxed out your credit card again?'

'No chance. It's just the joint's famous for its spaghetti bolognese and I'm wearing my best white shirt, innit!'

Jack gathered Taylor on the way out, she grasping a dozen or so unruly manila folders under her arm. 'Anything interesting in that pile of papers?'

'Sure is. The sales receipt, warrantee and instruction manual for the drone. He bought it from a hobby shop here in Yorkville four years ago, no wonder it's dusty. Details of share portfolios, cryptocurrency assets. His rental agreement for this house. Odd that a man on his income would rent rather than buy property.'

'Maybe he knows something others don't,' Jack suggested.

'Still seems bloody weird to me. Bricks and mortar, it's supposed to be a no-brainer when it comes to your financial security.'

'Is that it?'

'No. The most interesting thing I found was a couple of love letters between Keenan and Dervla. The ones she sent have Irish stamps on them. They must have been head over heels for each other.'

Jack opened the front door for Taylor. 'Writing letters is bleedin' unusual in the electronic age. Can't remember the last time I did that. Probably a complaint to the Croydon Council about rubbish collection.'

'Rather romantic, I reckon.'

'Rubbish collection ain't the slightest bit romantic.'

'I mean them writing to each other.'

'Can't argue with that, Claudia.'

The journey to Luigi's took fifteen minutes, during which Taylor scrolled through her mobile phone admiring pictures of her sister Annie's vegetable garden on Instagram and having a text conversation with her at the same time. Annie had undergone surgery to remove a melanoma a couple of years ago. It was benign and everything was rosy, but recently a malignant one was discovered, of all places on the sole of her foot. Things were unclear about her future, with suggestions of aggressive chemo and radiotherapy. Jack knew not to interrupt Taylor when she was communicating with Annie. Besides, he was busy mentally composing a fantasy love letter to the DC that he would never physically write.

Or would he?

The car park at Luigi's was full. A recent five-star review in the local rag had seen a big uptick in patronage. With only a couple of motorcycle spots and two for disabled customers free, Jack had to exit the parking lot. Swearing under his breath, Jack drove around the block and parked in a No Standing zone at the front of the restaurant.

'You can't leave the car here,' said Taylor. 'We're not attending an urgent matter.'

'Says who? We're conducting a murder investigation. I'd say that's pretty important, wouldn't you?'

'Seriously?' She flashed him her look of virtuous indignation, the one he found rather cute. 'What would the Inspector say?'

'Very well', he huffed, throwing the Territory into reverse. They parked two blocks away, which wasn't such a bad thing. They walked in fresh, warm air redolent of frangipani, the soft blushing pink, yellow and white flowers covering the trees' branches, some fallen to the ground.

Taylor bent to pick a flower off the footpath. 'When I was a little girl, I used to make lei necklaces out of these.'

'When I was a lad in South London I don't think I ever saw flowers outside of a florist.'

Taylor handed him the little flower. 'Then it's a good thing you moved here, innit?' She laughed, her attempt at a Cockney accent appalling.

Jack looked away from her so she didn't see his blushing cheeks. It was a very good thing indeed.

Chapter Twenty-Nine

THE OLD-FASHIONED PEARL necklace she wore on a background of tan, freckled flesh contrasted with her youth. Jack pegged her at about thirty-five. Much too young to have attained her level of success without bending the rules here and there. Jack chided himself for his cynicism; for all he knew she'd played a straight bat and her riches had been honestly obtained. *Yeah, right.*

Glenn Farr was sitting back far enough from the table for the detectives to see the woman's infamous emotional support animal. Farr, with calm, repetitive motions, stroked the head and back of the small black poodle curled up on her lap. The scene put Jack in mind of an evil criminal mastermind from a B-grade movie. The dog snored softly, eyes twitching under closed lids. Perhaps dreaming of a free life, out in a paddock chasing birds and lizards.

'You're lucky to be able to bring a dog into a restaurant,' said Jack as he pulled out a chair for Taylor, then tucked her in. 'I wasn't allowed to have one in my apartment.'

Farr smiled even white teeth. 'Yes, it's a shame landlords

take such a harsh attitude. As far as my situation goes, I got this little treasure to help keep me calm, to stop the crippling panic attacks. And,' she tapped the table with a fingernail, 'so far, so good. You can't register them like seeing eye dogs, but if you explain the situation, most people warm to the idea and you can take them to lots of places.'

'The owner of Luigi's certainly has a liberal attitude,' Taylor observed as she placed her phone on the table. 'Please excuse my bad manners,' she said, 'but there could be an important update coming from the magistrate's office.'

'No need to apologise. And yes, this restaurant is totally obliging. Mainly because *I* am the owner of Luigi's. Well, one of them. A sleeping partner, if you will.' She smiled again. It was the default setting for her face, yet there were subtle nuances. This one was a smile of self-satisfaction.

'You said the little fella—' Jack started.

'Girl. Her name's Brie. Like the French cheese.'

'Got it,' Jack nodded. 'You said she keeps you calm. Does golf also keep you calm?' He seated himself, picked up a linen napkin and flicked it open across his lap. He rubbed the material between his fingers. It was thick enough to protect him from spills; he'd take the risk and order the bolognaise after all.

'Yeah, she keeps me grounded. In day-to-day life, that is. Golf's a different story. On the fairways and greens I let my emotions out. I don't care if I lose my rag. Sometimes I'll muff a shot, hurl my club and swear like a trooper. I'm actually known for my bad temper on the golf course.' Another smile that belied the words she could ever lose control.

'An interesting admission,' said Jack.

'But a qualified one. In every other aspect of my life I'm

chill. Don't you have an outlet like I do, DS Lisbon? Some way to let off steam?'

'Yeah, I do 'n all.' He described his background in pugilism and his lifelong love of physical combat. He left out the part where the violence of the ring sometimes crossed over into his professional life. Not often, but occasionally it was the only way out of a pickle.

'And you, DC Taylor?'

Taylor paused for a moment. 'No. Somehow I don't seem to need it.'

'Half your luck,' said Farr, looking down at the dog and making faint cooing sounds.

'Does Brie accompany you around the golf course while you're playing?' said Jack.

'When I'm hitting a round by myself I take her, definitely. She loves riding in the golf cart.' A soft puppy noise came from Farr's lap, as if in confirmation of her words. 'But not when I'm playing with others. Imagine if she barked when a player was lining up a tricky putt, well, you can imagine how that'd go down!' A quick laugh. Farr ran fingers through short, dyed-grey pixie cut hair that gave her a slight resemblance to Jamie Lee Curtis. Jack couldn't understand the trend of young women deliberately going for this look. When the natural greys started springing from her head, she'd no doubt be trying to cover them up. 'But outside of the golf course,' she continued, 'there are always people around me. People who need my attention. Business partners, clients, builders, contractors. Not to mention my demanding husband and kids. It was either stay on the Valium to combat the panic attacks or try a new approach. Since I got Brie, I've found myself in a tranquil place I never thought possible. I'm also making the best decisions of my life. And I've never been happier.'

Jack analysed Farr's face. Her appreciation for the animal was touching. How hard would she crash when the poodle died? Or would she brush it off and replace her with another, take the hard-nosed pragmatic path? He was tempted to vocalise the thought but reigned himself in. Instead he asked, 'Do you play competitively?'

'When I get the chance. A friendly ladies' competition. I'm playing off scratch these days.'

'What does that mean?' said Taylor. 'I'm not up on my golfing terminology.'

'It means I have a handicap of zero. When I step onto the course, I can expect to make par over eighteen holes. It took me a long time to get this level, but I'm a very determined woman. Once I set a goal, nothing stops me from achieving it.'

'What about that temper you spoke about?' said Jack. 'Must get up the other players' noses.'

'They make allowances for me,' she said flatly. 'And I only ever get mad at myself.'

A waitress in a black apron that almost reached the floor interrupted, handed the huge fold-up wine list straight to Farr. She scanned the offerings, ordered a bottle of Tasmanian pinot noir, sparkling mineral water and a round of antipasto to nibble while they perused the menu. The dog remained completely calm under the table despite the ear-jarring acoustics created by a slate tile floor, bare brick walls and an absence of soft furnishings. Jack began to wonder if the mutt had been slipped a tranquiliser.

Enough of the small talk; time to push the envelope. 'It must have pissed you off when the Trust Bank refused to advance you the loan for your latest project. The rejection would have hurt, especially for a woman with your great track record.'

Farr gave a scratchy laugh, pulled the ubiquitous smile into a grimace. The dog stirred finally, its head popping above the edge of the table for a moment before it leapt from its owner's lap and took up a position on the floor. 'You've got to be kidding right?'

'What do you mean?'

'How would you have even the slightest clue about my financial arrangements?' Jack leaned back in his chair, the woman's suddenly feisty attitude catching him off guard. 'Especially with the bank. If that Fong blabbed to you, I'll have his guts for garters. Or maybe it was Salesa, after he got the flick.'

Taylor smiled amiably at the waitress, returning with, in one hand, a groaning platter of antipasto comprising assorted olives, cheese, cured meats and sun-dried tomatoes, and a basket of sliced focaccia in another. Once she'd departed again, Taylor said, 'Like journalists, sometimes we cops get tips from informed sources.'

'And,' said Jack, forking a piece of salami onto a slice of bread. 'Just like journos, we have to respect the confidentiality of those sources.'

Farr gave an understanding nod. 'Doesn't matter. Now I think of it, the guys I mentioned would probably respect my privacy. I've got a hunch it was someone at the club, someone who gets to hear a lot of loose talk, maybe someone who pours beers and wipes tables because that's about the only job he's fit to have. Am I right?' She stared hard at Taylor, who, Jack thought, did a creditable job of keeping a straight face.

'Like DS Lisbon said, we can't reveal things like that.' Taylor absently spun her phone in a circle.

Farr reached into a clutch bag, pulled out two business cards and handed them to the detectives. Jack studied his. It was emblazoned with the logo of her company, Farr and Away Developments. 'Why are you giving us these?' he said. 'We already have your contact details.'

'If you look closely, there's an image of a massive apartment block in the background. It's a bit like a watermark, quite faint.'

'Yes, I see it,' said Taylor. 'What is it?'

'That's the project I'm going to finish by the end of this year, perhaps as early as September if everything goes smoothly. You see, the Trust Bank isn't the only lender out there.' She stopped for a moment as a waiter came back with a bottle. He opened it, poured a tiny portion for Farr to sample and obsequiously waited for her to approve. He spent a couple of minutes explaining the wine's provenance and its brilliant qualities, ascribed to it a myriad of flavours – strangely, none of them being grape. Jack guessed he probably called himself a sommelier. For a moment, such was the enthusiasm with which the bloke imparted his knowledge, Jack almost regretted having given up the booze for good. He followed his usual routine, allowed the man to pour him a glass – it was his test whenever he was at a restaurant or pub. Have alcohol in front of him, but resist the temptation to drink it. So far, he'd been able to hold out for four solid years going on five.

'When did you get the financing to complete the project?'

'Six weeks ago. If you're thinking I had some kind of motive to kill Paul Keenan…well…I'm actually rather flattered.' She swirled the pale red alcohol around in her glass, took a long sniff through a slightly upturned nose and then a dainty sip. She picked a slice of prosciutto from the platter and dropped it on the floor. The sounds of Brie gobbling up the treat made Jack smile and shake his head at the same time. Farr had chutzpah by the bucketload. He couldn't help but like her.

Jack wasn't giving up the fight before mains had been served, though. 'Perhaps there was a lingering anger? Yes, you got the money, but it's caused you extra work and lost time and...'

Farr held up a hand with rings on every finger, thumb included. 'The bloke actually did me a favour, you know? I was able to get the money from another source at a much lower interest rate over a longer term. Not that I'll need the extra time. Lots of the apartments have sold off the plan. There are plenty left, though. Perhaps I can interest one or both of you lovely officers in an affordable condo by the sea?'

'I've recently bought an old farm property,' said Jack, stabbing food off the platter and transferring it to his own plate.

'How much?' said Taylor, locking eyes with Farr.

'Prices start at seven hundred thousand for a ground-floor unit.'

'I thought you said affordable?'

Farr shrugged. 'It's all relative, I guess. Similar properties to mine are selling for a lot more.' She chewed an olive, washed it down with a mouthful of pinot. Taylor followed suit, Jack sipped water.

'I've almost cleared you from suspicion. In my mind at least,' said Jack.

Farr beamed, topped up her own glass of wine. 'Thank you. So I don't have to surrender my passport or anything like that?'

'No, no. Of course not. But please tell me one thing. Why would Paul Keenan not approve the loan?'

'Technically, there's a separate loans office down in Brisbane where applications are processed. He may have made a recommendation against me, but maybe not. They have their procedures, ones that you and I will never be privy to.'

'But let's suppose he did make a recommendation against you, why d'ya reckon he would have done that?'

'Six months or so ago I was playing one of the holes on the back nine. On a parallel fairway I saw Keenan getting hot and heavy with Dervla Morris behind a tree. He came up for air, looked to his right and spotted me watching them. He quickly let go of her like she had the plague.'

'Oh dear,' said Taylor. 'Caught red-handed.'

'I was appalled because barely 50 metres away poor old Lachlan Morris was bashing about in the long grass with an iron, trying to locate his ball.' She tilted her head back. 'Meanwhile, Dervla's already found Paul's balls!'

'Did you mention this to anyone.'

'I…I may have mentioned it to my playing partner.'

'May have?'

'OK, I did. Who wouldn't have shared such a juicy morsel?'

'And who was that person? Anyone we might know?'

The answer was not what the detectives were expecting. Not even close.

Chapter Thirty

DESPITE WEARING the napkin across his chest and stomach like a bullet-proof vest, tomato sauce stains adorned the cuff's of Jack's precious white shirt. He tried to clean it off in the restaurant's bathroom with liquid soap and water, but only managed to spread the area of damage. It was worth it though, the meal was a knockout. The tiramisu and espresso to finish, perfection.

Back at the station, his immediate plan of action was twofold – write up a report of the interview with Glenn Farr, and conjure up an excuse for accepting largesse from a member of the public when he'd been told specifically not to. Farr ended up paying the entire bill and wouldn't accept a cent from the detectives. Jack decided he would keep quiet about it and hope the Inspector wouldn't ask questions.

Taylor appeared as he was putting the final touches to his report. She loomed over his desk, hands on hips. 'Newsflash. I've just got word from the magistrate on the production notice applications.'

Jack stopped tapping at his keyboard, looked up

obliquely with his "please tell me some good news" expression.

'Every single request has been denied. That magistrate is a…I'm too much of a lady to say it.'

He rubbed a palm across his face. 'Not unexpected, although I thought at least one of them might get over the line.'

Taylor shook her head slowly. 'No dice. On another note, I've had a quick look at the paper statements that Sabrina handed over for her bank and phone accounts. Nothing unusual that I can make out. She's clearly taking cash for her services, and that's how she pays the rent and affords the fancy gin. You think she's dealing to boost her income?'

'Ha! I'm almost sure of it. Hookers in this town don't make that much money. This isn't Vegas, or even the Gold Coast.'

'So.' Taylor blew out her cheeks. 'What now?'

'I guess we'll have to take a closer look at Ruby. After what Glenn Farr told us.'

'I agree,' said Taylor. 'She already hated Keenan for badmouthing her father. Add to that his lurid public behaviour, behind Lachlan Morris's back, and it may have spurred Ruby on further.' She paused for a moment. 'Then again, maybe it wasn't behind his back. Remember, Dervla asserts her husband gave his blessing to…'

'Bullshit, Claudia. If that was the case, why the secrecy of making out behind a tree, why did Keenan act shocked when he saw Farr watching them? I'll bet London to a brick the old bloke *never* approved of this.' He twirled a pen between his gnarled boxer's fingers. 'Ruby struck me as a person of principle. What if she went running to old man Morris and…'

Taylor rested her hands on the edge of Jack's desk. 'You're not seriously suggesting he organised the kill and made sure to get himself shot to throw suspicion? A big gamble, considering he nearly died.'

'I'm not suggesting anything of the sort. Let's push Ruby a wee bit harder. I think she knows more than she's letting on.'

'Perhaps Kylie Smith could follow up. She's already established a rapport with the woman.'

'Yes, but Kylie had that look in her eye when she mentioned the invitation to go trap shooting. She made it sound more like a potential date with Ruby than a chance to get some answers.'

'C'mon, Jack. Constable Smith's professional enough to keep a level head, you know that.' She tapped the top of a stack of folders on Jack's desk. 'I reckon you're writing Ruby off as a suspect too fast.'

'Why?'

'She's an experienced shooter. She could have transferred that marksmanship across to a drone. Maybe she was able to do some sneaky practice with the one in her dad's shed, then she's gone and got herself a bigger rig from somewhere. She's a good golfer, which requires excellent hand-eye coordination. In other words, she's got all the skills. And motive.'

'Geez, Claudia. You're right. How's about we–'

Before they could debate the point any further Jack's mobile erupted. It was the ring tone that could only mean his daughter was calling from London. Rick Astley's "Never Gonna Give You Up." The screen of his mobile phone said it was 14:40 Australian Eastern Standard Time, which was 03:40 in the UK. 'What the..?' He looked up at Taylor with big eyes. 'Excuse me, this is weird. I've gotta take it.' She nodded understandingly and retreated to give him some privacy. Something in the pit of Jack's stomach told him this wasn't a random call to say hi. Skye's opening words confirmed it.

'Dad! It's so…terrible. I can't even…' He could hear her sniffling, trying to get her breath. 'It's mum.'

'What? Has something happened to her? Did she have an accident?'

'She's really sick.'

'What, sweetheart?' He was already on the march, heading for the back landing where the Inspector and Noah Semmens took their smoke breaks.

'She's…dying, Dad.' The kid gushed garbled words through choking sobs. 'There's nothing they can do to save her.'

'Slow down, sunshine.' Fear was rising in his chest. Skye was a sensible kid, not one for making up stories. And to be calling in the middle of the night was doubly alarming. 'Tell me from the beginning.'

With a couple of false starts, Skye managed to explain. Earlier in the day, Jack's ex-wife Sarah, the Jamaican beautician he'd married fifteen years ago, collapsed in the kitchen while drying dishes. Skye didn't panic, she called 999. *Good girl.* Then she rang her Aunt Jocelyn, Sarah's sister, who was at the flat in a flash. The paramedics arrived within half an hour and rushed Sarah to King's College Hospital, daughter and sister following in an Uber. Sarah had been complaining about a lump in her lower stomach for a while, but done nothing about it. She'd even asked Skye to feel it. *It was huge, Dad! I told her to go to the doctor but she never listens to me.* At the hospital, Sarah was diagnosed with aggressive stage four ovarian cancer. The oncologist informed Sarah she would live another two months maximum.

Jack patted his pockets, looking for cigarettes he hadn't smoked in years. He located their substitute, unwrapped one and chewed hard. 'My God, where are you now?'

'I'm at Aunt Jocelyn's place. She told me not to worry you with this news, but it's wrong to keep you in the dark.'

'You did the right thing, sweetie.'

'I waited till I was sure she was asleep to call you so she doesn't get mad at me.' The sound of a nose being blown softly. 'I don't like it here, Dad. I want you to come and get me.' She broke down and sobbed steadily for more than a minute. Jack could only stare at the steel wall of the neighbouring warehouse.

When he finally spoke to her again, Jack realised his cheeks were wet. 'I will come and get you.'

'When?'

'As soon as I can.'

Chapter Thirty-One

SLUMPED IN HIS SWIVEL CHAIR, he gratefully accepted a steaming cup of coffee from Taylor. The pungent aroma of the brew was a comfort, one he used to get from whisky fumes when he was a deadbeat South London copper. She patted him awkwardly on the shoulder the way an older sister might buck up her kid brother when he'd fallen off his bike and scuffed a knee. Batista sidled up. When Smith and Trevarthen started approaching with expressions like grief-stricken zombies, it was too much. Jack stood and said, 'Thanks for the sympathy guys, but my ex-wife isn't dead yet.'

'We can handle the case, Jack,' said Taylor. 'The way it's going, we might still be working on it by the time you get back.'

Jack winced. 'That's not the defeatist attitude I'm used to hearing from you, Claudia.'

'She's right,' agreed Batista. 'You need to be with your daughter at this time.' The Inspector clasped his hands together like a priest.

'Sorry, but I'm not going anywhere until we arrest whoever killed Paul Keenan. End of.'

'Nonsense,' Batista insisted. 'You can be on a plane tomorrow. Special leave.'

'Thanks sir, but it makes no sense. I can't hang about for two whole months waiting for Sarah to pass away. Besides, I know her, she's tough and stubborn enough to defy the prognosis. Heck, if I was cancer I'd be too scared to take up residence in her body.' He offered a grim smile.

'What's your plan then?'

'When Sarah's time is coming, say a week left, I'll go then. Skye's a tough cookie like her mum. Don't forget she survived a kidnapping, with no lasting PTSD or anything like that.' He knew there could be a delayed onset of the condition, but if it never happened he wouldn't be surprised. His words about his daughter's toughness were no mere exaggeration, they were the truth. 'I'm assuming I'll get custody of her when Sarah dies, and I...'

'Don't bank on it,' said Trevarthen. 'A mate of mine assumed he'd get his son back after his ex died, but she'd made a provision in her will for guardianship to transfer to her parents. My friend contested the will in court and lost. They boy's living with his grandparents as we speak.'

Jack ran a hand through his hair, long due for a trim. Trust Aden to bring on a reality check. 'I never bleedin' thought of that.'

'Would she do that to you, Jack?' said Taylor. 'Surely the resentment must have mellowed over the years.'

'I'm not the same person I was when we parted, and she knows that.' He took a long draught of coffee. 'The man of those days didn't deserve to have his kid back. To be fair, she has treated me with less hostility as time's passed. If she was still harbouring a grudge, the only person I imagine she could appoint guardian is her sister, and Skye doesn't like her much. She'd object strongly to any direction to be handed over to Jocelyn.'

'I'll write a glowing letter of recommendation,' said Batista with an avuncular smile, finally unclasping his hands. 'If that'll help.'

'I'm sure it will, sir.' He stood and shrugged on his trusty, threadbare grey jacket. 'Oi, Smith!'

The constable, about to head out the main door with Trevarthen, strode back to where the senior officers were gathered. 'Yes, sir?'

'Have you organised that meeting with Ruby Brownstone yet?'

'Um, no sir. I'm waiting for her to make the invitation. It was her idea, after all.'

'Need I remind you that we're investigating some serious shit here. We do NOT wait for things to happen.' He locked his eyes with hers, which flickered like an old-fashioned TV warming up. 'Get onto it. I want you to get right up in her face and hit her with questions based on this.' He pushed a piece of paper against her breastbone. On it, the points about Ruby Brownstone that Taylor had raised earlier. Out of the corner of his eye he saw Taylor crack a broad smile.

'Come with me, Claudia. I think we've been concentrating too much on the murder victim and not enough on the bloke left alive.'

LACHLAN MORRIS LAY on his back, arms straight by his side on the outside of the hospital blanket, jaundiced eyes wide open. A bouquet of gerberas and chrysanthemums poked out of a glass vase, a modest card propped up against it. Jack coughed. 'Excuse me.'

'Wha...?' The head jerked in the nest formed by a soft pillow. 'Who's there?'

'The police again. Sorry to disturb you.'

'What do you want?'

'Same as you, probably,' said Taylor. 'To find who shot you.'

'And Paul, don't forget about Paul.'

'Indeed we won't,' said Jack reassuringly. 'D'ya mind?' He grabbed the card from the side table without waiting for permission. Inside was written. *Wishing you a speedy recovery, Mitch, Sally and Oliver.* Two signatures. 'I see your son's popped around, even when your wife neglected to.'

'Actually, no.' Morris reached out for the card, Jack handed it to him. 'It was my daughter-in-law, Sally, bless her. She brought the little chap in. He's such an adorable fellow.' A faint smile brightened his pallid face.

'Why didn't Mitchell come with them?'

'Apparently he's got a tummy bug. He didn't want to jeopardise my recovery. He's a good lad that one. He'll be in when he's feeling better.' Morris opened the card, read the message, put it back on the side table. Jack wondered what that little performance was all about. To show how much he loved his son?

Jack pulled up a visitor chair, went to sit down but had second thoughts. Better to reinforce the psychological dominance by staying above Morris. He leaned over at a slight angle. 'One of our officers has done some digging into your public profile.' *Thanks, Wilson.* 'It seems some people have been accusing you of using your position as president of the Rotary Club to get extra benefits. In particular, for that terrific son of yours.'

'Rubbish.' Morris blinked slowly, turned his head away sightly.

'His property was magically rezoned after you made representations to the Yorkville Council. Theoretically, this allows him to divide and sell his acreage to developers.'

Silence.

'The person affected was his neighbour, Ivor Quaid. Now, here's the interesting part. Mr Quaid's got a very similar plot of land, but the rezoning application he made after he learned what happened with Mitchell's acreage was rejected out of hand.'

More silence.

'Look, Mr Morris. I'm not interested in getting you into trouble for this, even if it's true you influenced the decision. I'm simply fleshing out potential enemies who may have wanted to, I dunno, kill you?!'

'OK, OK.' He gestured towards a plastic jug, Taylor poured him a glass of water and handed it to him. He could only manage a small sip with fumbling fingers before Taylor took the glass away. 'One of the town planners did me a favour. Yes, that neighbour of Mitchell's might have a point, but surely he wouldn't…'

'No? Our estimates put the potential profit your son can make in the millions. Quaid misses out.'

'Mitchell's got no intention of subdividing. He loves having all that space around him. It was me thinking about their financial future, Oliver's future.' Morris gave an exaggerated yawn. 'Do you mind if we stop the questions for now? I'm exhausted. And, to be honest, I can't think of anyone who'd want to hurt me. It's something to do with Paul's business, I'm sure.'

'We'll be calling in on Mr Quaid, though.'

'He won't be very welcoming.'

Jack laughed. 'Us cops are pretty used to that.'

'I can imagine.'

'Are you aware Dervla had a fit at your home yesterday and was brought here in an ambulance?'

'Yes. A doctor told me.' His voice was barely a croak now. 'Thanks for asking. I'm so glad she's on the mend.'

'We're going to speak to Dervla shortly. Now, I don't know if it's a coincidence or not, but the fit came on suddenly when I started asking about her affair with Mr Keenan.' Jack scratched behind his ear, waiting for Morris to respond. When he didn't Jack said, 'Did you hear what I said?'

'You didn't ask me a question.'

The old boy's got all his marbles, all right, Jack noted. 'Quite correct. Then let me reframe it as an unambiguous question. Did you know about the affair between your wife and the deceased?'

'No comment.'

'C'mon, Mr Morris Dervla has told us you, and these are her words, gave your blessing. Yes or no?'

'I'm very tired now.' He clicked the button on the device to summon a nurse. 'Please don't visit me again. I'll be happy to talk to you once they let me out of here.'

Out in the corridor Taylor said, 'He knew, all right.'

Jack shook his head. 'I'll admit I was wrong. But whether he approved? The jury's still out on that one.'

SITTING in the recliner chair in her private room, Dervla looked like a vampire had sucked the lifeblood out of her. Her cheeks seemed to have shrunk as well, the eye sockets jutting out. The eyes within those sockets glowed red raw.

On the wheeled table beside her chair sat an enormous pile of crumpled tissues. Jack didn't care if she was miserable. People were hiding things from him, and he didn't like it. 'How much longer are you staying in the hospital?'

'Another couple of tests and I'll be discharged.' She grabbed a fistful of tissues, let go with a trumpeting blow. 'Depending on the results, of course.'

'That fit you had was pretty serious,' said Taylor.

Dervla sighed. 'I'll be taking medication for a while, a nurse will come and check on me from time to time. Drugs might be replaced by psychological treatment later. Perhaps a combination of both. But it's early days. All I can think about is…oh, dear,' she sobbed. 'Sorry.'

Jack thrust his hands in his pockets, walked to the window, stared at the rolling green hills to the west. Low clouds hid their peaks, a grey curtain of gloom descended, the perfect match for his current mood. Without looking at Dervla he said. 'We're running out of ideas and I'm getting a tad frustrated.' He turned back around, resumed his position next to Taylor. 'What's your take on Michael Salesa and Glenn Farr? What did Paul tell you about them?'

'Not much.'

'Really?' said Taylor doubtfully.

'Really. He rarely talked business with me. Outside work hours, Paul was quite the romantic. He enjoyed talking about art, literature, loftier things, you know?'

Jack unwrapped a stick of nicotine gum and placed it in his mouth. Her assertion tallied with the high-brow reading matter on the victim's book shelves, so maybe he did leave everything at the office when he clocked off. Jack would give anything to have that luxury.

'You said not much.' Taylor wouldn't let go easily. 'Which means he did say something.'

'Let me see.' Dervla wrinkled an eye as she gave the matter thought. 'All I remember was the man, Michael was it? Yeah, he was asked to resign because he got super drunk on the job one too many times. Paul said he liked him and he was good at his job but it was a shame he was a slave to alcohol. As for the woman, nope, nothing, sorry.'

'I find that hard to believe,' said Jack. 'Glenn Farr admitted to us that she saw you and Paul canoodling on the golf course a while back, and when you realised you'd been caught, you broke it up pretty quick.'

Dervla put her hands over her eyes. 'Yes, we were ashamed to get caught like that. If Paul recognised the woman, he didn't let on to me.'

'Claudia, you got any more questions for Ms Morris? If not, we can leave her in peace.'

Taylor fixed eyes on Dervla, who was again reaching for a tissue to wipe away a couple of stray tears. 'What about your husband? Can you think of anyone who would want to hurt him?'

'Everyone who knows Lachlan adores him. I just…'

'We've recently learned of his son's neighbour getting uppity over a rezoning incident. What do you know about that?'

'Fook all. You may as well be talking Chinese; as far as that stuff goes, I'm clueless.'

'I guess we're done then,' said Jack, offering a half smile. 'We wish you a speedy recovery.'

As he turned the door handle to let himself and Taylor out, Dervla called them back. 'Listen, there's one thing I think maybe I should've mentioned before. Some bloke had a go at Paul in a shopping centre car park.'

'What?' said Jack.

'All in your own good time,' said Taylor, notebook out and pen poised.

Dervla closed her eyes tight, then they sprang open again. 'It was a Friday. Last week of January. I remember because I was desperately looking for a birthday present to send to my brother Ardal in Ireland. Something distinctly Australian.' Dervla explained she and Paul had agreed to meet at the Yorkville Mall for lunch, with Paul helping her choose a gift. 'I'm terrible at buying presents,' she said. They arrived in their own cars. She was lucky to score a spot near the entrance, and as she got out of her car, she heard shouting from a distance of about 50 metres. A tall, swarthy man with a short-cropped beard and dark curly hair was screaming at Paul, waving his arms around. Dervla locked her car and marched towards the two men, calling out Paul's name. As she got closer, she pulled out her mobile and held it up as if she was filming. 'The man saw me coming and took off like a startled fookin' rabbit.'

'So you weren't actually filming the incident?' said Jack, a little too tetchily.

'No. I had no time to set it all up. I just wanted the man gone.'

'Well done,' said Taylor. 'Who was the man yelling at Paul?'

'No idea.'

'Didn't Paul tell you who it was?'

'He had no idea either. Never saw him before. He said the man was yelling vague threats, saying he knew where he lived and he'd better watch his back.'

'Do you think you could describe the bloke for one of our sketch artists?' said Jack, the friendly tone returning. This was shaping up as the best lead they had.

Dervla nodded. 'I'll give it a try. Anything to help.'

Jack took the Kia Stinger well beyond the speed limit, sirens and lights encouraging the good citizens of Yorkville to make way for the law. Taylor shook her head most of the way, but held her tongue. A block before arrival at the mall, Jack dropped the speed back to a smidgin over the limit and killed the audio-visual spectacular. After a quick word with the ultra-cooperative manager of the shopping centre complex it was ascertained that CCTV footage was retained for a period of two months before being erased. A quick mental countback to the last Friday of January – the 31st – meant the detectives were in luck. Just. They grabbed a copy of the footage they needed on a USB flash drive for the date in question and took it back to the station for a private screening among friends.

Chapter Thirty-Two

IT WAS five minutes to official knock-off for most officers, with Damien Wells and Kylie Smith rostered on for evening patrol. Even they'd be ending their shifts before midnight – Yorkville simply wasn't big enough to warrant round-the-clock police operations: if any serious shit went down, backup could always be relied on to come from Cairns. This evening, all hands were on deck as Jack summarised the outcomes of the day's activities. Ears pricked up when he got to Dervla Morris's revelation of the aggressive stranger in the car park. Taylor took over briefly, read the description from her notes. 'And if that wasn't enough, we got hold of some interesting CCTV footage showing the incident. It's not the greatest quality, but it backs up Dervla's claim.'

The team sat in silence, watching the four minutes and thirteen seconds of the video, which, although blurry, was of a higher-quality than Jack was accustomed to from commercial security cameras. Kylie Smith stood abruptly as Jack switched off the video. 'I know who he is, sir!'

'What?' said Jack, Taylor and the Inspector one after the other, like an echo in a canyon.

'He was the man at the window at Sabrina's house. When we first reviewed the footage from our body-worn cameras, we didn't watch my video all the way to the end.'

'Who cut it short?' demanded the Inspector.

'Sorry, my bad,' said Wilson with a sheepish frown.

'Be more attentive in future,' Jack snapped. 'This has cost us valuable time.'

'Yes, sir.'

Smith continued, 'Only the guy was wearing boxer shorts at Sabrina's instead of the cargo pants and tank top we can see on that clip.'

'Anyone recognise him?' said Jack.

Mumbles of negativity.

'Let's take another look at Smith's BWC footage,' said the Inspector.

The equipment hurriedly assembled, the clip replayed, the entire CIB crew was in agreement. The man in the car park and the man at Sabrina's window were one and the same person.

'Get onto Sabrina immediately,' said Batista, the fire back in his eyes. 'She's been taking us for idiots the whole time.'

Jack stormed to his desk, snatched at the receiver and punched in a number. It rang out and he tried again with the same result. He slammed the phone down, rattling an assortment of plates and coffee mugs. A manila folder nestling precariously atop a mountain of others slid to the bottom of the pile, continued across the surface of the desk and onto the floor where its contents of loose sheets spread out in all directions. He let rip an oath of frustration. Taylor loomed beside him, the keys to the Kia Stinger clutched in her fist. 'Let's go, sunshine,' she said in a tone that brooked no argument. 'I'm driving.'

Riding shotgun for a change, Jack switched the radio to a popular music station. He hated its contemporary playlist of ephemeral tunes that were on high rotation for a month and then consigned to the dustbin of history. This week, though, a stroke of luck. The regular vacuous DJ was ill and an old-school announcer had been called up to fill the breach. Jack edged the volume up as The Clash belted out their genius cover of "I Fought the Law". Taylor side-eyed him with a frown, nevertheless her fingers tapped the top of the steering wheel in time to the rollicking tune. Jack avoided her gaze and stared at palm trees and brick-and-tile suburbia flashing by.

Taylor calmly pulled up in Sabrina's neat driveway, the Corolla parked obediently in the car port. No need to leap over fences this time. The occupant appeared at the door on the second knock, clear eyed and dressed in a modest summer frock. She cheerily admitted the cops with a wave of her hand. Moments later they were in the cool, dappled shadows of the outdoor entertainment area, seated on chunky benches behind a picnic-style table. 'Back so soon, officers?' said Sabrina. 'Come to apologise for your earlier break-and-enter performance?'

'Not on you life.' Jack could feel the tendons in his neck flexing. 'And we broke nothing.'

'My financial records were all in order, I take it?'

'As far as we can tell,' said Taylor, 'there's nothing untoward.'

'Although,' said Jack, 'with new information come to light, I'm about to convince the magistrate ALL your sneaky affairs need going over with a fine-tooth comb. Right down to the very last text message and email.'

'I beg you pardon?' Sabrina stirred a swizzle stick around a tall glass. She made no move to offer refreshments to the detectives.

A coloured photo fell to the table – a still image from the CCTV footage. Then another, this one reproduced from Smith's body camera. 'You know this bloke?'

She shook her head rapidly. 'No.'

Jack waited for a moment, Taylor said nothing and kept her eyes focused on Sabrina. The woman began to squirm ever so slightly in her seat.

'Can it, Ms Keenan.' Jack rolled up his shirt sleeves, the dotted spatters of bolognese sauce disappearing as he made the folds. 'Don't bullshit me, today of all days. I've received some rather bad news from back home in the UK and you playing games isn't making it better. When people tell me lies, I have this tendency to lose my temper. Luckily, young Claudia here is on hand to make sure I don't tip this effin' table on its end!' He banged his hand hard on the tabletop, a couple of blue-headed lorikeets flew from a hibiscus bush with a squawk.

'What's the meaning of this?' Her eyes bulged like one of the hundreds of cane toads that had taken up residence in Jack's dam. 'If I said.. '

'Ms Keenan.' Taylor pushed across the photo from Smith's body cam. 'This man is standing at your bedroom window. You can't deny it. A jury would agree.'

Sabrina held shaking hands up in front of her. 'Whoa! Jury? What are you talking about? Are you going to arrest me?'

'I'm seriously thinking about it,' said Jack.

'OK, OK. He's a client. The one at my window, I mean.'

'The one in the car park's the same guy!' said Jack. 'Same hair, same short beard, same height and build.'

'I'll admit,' said Sabrina. 'The similarity is striking, but I don't think you can be a hundred percent certain the one in the car park is the same man. It's rather blurry and taken from quite a distance.'

'Come off it!' Jack was on his feet, pacing behind the bench seat.

'Is the bloke at the window a regular client?' said Taylor.

'Give us his name, dammit,' Jack thundered. 'If he ain't the bloke in the car park, let him clear himself. Otherwise, we're throwing all our resources at IDing him. We might even hand these images over to the press. Your name will be linked to the appeal for information, of course.'

Sabrina cleared her throat. 'I'd love to help, but integrity's vital in my line of work. I have to respect the man's confidentiality. He's got nothing to do with what happened to Paul and Lachlan, I swear it.'

'Then can you explain why he was berating Paul in the car park of the Yorkville Mall on the 31st of January?'

Sabrina shook her head, said with clear exasperation. 'You're making a mistake, seeing what *you* want to see.' She tapped the photo of the gesticulating man in the car park. 'I'm telling you, these are different men.'

Jack scooped up the photos, placed them side by side, stared hard at one photo, then the other. 'I can't see no differences. Height, build, hair, skin tone. Neither of 'em have any tattoos that are visible. You look, Claudia. I'm going bleedin' cross eyed here.'

Taylor lined up the pictures as Jack had, analysed them for a minute each, running fingers through her hair as she concentrated. Jack resumed his pacing, Sabrina sipped her drink. 'I think I see it now,' said Taylor softly. 'Their noses are slightly different.'

'What?' Jack stopped. 'No they ain't!'

'Yep. See car park man? His nostrils are quite wide, almost flared. The man in the window, I reckon he's got a thinner nose.'

'Dammit to hell!' Jack grabbed up the photos, shoved them back in the envelope. 'Let's go Claudia, before I have a bleedin' stroke.'

Chapter Thirty-Three

GENTLE, knee-high waves broke onto the beach, lapped gently amid hermit crabs and scattered shells. In such an idyllic location, the sign in five languages that warned against swimming in these crocodile-infested waters seemed to be spreading unnecessary fear. The fatality statistics recorded for this spot – five in the last decade – said otherwise. Jack held his hand up to block the sun as it crested the horizon in the east, bathing the still morning in a warm, golden glow. Jack rubbed Daisy behind the ear, adjusted her collar and double-checked the clip to her lead. Good to go. He took a dozen or so running strides, then pulled up to observe a pair of nonchalant kangaroos, almost camouflaged against the background of dark green trees. They glanced at Jack and Daisy before hopping languidly into the thick jungle that lined the two-metre-wide ribbon of sand. Daisy barked twice and lunged towards the spot where the roos had been, but Jack gave a gentle tug on the lead and set off once more. It quelled the animal's curiosity for now, as Daisy resumed her ungainly, loping run beside her master.

Jack covered the 3 km in either direction in less than thirty-five minutes. Sweat pouring off him, he breathed in and out like a busted bellows. Despite the knowledge, the warning sign and common sense, he stripped down to his underwear and dived headlong into the water. He ducked under a couple of times before deciding he'd pushed his luck far enough. Trudging through the sudsy backwash, something hard and heavy brushed against the outside of his calf. Jack couldn't remember the last five steps to escape the water, although the image of his grinning, sopping wet dog trotting alongside as he reached the shore would stay with him forever. He grabbed Daisy's face in both hands, looked into her brown eyes. 'You scared me to death, you bleedin mutt!' Skye would have roared with laughter.

Jack spent the morning at his desk, going over every scrap of information they had found relating to the case. By midday his head was spinning. Nothing was making sense. The car park man was giving him the biggest headache. Was it some random altercation between Paul Keenan and a member of the public? It was the version Jack was leaning towards. The only wrinkle: why didn't Paul simply come out and tell Dervla what it was about? He requested the video of the man at Sabrina's window be posted internally to a QPS webpage. Perhaps another officer somewhere in the state might recognise the person and call it in. By lunchtime, crickets on that score. He bailed up Smith before she went on her rounds, confirmed a trap shooting "interview" with Ruby Brownstone, unfortunately not until the end of the week. Still, better than nothing.

At 13:45 he received a preliminary report from Margaret Proctor, cc'd to Taylor and the Inspector. Unfortunately, it contained more questions than answers. Proctor had sent the sex toys gathered from Keenan's home to the lab for DNA testing, but she didn't expect a response for at least a week, maybe two. Full autopsy on Paul Keenan revealed the obvious: a supremely healthy man cut down by bullets. ETA on the ballistics report – three weeks. Frustrated, Jack grabbed his jacket, headed for the exit. The plan – grab a double espresso from the Good Bean café and a latte for Taylor, sit down at his workstation and trawl, trawl, trawl. The most unglamorous part of policing, but the part that often produced breakthroughs.

At the door, his plan changed. On the way in was a figure in the drama he'd thus far not spoken to. Jasper Keenan. 'I need to talk to someone.' The whites of his eyes had acquired a pale pink tinge, his posture was limp.

'Will I do?' said Jack, channelling rarely used Good Cop.

Jasper pointed to Taylor, studying something intently on her computer monitor. 'I spoke to her last time. She's nice.'

'Cool. She can join us then.'

The detectives ushered Jasper into Interview Room 1. The witness straightened his shoulders prior to taking a seat, accepted a cup of tea with milk and two sugars and readily agreed to being recorded. 'I'm done crying. I wanna do whatever it takes to get justice for Uncle Paul.'

'You sure you don't want another person present?' said Taylor.

'I'm an adult,' said Jasper matter-of-factly. 'Twenty-two in July.'

Jack adjusted the camera, resumed his seat. 'It's nothing to do with your age, sunshine. Sometimes it's useful to have someone you know and trust sitting beside you.'

'No need. What I'm going to say would probably piss off every person I know and trust.' He offered a weak smile, but Jack knew the lad's heart must be pounding. The interview room was stark and foreboding even for the toughest crims.

Half an hour later, Jasper had left the station, returned to the home he said he hated, but with a smug look of satisfaction on his face. Jack sat scratching his jaw, Taylor and Batista crowding his desk. 'He's not the kind of son I'd be wanting. Asking us to arrest his own father!'

'Maybe there's something in what he says, though,' said Batista. 'The feud between the brothers goes back a long way. Perhaps Rohan should figure higher as a potential suspect. I'm thinking back to Trevarthen's report; he said the man started acting weird all of a sudden and sent him packing.'

Jack shook his head. 'Nope. He'd just lost his brother, bad blood aside, so strange behaviour is understandable. As for Jasper, the kid's blind to reality. I mean, he claimed he had no knowledge of his uncle's affair with Dervla Morris. Fuck's sake, half the town knows about it! My guess, the uncle's been slowly poisoning Jasper's mind with nonsense about his father. That kind of psychological drip-feeding is gonna have a cumulative effect, innit.'

Taylor looked at the Inspector. 'Jack's right. Jasper has this unwavering loyalty to Paul. Even when we told the kid we had corroboration from several sources that Paul was fooling around with a married woman, he refused to accept it. Said everyone was making it up because they hated Paul, they were jealous of him, you name it.'

'Nevertheless, perhaps we should bring in Rohan to rattle his cage,' said Batista.

'Maybe later,' said Jack. 'We've got better things to be putting our efforts into.'

'Such as?' said Batista. 'I don't see a lot of options right now.'

Jack explained how he had planned to delve into the databases and hit the phones when Jasper had strolled in to denounce his dear old dad. Batista summoned the two detectives into his office to brainstorm, a tactic that had opened up new perspectives on previous cases. Jack agreed: alone, he wasn't seeing the forest for the trees and it was pissing him off.

'Let's start with the nuts and bolts.' said Batista. 'Have you seen Proctor's report?'

Both detectives had, but discounted it as a formality. Everything in it, they knew already.

'What about your man in the UK, Micky Knox? Has he come up with anything?'

'Nada.'

'On a similar negative note,' said Batista with a frown. 'Our technical experts at HQ haven't been able to find evidence of the purchase of a top-of-the-range drone in the Yorkville area during the last twelve months.'

'Another long shot,' said Jack. 'The equipment could have been bought anywhere and driven here!'

Batista sighed. 'This morning I spoke with the head of the Federal Police, asked him to do me a favour and expedite enquiries into possible links between Keenan and terrorist organisations.'

'I'll bet you my Hilux that's nothing but a wild goose chase, too, sir.'

Batista twisted a paperclip until it snapped in half, immediately grabbed another and repeated the process. 'What do you base that assumption on?'

'Logic. If the IRA or similar was going to take out Keenan they'd have put a bomb in his car. They're pretty predictable when it comes to MO.'

A glum silence fell on the trio. Batista broke it. 'I'd like to interview the Country Club President and the Operations Manager. Ballistics are going to the course today to take photos, measure angles, hunt for any remaining evidence. After that, I don't think it's fair or productive to keep the Club shut. I'm going to give them permission reopen tomorrow.'

'Wise decision,' said Jack with a nod.

'You don't suspect the President or the Ops Manager had a hand in this, do you sir?' said Taylor.

'No. But they're sure to have their own theories. I reckon they know me well enough to open up.'

Jack picked at a tiny spot of dirt under a fingernail. 'I'm sure they'll cooperate, sir. That charm of yours is irresistible.'

The Inspector ignored the flippant remark. 'They'll have insider information about members of the club we haven't canvassed yet who disliked Keenan.'

'Or Morris,' said Jack.

Taylor walked to the window, prised the venetian blinds apart and looking out onto the street. 'Jack's right. We've been focussing too much on Keenan and not enough on Morris. The fact he was hit was no accident. The shooter deliberately took aim at both of them. In fact, more bullets went into Morris.'

'True,' said Jack. 'Three slugs as opposed to two.'

'I hadn't looked at it that way,' admitted Batista.

'Therefore, I propose getting close and personal with Mr Ivor Quaid. It was on the to-do list, but now I'm seeing the absolute urgency of it.'

'Who did you say?' Batista spun a pen in circles on his desk. 'I've missed the memo on that guy.'

'Wilson dug up the information. It'll be in the online file, sir.' Taylor explained the rezoning gift bestowed upon

Morris's son, Mitchell, and the neighbour's failed application to council seeking the same decision. 'The bloke's potentially missing out on a lot of money, so he may've wanted revenge.'

'What do we know about him?' Batista pressed. 'Anything to suggest he's volatile?'

'A retired postal worker who's a bit of a loner and a crank. Lachlan Morris said we wouldn't get a warm welcome.' Jack was on his feet. 'C'mon, Claudia. Let's visit Morris Jr and his neighbour. The effin' deskwork can wait.'

Chapter Thirty-Four

MITCHELL MORRIS and his family lived in a small log cottage 43 km inland from Yorkville. Ten acres of mixed farming land and native bush bisected by a long, winding dirt road that was bordered either side by thick scrub. As Taylor slowed to swerve around a fallen log, a mother cassowary and its three chicks crossed in front of the vehicle. In a country full of bizarre wildlife, the adult of this species was a standout – almost as big as an ostrich with a lustrous blue head crowned by a kind of horn, red flaps on its neck. The fuzzy black-and-tan striped babies looked like they belonged to an entirely different species. Taylor explained it was a stroke of luck to glimpse them; the Australian cassowary was classified as endangered. 'Could be an omen we're going to get lucky with this case,' Taylor suggested with a half smile.

'Let's hope you're right. Pity it all happened too fast to take a photo. Skye will never believe me when I tell her.'

'I'll corroborate your story.'

'Bleedin' heck, Claudia. Do you ever drop the cop speak?'

Curtains at one of the windows twitched as the Ford Territory bounced ever closer to the end of the track and the turning circle at the front of the house. A stocky man in a broad-brimmed leather hat, blue overalls framing a black-and-white checked shirt appeared on the bullnose veranda. He beamed a smile of welcome, placed his large hands on the railing and waited for his guests to climb the stairs.

'Howdy,' he thrust out a calloused paw, first to Jack, then to Taylor. 'You guys look like cops.'

'No fooling you, is there,' said Jack without a trace of sarcasm. 'I guess it's the clothes we wear.'

Mitchell nodded. 'And the fact my old man's been the target of a murder attempt.' He pursed his lips, almost hidden in a luxurious woodsman's beard. 'And poor Paul, too. I almost forgot him. I expect you'll be wanting to know what I make of the whole tragedy. Shocking.'

'Indeed,' said Taylor. 'Now, are you sure you're up to talking. Your father told us you had a bad tummy bug.'

'The operative word being *had*. I picked some wild mushrooms and fried 'em up, but there musta been a sneaky toadstool amongst them. I was crook as a dog for a couple of days.'

Jack had seen a few mushrooms growing on his own property. Whether they were edible or deadly, he had no clue. He resolved to do some research. 'Unlucky.'

Mitchell laughed, his florid cheeks shaking. 'I'm usually good at identifying the rogue fungi, but there are some lookalike false friends that can slip through. Luckily, they're not of the lethal variety.' He wiped his hands on a towel he retrieved from a back pocket. 'Please, you've driven a long way, come inside and take a load off.' As they walked down a bright hallway, a skylight letting in sunshine, Mitchell said, 'The surgeons have done a wonderful job. That Dr Pereira, he's a marvel. I'll be popping in to see dad after work tomorrow.'

'Where do you work?' said Taylor. She side-eyed Jack, who was frowning at the compliment given to the doctor.

'Varney's in downtown Yorkville. You know it?'

The officers nodded in unison. Varney's was a vacuum cleaner specialist store. Its TV adverts were famous in Far North Queensland for their catchy, cheesy jingles. 'What do you do there?' said Jack.

'Very boring, I'm afraid. I sell bloody vacuum cleaners. And I help out with the accounts from time to time. Not very glamourous.'

'You were worried about *us* having a long drive to get here,' said Jack. 'You've got a 90 km daily commute.'

Mitchell waved his hand dismissively. 'Not really. I listen to audio books as I drive and the time flies by.' Jack chided himself — he'd lived four years in this vast country but his Englishman's brain still thought a drive like that was an odyssey. For Aussies, it was like a walk to the letterbox.

They reached a sprawling open-plan kitchen-diner-living room, where a woman in a paisley headscarf stirred a large pot, steam climbing towards an extractor fan where it narrowed before being sucked away. The aroma of a hearty stew reminded Jack of how little he'd eaten today. A chubby-faced baby lay sleeping in a bassinet within arm's length of his mother.

'We've got company, Sally,' said Mitchell. 'The police have decided to pay us a visit.'

The woman turned the gas down, rested a wooden spoon on a small plate, and joined the others at the kitchen table. 'I wondered when you'd finally get here. We're desperate to help you catch the bastard who did this.' She spoke the last words through slightly clenched teeth. 'I've cried a river. Mitchell too, although he puts on a brave face.' She turned a warm smile towards her husband. 'Lachlan is the best father-in-law I could have wished for. I've been married before, and that whole family was a disaster, let me tell you! Lachie is a treasure. He'd do anything for us, so what happened is an absolute tragedy.'

Jack marvelled as the woman spoke so effusively. They'd come to talk to Mitchell, but it seemed he was going to have to wait his turn. As she rambled, Jack took in the copious decorations and *objets d'art* scattered about the house. He counted a dozen intricate laminated jigsaw puzzles in frames, each containing at least a thousand pieces, sailing ships in bottles perched on free-standing shelves, a collection of famous landmarks made of matchsticks. He recognised the Taj Mahal and Angkor Wat among them.

'Sally, would you get the detectives a drink?' interrupted Mitchell. 'How about some of that delicious mango and paw-paw juice you made?' The beverages appeared together with a towering plate of biscuits, also bearing the rustic appearance of being homemade.

'Mr Morris,' said Jack, turning his body square to the man. Time for his missus to cede the floor, at least for a few minutes. 'First of all, who do you think would want to harm your father?'

Mitchell shook his head slowly. 'You know, I've been asking myself the same question since we heard the awful news. Racking my brain. Now, I'm not a sticky beak by nature, so I'm not up to speed with all of dad's business dealings. I mean, he's retired now, but he still has mates in Rotary and at the Country Club who…geez, I dunno. Everybody likes dad!'

Sally nodded enthusiastically. 'The only person who might have got his nose out of joint over Lachie is our neighbour, Mr Quaid.'

Jack asked about the rezoning situation, and Mitchell's answer caught him by surprise. 'I'm going to try and get the decision reversed.'

'Pardon?' said Taylor.

'Exactly what I said. You've probably done your homework on us. This is a big property. Lots of pasture, but also plenty of bush. Now, when people buy large acreages like this, they tend to do it for one main reason. Solitude. Sally and I plan to live out our days here, raise Oliver in a healthy environment.'

'And having an angry neighbour isn't conducive to that,' said Sally. 'We've got no reason to want to subdivide. Sometimes Lachie's generosity can go to extremes.'

'We'll definitely be talking to your neighbour.' Jack turned to Mitchell. 'Do you know if he flies drones or does much shooting?'

'No idea.' said Mitchell, helping himself to two biscuits at once. 'You'd have to ask him yourself. I'd guess he's got a rifle, but we've never seen or heard any drones hovering about, have we love?' He glanced at his wife, who gave a shake of her head.

'And you?' said Jack. 'Got any guns we ought to know about?'

'If you checked your database, you'd have seen I have two registered shotguns. I use them to keep the roo and possum numbers under control. The odd feral dog and cat, too.'

'Gotcha,' said Taylor, scribbling on her notepad. She had checked the records and the man was telling the truth. 'Pistols?'

'You gotta be kidding. No one has pistols out in the countryside.'

'What about drone flying?' said Jack. 'Ever had a go at that?'

'Ha!' Mitchell gestured at the numerous pieces of artwork. 'Apart from the odd round of golf, those bad boys take up all my spare time. I've been making models since I was a kid. You like them?'

Jack had to admit they were of the highest quality.

'He spends hours fiddling with them,' said Sally. 'It's almost an obsession.'

'I wouldn't go that far.' The big man blushed as he dunked a biscuit in his glass of fruit juice. 'I still manage to keep this property in order, don't I?'

Sally reached across and touched the top of her husband's hand. 'Of course you do, babe. But meeting up with your cronies once a week without fail has gotta be close to an obsession.'

'I'd call it dedication to my passion,' said Mitchell with a broad grin.

Sally smiled across the table at her husband. 'I can agree with that.'

As much as Jack was enjoying the small talk, the interview was meandering down the plug hole. 'Mrs Morris, you said you were glad we'd finally come because you want to help us catch the killer.'

'You bet!' she said with a forefinger thumping the table.

'Exactly how are you going to do that? What information do you have?'

'Um…wow. I hadn't…' She tucked her lips together, tilted her head apologetically. 'What I meant was, we'll do anything we can, but I guess I hadn't thought it through.'

'Let's talk about Paul Keenan.'

Mitchell shrugged. 'Happy to.'

'How about the rumours he was having an affair with your father's lovely young wife?' Jack stared hard into Mitchell's eyes, looking for a tell. Nothing.

'We've all heard them. It's bullshit made up by troublemakers. Dad and Dervla are as much in love today as they were when they got married.' He pointed at a portrait of a younger version of Lachlan Morris with a blonde woman and a teenage boy. 'She'll never, ever, replace my mother, God rest her soul, but she seems to make dad happy.'

'I hate to burst your bubble, sunshine, but Dervla and Keenan were getting it on.'

'Rubbish!' interjected Sally. 'We've had Lachie and Dervla over for dinner several times, and they never stop holding hands and smiling at each other.'

'An act on her part,' said Jack with no emotion. 'When a fellow officer and I raced to the crime scene we found Dervla cradling a dead Paul Keenan in her arms, your father lying bleeding just metres away. She told me Keenan was the man she loved.'

'Means nothing,' said Mitchell. 'She would have been in deep shock, behaving out of character. No, I won't be having any talk of her cheating on dad, you get me?' His eyes glowed. 'Besides, I've played golf with the three of them myself, and from what I could tell Paul and her were nothing more than good friends.'

'OK,' said Jack in a conciliatory tone. 'Let's assume the people who have sworn to us that Paul and Dervla were having an affair are all lying. Including Dervla herself. It's possible, could be a conspiracy. To what purpose, I have no idea. But let's assume all of that is true.'

'Because it is!' The first sign of heat coming into his voice. *The man loves his father so much he's in complete denial.*

'Right. Is there anyone you can think of, from the Country Club for example, who may have wanted to hurt Paul Keenan.'

'Easy. Reg Brownstone. For one thing, he flies the drone to survey the course…'

'Not any more,' said Taylor. 'He kept crashing.'

'Ha! That could have been a distraction. Fact is, Paul let rip – unfairly, granted – against old Reg in public. He's a proud man. I'd be looking at him.'

'I can assure you, we are,' said Jack.

'And if not him, his kooky daughter could've taken it upon herself to exact revenge.'

'Why kooky?' said Taylor.

He shrugged. 'I dunno. Her relationship with Reg is way too close.'

'You're not suggesting…?' said Taylor, eyebrows arched.

'No, no,' said Mitchell, writhing slightly in his seat. 'Nothing like that. It's just at her age, you'd think she'd have struck out on her own by now.' He paused, took a drink. 'I know Paul upset some people in the business world with decisions that went against them.'

'How do you know that?' said Taylor. 'That's confidential information.'

'The Yorkville Country Club is the kind of place where people have a few drinks, spill their guts in the bar, sometimes exaggerate, sometimes not. But there's no smoke without fire.'

'Yet that somehow doesn't apply to Dervla and Paul's little affair?' Jack studied the man's face for a traitorous tell. Mitchell remained impassive.

'I told you, I've been with them all together. If there was something afoot, I'd pick up on it.' He took a deep breath. 'And another thing. Paul's been a great friend to Dad over a number of years, which means he's a great bloke. Whoever killed him and nearly killed my father is an absolute arsehole!' The man's face turned a light shade of beetroot.

'Mitchell!' cried his wife. 'Language!'

'It's all right,' said Taylor. 'Technically, your husband is correct.'

'And I'll tell you who fits that definition perfectly,' said Mitchell. 'Paul's ex, Sabrina. A complete bloody fruitcake.'

When the pile of biscuits had dwindled to crumbs and the jug of juice was empty, the two detectives thanked the Morrises and took their leave. A quick check on neighbour Ivor Quaid revealed a lonely and grumpy old man afflicted with horrific arthritis. The man hobbled about with a walking cane, a faithful border collie at his heel. The property had been in the family for years, he said, and he was the last descendant with no heirs.

'When I got wind of that whippersnapper next door getting his land rezoned I hit the roof!' There was a spark in his cloudy eyes, in contrast to the fragile physical shell.

'What do you plan to do now?' said Jack.

'Dunno,' Quaid said. 'Write a letter of appeal to the mayor, I guess. I was hoping to sell off parcels of land and get meself into a nice nursing home. I got no one to look after me, 'cept Molly here.' He reached out a gnarled hand, gently patted the dog on the head.

'Did you have any anger towards Mitchell's father?'

'Why? I don't even know the bloke.'

'He's the one who got the rezoning application through.'

'He did? I had no idea. Just got a letter from the council telling me about the new status of the Morris place next door. I thought young Mitchell had done it. Anyway, I got an old mate, a retired solicitor, to help me write up my own application. Didn't help, though, it came back with a bloomin' great red stamp on it saying rejected!'

'Did you approach Mitchell Morris with your grievance?' said Taylor.

'Yeah. I rung up to give him a piece of my mind. I was swearing me head off, which maybe wasn't too smart, and he hung up on me. He must reckon I'm a crank. Sometimes I think the same thing.'

A quick look between Jack and Taylor. They were wasting time with Quaid. Jack touched him gently on the forearm as he slipped on his jacket. 'Mitchell tells us he's going to have the rezoning decision reversed.'

A weak smile accentuated Quaid's network of crow's feet. 'Still, I was hoping I'd be able to subdivide and make a fortune.'

'Don't despair,' said Taylor. 'Even as a rural listing this place would be worth a mint. Enough to pay for twenty years in a retirement home.'

'You reckon I got that long?'

'Sure,' said Jack. 'Probably more.'

As they turned left to enter the highway, Taylor said aloud what Jack was thinking. They were down to three contenders – Reg and Ruby Brownstone and Sabrina Keenan.

Chapter Thirty-Five

JACK DISCONNECTED the call to Constable Smith, twiddled a dial to boost the radio volume. Taylor's hand darted to the dash to turn it down again, but only a fraction. Driver's choice was the rule when it came to music, but the DC generally let Jack have his way. Jack grunted his thanks. The old-school announcer was on again, playing pioneering punk classics from the bottom of the archive. The Saints were belting out "Stranded", a high-octane number with the melodious qualities of a rusty chainsaw. That this Australian band didn't become one of the biggest punk acts in the world was a travesty in Jack's mind.

'I understand Friday's a long way off, but Kylie's going to sound desperate hitting up Ruby again so soon.'

'Nonsense.' Jack wound down his window, inhaled a lungful of sweet, tropical air. 'If anyone's desperate, it's me. I need to get to London ASAP, preferably not with this effin' case unsolved.'

Taylor shifted down a couple of gears, nursed the vehicle over a speed hump. 'That's your pride talking.'

'The longer this drags on, the less chance there is of cracking it. You know the statistics.'

'Whatever.'

'I'll forgive you that petulant attitude only because I know you won't give up, even if I have to abandon ship.'

'Damn straight.'

Jack kept his mouth shut, savoured the last minute of the song until it ended gently, with a soft one-two drum strike and a tinkle of cymbals. He looked up, realised they weren't heading back to the station as he assumed they would. 'Where are we going, Claudia? I'm hoping it's that new café on Strudwick Avenue. The reviews are terrific.'

'Close, but no espresso.' She drove another three blocks before turning into the now familiar Lang Street, Yorkville West. She guided the Territory behind a Jeep parked four doors down from number 28, on the opposite side of the street.

'What are we doing here?' said Jack. 'Stalking?'

'Stakeout.'

'C'mon, Claudia. This is ridiculous. This car has the word POLICE written on it in massive capital letters. If you wanna do a stakeout, let's go and grab your Honda Civic, a bag of treats from the bakery, a thermos full of coffee, and do it properly.'

'I hate it when you're right.' She made a hasty U-turn and headed for the station.

Car swap completed and refreshments on board, they returned to the same spot behind the Jeep in under thirty minutes. On the way, Taylor fleshed out her scheme.

'Are you seriously going to do this?' said Jack.

'Yep. I've had a rethink about car park man and bedroom man.'

'And what's your conclusion?'

'I saw a difference that I wanted to see. The flared nostrils weren't some natural feature, it was because the bloke was angry. Or at least pretending to be.'

'The main problem I have with this idea — if you're right — is the timing.'

'It's not a problem. Remember, Semmens and Smith turned up at her house around lunchtime and Sabrina and the escort were already going at it. According to Smith, Sabrina said the guy was called Chip. Probably a stage name.'

Jack unbuckled his seatbelt, wriggled his back into the seat. 'You ready for a bit of devious fun?'

She sucked in a deep breath. 'As the old Elvis song goes, it's now or never.'

Taylor pulled out her mobile, activated loudspeaker. Jack turned on the iPad that went everywhere with them, pulled up a webpage displaying about a dozen ads: men offering escort and massage services. Ages from early twenties up to late forties. 'Bloody hell. I had no idea there was this kind of a demand for male sex workers.'

'Is there one called Chip?'

'Lemme see.' He scanned the ads, eyes widening as he read the descriptions of services offered. Some were graphic, nothing held back. 'Nope. The first five are agencies, then the lone operators.'

'Start at the top and work your way down,' she said flatly.

Jack bit back an inappropriate rejoinder. 'Righto.' He read out the first number. Taylor rang it and the call went to voice mail after one ring; she left no message.

'Next,' she said.

Same result.

Third call. 'Hello,' said a friendly female voice. 'Max Longo Premium Escorts. How can I help you?'

Taylor spoke in a voice with a slightly higher pitch than her own, emulating Sabrina Keenan. 'I'd like you to send around my regular man, the lovely Chip. Right away. I'm in desperate need of a...massage.'

Jack rolled his eyes, but the performance was creditable. Taylor did manage to sound a lot like Sabrina.

'I'm sorry, he's currently showing on our system as off-duty. He won't be available for another two hours.'

'Book me in. Tell him Sabrina can't wait to see him!' She gave the address, ended the call, turned to Jack. 'See, I was right. She *was* playing the double bluff.'

'How did you know?' Jack tipped coffee into a plastic cup, handed it to Taylor, then poured himself one.

'I didn't. It was purely a hunch.'

'This firm charges $300 per hour. How does she afford it?'

'Let's find out.'

Jack cracked his knuckles. Taylor had done her bit, now it was up to him. *Let's hope Chip plays ball.*

SUNSET WAS FAST APPROACHING when a late-model silver Hyundai Elantra sedan pulled up in Sabrina Keenan's driveway. Sabrina's car had departed fifteen minutes prior, heading north along Lang Street away from the detectives. She could return at any moment. Jack felt his pulse quicken, he noted Taylor's eyes blinking rapidly.

The target moved about in his seat, made some hand gestures, clearly speaking to someone hands-free.

'Shit,' said Taylor. 'What if he's ringing her to confirm? I didn't think of that.'

'Let's hope he's touching base with the agency to say he's arrived safely. If he's calling her and she denies making the booking, they'll figure it's a ruse and he'll drive away. Let's wait a bit.'

The target opened the car door and stepped out, a shopping bag in his right hand. He stared at the spot where Sabrina's Corolla should have been parked, scratched his head for a moment. Jack pegged him at a couple of inches taller than himself. The man's muscular chest and arms filled out a navy blue polo shirt, faded jeans encased bulging thighs. No pushover. In the fading light, the man turned slightly, the DS caught his profile and recognised him as the star of the two videos.

A word of encouragement from Taylor before Jack opened the car door, closed it gently, crouched and scooted across the street. He walked briskly across the concrete driveway and tapped Chip on the shoulder. 'A word, if you don't mind.'

The target spun around and adopted a boxer's defensive stance, dropped the paper bag, which toppled over and spilled its contents. Out of the corner of his eye, Jack registered a large jar of lubricant, packets of condoms and a pair of fluffy pink hand-cuffs. He thrust out his ID, but Chip chose flight over fight, and in a heartbeat was halfway down the driveway, arms and legs pumping.

Jack swore under his breath and gave chase. Tyres squealed as Taylor gunned her Honda Civic across the street and into Sabrina's driveway, bumping over the gutter in her haste. The DC leapt out of the car, Glock gripped firmly in both hands and pointed directly at the oncoming gigolo. 'Stop, police!' she screamed.

Chip slowed to a walk, put his hands behind his head. 'OK, don't shoot me.'

Taylor looked down and holstered her weapon; Chip took the opportunity of her momentary distraction to vault over a neighbour's breeze-block wall and hare off down the street.

Jack sucked in a deep breath, summoned his inner Olympic sprinter and turned on the afterburners. He gained on the lumbering ox with every stride. Chip had spent too much time developing his muscles at the expense of aerobic training. At the T-junction at the end of Lang Street, Jack dived at the man's legs, driving his shoulder at a point inches above the left thigh in a classic rugby tackle. Chip expelled a loud "oof" as his hundred-kilo body crashed head-first into the concrete footpath. Jack neatly applied a wrist lock and hoisted the oaf to his feet. Chip, face scratched and bloodied, protested in pain as the DS tightened the restraining hold without mercy. 'No wonder you don't have a proper job,' said Jack. 'You're too effin' stupid.'

Chip uttered a guttural groan before finding his voice. 'This is…police…brutality.'

'Shut up or I'll arrest you for failing to obey a lawful instruction and resisting arrest. Answer a couple of easy questions down at the station, and you'll be home in time for tea. Now, hands behind your back before I snap your wrists.'

Chip meekly surrendered and Jack deftly applied zip-tie handcuffs. 'Not as sexy as the ones you carry around,' he whispered in the man's ear. 'But very effective.'

Taylor pulled up beside them. 'Need a hand?'

Point Blank

THE DIGITAL CLOCK above the door of Interview Room 1 said it was 6:23pm. Jack was keen to catch up with Trevarthen at the Iron Horse for a round of sparring at 8:00pm, but he'd postpone if necessary. Something told him young Chip could provide valuable insights. 'Thanks for coming in to assist with our enquiries,' Jack said amiably. 'We appreciate co-operative members of the public, don't we DC Taylor?'

'Indeed we do.'

'Now, for the camera, could you please state your full name, address and occupation.'

The witness dabbed at his face with a tissue, looked briefly at the spot of blood, held it up to the camera. 'I'm co-operating because I was assaulted!'

'Name, address and occupation, please,' said Jack, arms folded across his chest.

'You weren't assaulted,' said Taylor. 'You were apprehended while fleeing Detective Sergeant Lisbon. Now, please answer the question.'

The man expelled a lungful of air. 'Nathan Amos Weaver, flat 4, 12 Gould Parade, masseuse. I'd like a lawyer please.'

'What for?' Jack stood, spun the metal chair around and sat astride it, arms resting on the spine. 'You're not under arrest. But we could proceed with charges if you like, in which case I'd strongly advise you to seek representation. Your call, Chip.'

'Please call me Nathan. Chip's reserved for clients.'

'Oh, do forgive me,' said Jack in a voice dripping with sarcasm. 'We won't keep you long. First, why were you yelling at Paul Keenan in the shopping centre car park?'

Weaver frowned. 'He stole my spot. I had it all lined up when he sneaked in there.'

'Bullshit!' Jack thundered. 'I don't believe in coincidences. You just happened to bump into the ex-husband of your "client", a man who only weeks later winds up dead. Pull the other one, sunshine.'

'He's dead?'

'You bet he's fucking dead! Murdered. And I have a feeling you've got something to do with it.'

'No, no, no! Who is he again?'

'Paul Keenan. Like I said, your client's ex. The story's been all over the news.'

'She never told me he was her ex. I thought, I dunno, he was someone who might've ripped her off on a business deal or something. And I don't watch the news. I'm too busy.'

'Too busy taking advantage of lonely women and pumping yourself full of steroids, more like it,' said Taylor.

The big man's shoulders slumped, his hands darted to his face. 'I knew that nutty woman was trouble. I should have…'

'Should have what?' demanded Jack.

'Should have told her to take a hike.' He paused to scratch the underside of his forearm. Jack looked for needle marks indicating steroid abuse, saw none. 'Look, she paid me $500 to follow the bloke from the bank, told me what car he drove. All I had to do was get up in his face and make some nasty threats. I knew it was a bad idea, but five hundred's five hundred, right?'

'And why did she want you to do that to this poor man, a man who's done nothing to you?' said Taylor. She shot him a look of seething contempt.

Weaver shuddered, his breathing came in fits and starts. 'I didn't ask. Discretion at all times is how I operate.'

Jack believed the man was ignorant of Sabrina's tangled

web of a life. But there were a couple more burning questions to be answered. 'Do you think Sabrina is capable of murder?'

Weaver looked up, one eye closed as he pondered the possibility. 'In the heat of the moment, I reckon she could grab a meat cleaver and hack someone up. She's...unpredictable. But for anything that required a lot of thought, forget it.'

'The car park ambush required thought,' countered Taylor.

Weaver laughed. 'I said *a lot* of thought. That idea came to her out of the blue. I didn't like it, but as I told you, money is money.'

'As far as we can tell,' said Jack, getting to his last question. 'Sabrina's existing on a supporting mother's benefit. If you can tell us how she's able to drop so much cash on gin, intimate services and the odd act of intimidation, I reckon I'll let you walk out the door right now, free as a bird. You mentioned the words "business deal" before. Can you expand on that?'

Ten minutes later, Taylor was typing an application for a warrant to search for Schedule 9 drugs based on a statement by Nathan Weaver. According to the escort, the cops would find several kilos of cocaine neatly packed in a suitcase under Sabrina Keenan's bed. As Jack logged off his computer, one thought ran through his head. *So much for discretion.*

Chapter Thirty-Six

PULLING into the Iron Horse car park at a fraction after 8:00pm, Jack spied Trevarthen's black Harley Davidson motorcycle near the front entrance. With nowhere to park in the main area, the DS was forced to go around the back to the spill-over section. He grabbed his sports bag from the rear seat, his mobile phone from the console. A glance at the screen – a missed call from Kylie Smith. Aden could wait a few more minutes. 'Talk to me Kylie. Try and make it quick.'

'Yes, sir.'

Smith explained how she'd popped around to Ruby's on a social call, no uniform, no pressure. Nevertheless, the case was at the forefront of Ruby's mind and she wanted to divulge a detail she'd remembered. On the day before the shooting, a man had called and enquired about booking a 9:30am tee-off time for a solo round. Ruby had to tell him no, that slot was taken. The man asked if it was booked by some family or other, because he knew them and they might let him join in. Ruby believes he said the family's name was

Sawyer. Ruby can't be sure, but she thinks she told him no, it was booked for Keenan and friends. Ruby nearly broke down in tears, worried she may have sealed Keenan's fate. Smith assured her it wasn't her fault, but the words had little effect.

'Holy shit, Kylie. Do you know if the Country Club logs calls? We can—'

'Sir, she told me they use an old-fashioned system. Itemised calls won't show up until the next bill is issued mid next month.'

Jack rubbed his forehead. 'If the killer's as meticulous as I believe, he'll have used a payphone or a burner. Still, it's worth a shot. Tomorrow I'll seek an order to obtain the phone records before the Country Club gets the bill.'

'Sir. Anything else?'

'No, Kylie. Except well done.'

After he ended the call, Jack realised that although the killer may be clever, he couldn't resist the urge to drop a hint. *Sawyer* was a way to pronounce part of the name of a famous Swiss-German weapons make: Sig *Sauer*.

Inside the gym, in the crowded boxing section at the far end of the complex, Jack spotted Trevarthen sweating drops the size of dollar coins as he thumped the heavy bag. He hopped from one foot to the other, flailing away with combination punches. Jack smiled: his mate's strikes were getting stronger, jabs firmer and more decisive, each rip meeting the bag with a loud thwack, but his dancing skills were as appalling as ever.

'Hey,' Jack called out as he strode towards the first of three boxing rings. 'Don't wear yourself out before the main event.'

Trevarthen dropped his hands to his side, jogged to the ring and climbed under the ropes. He shuffled his feet while

Jack set up the boxing interval timer app – six three-minute rounds with a minute rest in between – and placed his mobile on a plastic chair. Jack joined Trevarthen in the ring, the two men touched gloves.

'I reckon you'll throw in the towel after round four,' said Trevarthen, before slotting in his mouthguard.

'We'll see about that,' said Jack.

At the end of round four, with sweat running from every pore and a stabbing pain arcing through his face, Jack held up his hands. Trevarthen raised his gloves, did a couple of mid-air half-turns. Jack yanked out his mouthguard, said through a mouthful of slimy spit, 'You got me, sunshine. I'm done.' He rested his hands on his hips, bent double at the waist and sucked in oxygen.

'Did you really surrender?' Trevarthen's tone was incredulous.

'You slipped a few through my guard, nailed me a cuppla times right where your elbow collected me down at the docks. Wouldn't be surprised if you've fractured my right cheekbone.'

'Geez, sorry, I…'

Jack put his hand on Trevarthen's shoulder. 'Don't be sorry. This is boxing, not a friendly round of golf. Speaking of which, I want to run something by you.'

'Isn't DC Taylor the one you should be–?'

'She ain't here is she?'

'No, but…'

'But nothin'. C'mon, let's hit the showers and get out of here.'

JACK POKED fat pork sausages around the barbecue, scraped frying onions into a pile. Scorched black remnants of meat from past meals lined the sides of the metal plate. Trevarthen observed keenly. As did Daisy, who sat unblinking at Jack's feet in case a titbit fell to the floor.

'Is that your stomach I can hear growling, or the dog's?' said Jack.

'I reckon it's mine,' said Trevarthen. Jack wondered if his mate had taken the change of lifestyle too far and wasn't eating enough. Then he remembered the time – past 10:00pm. He picked up a snag with a pair of tongs, dropped it onto a slice of buttered bread sitting on the plate Trevarthen held in eager outstretched hands.

'Want a beer to go with that?' said Jack.

'I thought you didn't drink.' Trevarthen took a seat at the outdoor table on the back deck, tapped the bottom of a tomato ketchup bottle, releasing blobs of sauce onto the sausage.

'I don't, but I like to have some in stock for guests. It's a test of my resolve.'

'Like how you order booze in bars and don't drink it?'

'You noticed, huh?'

'We've all noticed. You think people don't observe the great Detective Sergeant Jack Lisbon?'

Jack shrugged. 'Never thought about it.'

The two ate in silence for a minute, Jack chewing purposefully on the left side of his mouth to minimise the pain throbbing away on the right side of his face. He laid down his knife and fork. 'I hate to admit it, Ade, but I'm gonna be flying out of the country without an arrest on this one.' He wiped his greasy fingers on a paper towel.

'Not necessarily. Who knows what's around the corner?'

Trevarthen picked up his banger sandwich, worked his jaws overtime on a piece of gristle.

'All I can do is think about the case. When I'm not agonising about Skye and her dying mum, that is.'

'Poor kid.'

'She doesn't deserve this. And neither does Sarah. As much as my relationship with the woman was caustic most of the time we were together, I'd never wish cancer on anyone.'

'You've never really spoken much about your ex.'

'And now ain't the time to start.'

Trevarthen offered an apologetic smile. 'I didn't mean to…you know…pry.'

Jack shook his head and shrugged. 'It's natural to be curious.'

Another brief silence reigned before Jack rose to clear their plates from the table. 'That escort me and Taylor pulled in said something pretty insightful for a toe-rag.'

'Need a hand?' Trevarthen gestured to the growing pile in the outdoor sink.

Jack waved away the offer. 'All under control, mate.'

'So what was it the toe-nail said?'

Jack burst out laughing. 'Toe-*rag*. Get it right.' He ran water on the plates, scrubbed them clean with a brush and rested them in a metal rack.

'Whatever. What did he say?'

'He said the killer would have to be a careful planner. On the basis of that, I'm ruling out Sabrina Keenan. She's too erratic.'

'Out of the other suspects, who would you rate as a planner?'

Jack returned to the table with fresh drinks. 'Kam Fong, the accountant from the bank, but he's not a serious contender. The Brownstones? Capable people, good at their jobs, but as far as this operation goes, I'm not buying it.'

'Glenn Farr?'

Jack frowned. 'Nope. Her need for that pooch tells me she's too sentimental. The temperament required is that of a...' He remembered the words of Mitchell Morris, '...an absolute arsehole.'

Trevarthen smiled. 'That covers a large percentage of the population.'

'Yeah, it does 'n all.'

'How'd the interview go with the Morrises? I bet Mitchell was fuming over what happened to his dad.'

'Him *and* his wife were livid. She's a huge fan of her father-in-law.'

'What do they think of Dervla?'

'The son said she'd never replace his mother but Dervla made the old man happy. He's got a family photo on the wall from when he was a teenager – Mitchell, Lachlan and the late Tessa. She was a plain looking woman compared to Dervla, I gotta say.' Jack sipped his coke. 'Mitchell's wife didn't say anything about Dervla, good or bad.'

'Sounds like they tolerate her more than accept her into the family.'

'Family,' Jack repeated the word in a monotone. 'What was it about that word? Oh yeah. That's the thing I wanted to run by you.' He related the information he heard from Smith; that a man had called the golf course reception the day before the shooting. 'He asked about joining the Sawyer family for a round at 9:30am. Ruby said no, that time was reserved for Keenan and his party.' Jack looked up as a shooting star fell to Earth. He turned his attention back to Trevarthen. 'There are no members with the name Sawyer, Ruby checked.'

'That was the killer calling, wasn't it?'

'Yeah. My instincts tell me the call was placed to find out when Paul Keenan would be on the course, and for no other reason.'

'But where did he pull the name Sawyer from? That's a bit random.'

'I had an idea it's a reference to the murder weapon. Sig Sauer.'

'Jack, I hate to break this to you, but it's pronounced "sour", as in "sour grapes", not Sawyer.'

'It is?'

'One hundred percent. Did you really…?'

'So it's nothing to do with the gun, huh?'

'I dunno.' Trevarthen sat his beer down so he could squash a mosquito that was feeding on his forearm. 'If you thought the word was pronounced a certain way, chances are someone else might too. But I gotta say, I've never heard that version.' He dabbed away the spot of blood and mashed bug with a tissue. 'Perhaps there's some other link.'

'Like what?'

'Hmmm,' Trevarthen pondered. 'Sawyer, foyer, lawyer. Any legal people figure in the enquiry?'

'No, sunshine. You know there ain't and I think we're clutching at straws with the word association.'

Trevarthen wouldn't be deterred. 'Saw…dust, saw horse, jig saw, chain saw, hand–'

'Give it a rest mate,' Jack interrupted. 'I think our best bet's gonna be the Country Club's phone records. Batista approached the president, got his permission to approach the club's telco.'

'That's something, I guess. Any chance of another beer?'

'How many have you had?'

'One more'll make it three.'

'You'll be over the limit.'

Trevarthen stretched his arms wide and yawned. 'They're only light beers. I can have a dozen of them without—'

A can was already sailing in the direction of his head, toppling end over end. Trevarthen's hand reached out reflexively and snatched it mid-flight, droplets of condensation spraying in all directions.

'Nice catch.'

'Cheers.'

'Y'know, Ade, it's a funny coincidence you said jigsaw before. Mitchell Morris had maybe a dozen of 'em all over his walls. Huge great things they were. All laminated, hanging there like priceless works of art. I'd say a minimum of a thousand pieces each, a couple were probably two-thousand.'

'Impressive.'

'Plus there was an assortment of those sailing ships in bottles, matchstick models of famous buildings. He'd made them all himself.'

Trevarthen cracked the can, the loud pop making Daisy sit up and prick her ears for a second before she flopped back to the ground. 'That would take a lot of perseverance and determination. More than your average punter has. Way more than I've got.'

'What are you suggesting?'

'I'm suggesting,' Trevarthen leaned his elbows on the table, effected a serious expression, 'that someone with the patience to spend countless hours on massive jigsaw puzzles and those tricky models might be prepared to spend countless hours learning to fly a drone and—'

'And fire a gun at the same time!' Jack finished the

sentence. 'Holy shit, Ade. It fits. His wife mentioned his regular meetings with other hobby enthusiasts. What if there were no such meetings? He could've been out there in the bush,' Jack waved a hand, 'practicing with drones and guns.' Jack told Trevarthen how Morris was dressed, in overalls, like a tinkerer. A man perhaps capable of modifying machines for his own lethal purposes.

'You should have had a poke about in his shed while you were there.'

'In retrospect, yes, we damn well should have.'

'But what's his motive?'

Jack thought for a moment. 'Resentment. He hated his beloved dead mother being replaced by young Dervla. And then to have her add insult to injury, she goes and cheats on the old goat.'

Trevarthen stood, tossed half the contents of the beer can down his throat. 'But why did he kill Paul Keenan and not Dervla?'

'He's old school. He can't bring himself to kill a woman, but he wanted to punish her for her brazen adultery. By killing the man she loved. She'll be suffering the aftershocks the rest of her life after what she witnessed. We've already seen the seizures starting.'

'But shooting his own father, Jesus. That's a helluva risk to take.'

'Ah.' Jack held up a finger. 'That's why he invented the story about the food poisoning, why he couldn't go and visit him in the hospital. He was ashamed he'd almost killed his father when he only meant to wing him a bit; he couldn't face dad until the old bloke pulled through.'

'So, what next?'

'Good question. We've got no evidence to hold against him. If he's as smart as I think he is, he's called the Country

Club from a pay phone. The drone and the gun will be... fuck knows where.'

'Then what? He would have covered his tracks perfectly. The purchase of the drone, the weapon, the ammo, everything.'

'You know what, mate? There's more than one way to skin a wallaby!'

Chapter Thirty-Seven

CONVERSATION WAS LIVELY once they'd left the station car park, the atmosphere in the 4x4 thick with anticipation of what lay ahead. Taylor, at first sceptical, now agreed with the men's conclusion that Mitchell Morris was the killer. On the drive she worked overtime on the iPad, dug up a video of a teenage Mitchell posted to Facebook almost a decade ago; his father had filmed the boy holding a two-iron in one hand, bouncing a golf ball up and down on the business end, a few under-the-leg moves thrown in for good measure. A woman's proud voice of encouragement in the background sounded like it could have been his late mother. Young Mitchell sustained the exercise for three entire minutes, the ball never missing the face of the club. Taylor also found a short video of the kid solving a Rubik's cube in rapid time, another of him juggling up to five tennis balls at once. The officers concurred, the dexterity needed to perform such feats would translate well to piloting a drone and firing the mounted gun from a remote location.

Whether the police's arguments – at best suppositions –

would find any support with the Department of Public Prosecutions, Taylor was highly doubtful. 'If he can get himself a half-decent lawyer, I reckon the DPP will laugh us out of town.'

'Let's see about that,' said Jack through the side of his mouth. His face was still sore, a trip to the doctor a distinct possibility.

Seven kilometres from their destination Jack turned to Taylor. 'Could you flick a text to the Inspector, tell him we're about to make an arrest? That'd be lovely. He can read it as he's having his breakfast.'

'What?' Her high pitched query reverberated inside the vehicle. 'He doesn't know?'

Trevarthen suppressed a chuckle in the back seat.

'Ah, no,' said Jack. 'Didn't wanna disturb him in the middle of his sleep, innit. He's been a bit tetchy, what with his wife giving him grief lately.'

'Maybe it's him giving her grief,' said Taylor. 'Ever think of that?'

Jack ignored the question, concentrated on the road ahead. Ten minutes later he took a right off the main highway and onto the suspect's rocky private road. The Ford Territory retraced the route the detectives took yesterday, this time in semi-darkness. The luminous clock on the dash said it was 06:02am; the sun would be peeking over the horizon in a little over twenty minutes. Jack guided the vehicle gently and slowly, not wanting to alert the residents of the property to their imminent arrival.

'If I remember rightly,' said Jack. 'The turning circle in front of his house should appear once we pass that big native fig tree up ahead.'

'Correct,' said Taylor, rubbing her eyes. 'Let's hope he's at home, otherwise I'm gonna be mighty cranky for the rest of the day.' She'd argued against the dawn raid with no physical evidence to arrest Morris, but Jack convinced her to come along. He'd made the call to her just before 11:00pm last night, Trevarthen on loud speaker adding his two cents worth at Jack's prompting.

'Course he'll be home, where else is he going to be at this time?'

'Do they have any dogs?' said Trevarthen. 'We don't want the bloke alerted by barking.' The constable had spent the night at Jack's farmstead after switching from light beers to a couple of full-strength ales which would have nudged his blood-alcohol level over the limit. The pair rose at 04:30, drove to Trevarthen's house so he could change into his uniform, then whizzed by the station to tool up with Glocks and a couple of tasers, and to pick up Taylor.

'I don't recall any dogs, do you Claudia?' said Jack.

'No. Doesn't mean…'

'Shush everyone,' said Jack. 'We're almost there.' The dark, shadowy outline of the Morris home looked like a giant doll's house in the faint morning twilight. He killed the engine, took a deep breath. 'On foot from here, folks. Aden, you go around the side and to the back door. Claudia, come with me.'

Jack watched Trevarthen adopt a semi-crouch position and silently trot towards the side of the house, gun already gripped in both hands. In a second, head ducked below window level, he was out of sight. The two detectives strode up the wooden steps. 'Let's do this,' said Jack. He raised his right hand and banged hard with the heel of his fist five times. 'Open up! Police!'

The sound of a baby crying carried to the officers. Jack knocked and called out again. Moments later, the door opened, a wide-eyed Sally Morris on the other side. 'What the hell's going on? Do you realise what time it is?'

'Please let us in, Ms Morris. We'd like to speak to your husband.'

'He's...'

'I'm right behind you, love,' came Mitchell's voice, then his hairy face appeared at his wife's shoulder, momentarily giving the impression she had two heads. 'Probably about dad.' He stared hard into Jack's eyes. 'Please come in.'

Once he and Taylor had crossed the threshold and entered the hallway, Jack made his move. He shoved his way past Sally, pushing her hard against the wall and eliciting a cry of shock. Jack chided himself for his carelessness, the woman was likely innocent in every conceivable way. He sensed Taylor leading a shaking Sally out the door to the temporary refuge of the front porch, speaking empty words of comfort. With the women gone, Jack backheeled the door shut, grabbed the man's left wrist and spun him around in one lightning-fast motion. He retrieved a pair of zip-tie cuffs, applied them before the suspect could even think about resisting. Morris may have excellent hand-eye coordination, but it was no match for shock and awe. 'Mitchell Morris, I'm arresting you for the murder of Paul Sterling Keenan and the attempted murder of Lachlan Troy Morris.'

'Fuck off!' Morris turned his head and scowled. 'This is a huge mistake that you're gonna regret. I want you to leave my property. NOW!'

The child wailed from a room off the hallway.

'No mistake, sunshine. And we will leave. After you've given me a tour of your shed.'

'Like I said, fuck off!'

Jack twisted the man's wrist like he'd done with the male

escort, only harder. Mitchell let out a piercing yelp. 'Take me to the shed or you'll be sharing a hospital ward with dear old dad, your broken arms in plaster. If you've got nothing to hide you've got nothing to worry about.' He called over his shoulder to Taylor, asked her to bring the lady of the house back inside to see to the baby, and to make her a cuppa while he and Trevarthen took Mitchell to inspect the tin shed at the back of the house.

Once inside the shed, a neat and orderly space with a polished concrete floor and gleaming steel racks laden with tools and all manner of materials, Jack cut loose the cuffs. He ordered Morris to flick on the lights and open every drawer and cupboard door, and then stand in a far corner at the back of the shed like a good lad. 'You attempt to run, you cop a taser to the balls, got me?'

Mitchell nodded, the bravado fading with every minute. While he and Trevarthen poked about, Jack said, 'I'm gonna want proof of these once-a-week meetings your wife mentioned yesterday.'

'I'm not prepared to do that,' Morris replied meekly.

'That's because there were no such meetings. You know, sunshine, it's a simple matter for me to run through your mobile phone records.'

'The group members don't ring each other.'

'I haven't finished. We'll be looking at your mobile phone data to discover all your movements. I'm rather friendly with the current magistrate,' Jack saw Trevarthen turn his head and raise his eyebrows at the lie, 'and she'll gladly approve any application I make to go over your entire bleedin' life with a microscope. It'll be interesting to see where you've been going on your days off.' He turned over several sheets of sandpaper and metal grinding discs. The search was now all about a show of strength; there was no evidence of drones or pistols to be found, although Morris had been truthful about the two registered rifles, stashed away in a gun safe.

Satisfied there was nothing incriminating to be found, Jack took Morris back inside the house to swap his silk dressing gown for a t-shirt and a pair of pants. He allowed the man to say his good-byes to Sally and kiss the baby on the forehead. 'I'll be back soon,' Morris said to his wife. 'These people have no idea what they're doing.'

She blew her nose into a handkerchief, nodded, wrapped her arms around Morris for a moment, but said nothing.

'OK, sunshine, that'll do. Get over here.' Jack applied a new set of zip-tie cuffs. 'We've got enough to put you away in Copperhead Jail for the rest of your life.' They had precisely nothing, nevertheless Jack could hear a jerkiness in Morris's breathing and sensed muscles twitching through his entire body.

Jack frogmarched the arrested man to the vehicle, where Taylor was waiting in the passenger seat, scrolling through her mobile. Trevarthen jumped in the back seat, ready to keep Mitchell Morris company on the red-eye express back to the station.

Chapter Thirty-Eight

'YOU SURE YOU don't want a lawyer?' said Taylor, pulling up a chair with a loud scrape. 'I'd strongly advise you to organise one.'

'Only guilty people need lawyers.' Morris leaned back, arms folded across his broad chest. 'And where's your bully mate, Lisbon?'

'He's speaking to the magistrate on the phone, seeing if we can't expedite things.'

'Whatever.' He blinked hard, ran fingers through his beard like a comb. His feet tapped rapidly under the table.

Taylor poured water from a jug into a paper cup, pushed it towards the latest guest of Interview Room 1. As Morris reached for it, Jack burst into the room clutching a folded piece of paper. He placed it on the table with a flourish, adjusted the tripod-mounted camera and switched it on. In a flat voice he stated the time, who was present, and asked the suspect if he was taking part in the interview of his own free will, which was answered in the affirmative. Jack changed his tone to upbeat. 'Awesome news! But not for you, I'm afraid, Mr Morris. Wanna know what it is?'

'Tell me.'

'We're going to get permission to access your phone, Internet and financial records. So I'm going to give you the chance to fess up now and save everyone a ton of time and grief.'

'Show me!' demanded Morris, his body shaking.

Jack handed over the paper he'd brought in, Morris studied it for a moment before exclaiming, 'This is instructions for a fucking electric shaver!'

'I never said it was anything else.' Jack smiled smugly.

'So where's the warrant or whatever it's called?'

Jack slowly rolled up one sleeve, then the other. 'That's gonna take an hour or two.' He glanced at his watch. 8:30am. Morris had been cooling his heels in a holding cell for an hour and a half while the detectives and Batista discussed the best way to approach the interview. 'My boss behind the glass there,' Jack gestured towards the panel, 'will be handling all of that official stuff. All DC Taylor and I wanna know is, why did you do it?'

'I did nothing.'

'Was it because your mother was replaced by an Irish bimbo?'

'Piss off.'

'You know, I can understand your anger, I really can. My father cheated on my mum, I'm sure of it. And when parents get caught up in their self-absorbed adult lives, it's not unusual for the kids to be...neglected.'

'Shut up!' Morris jabbed his finger. 'Both my parents loved me. If yours treated you badly, it's because you deserved it.'

'Fair call.' Jack chuckled. 'I was rather a brat. However

we do know that your mum did love you. We've seen those old clips of you juggling, playing keepy-uppy with the golf ball. You can hear dear old mum's voice in the background, overflowing with pride as she cheers you on. Very touching. Yep,' Jack sighed. 'Mums like that are to be revered and cherished. So sad she was snatched away prematurely with cancer.'

Jack and Taylor couldn't help but lean in as Morris turned his head, muttered something under his breath. He turned face on to them again, his eyes glistening with tears. A couple rolled down his cheek and disappeared into his bushy beard. 'Dervla will never replace my mother. No one will.'

'Of course not,' said Taylor.

'Dervla needed to be punished, didn't she, Mitchell?' said Jack.

The room fell silent for a moment, then Morris gave a micro-nod.

'For the benefit of the recording, please say the answer out loud.' Taylor exchanged a look of disbelief with Jack.

'Yes.' It was barely a whisper, but loud enough for the microphone to pick up. 'She needed to be punished.'

'And you did that?' said Jack.

The silence dragged on. Jack had gone too far, he'd have to backtrack.

But then...

'Yes.' Another whispered reply. Then, a shout: 'I punished the bitch all right!'

Taylor gasped, gripped her pen tighter. Jack's heart pounded like a trip-hammer. He'd hooked a huge fish, he had to be careful not to let it wriggle free. *Play to his ego.* 'The way you did it was pure genius. You had all of us baffled.'

Tears flowed freely from Morris's eyes, like a pipe had

burst. He grabbed a tissue from the box on the table, blotted tears away.

'Can you please tell us how you did it?' said Taylor.

'Will it reduced my sentence if I tell you everything?' He wiped away fresh tears.

'Telling the truth won't do you any harm,' said Jack, busting out the usual non-committal response for such situations.

'I'd like a lawyer present now, if you don't mind. But I'm telling you straight up. I'm not pleading guilty to the attempted murder of my father. What happened to him was a mistake, OK?'

Two hours later, with a criminal lawyer plucked from the yellow pages by Morris's side, the confession poured out in exquisite detail.

'I hated that woman even before she started fucking Keenan. When the two of them started their sordid little affair, something snapped in my head.'

'If you hated Dervla, why not target her?' said Jack.

'Don't think I wasn't tempted. But I was brought up not to harm women physically.'

'When did you decide to kill Paul Keenan?' said Taylor.

'I got the idea two years ago, after I learned about Dervla's cheating. Sally and I were in denial until, when was it, last October, I heard through the grapevine that someone saw the two of them kissing on the golf course, with Dad a few metres away. How disrespectful can you get!' He paused, exchanged whispered words with the lawyer, took a drink of water. 'That's when I started to practise drone flying. And then shooting targets until I could almost do it with my eyes shut. Hitting dad too many times showed I wasn't as ready as I thought I was. Another month of target practice with the recoil factored in better and he never would have wound up in hospital.'

'You sure about that?'

'Positive!'

'Where did you practice?'

'On an abandoned property 80 kms west of Yorkville. A mate of mine from the hobby group owns the land.'

Jack's eyebrows jumped. 'So there *were* meetings?'

'Yeah, but once a month, not once a week. I hated to deceive Sally, but, as they say, the end justifies the means.'

'What about the drone?' said Taylor. 'Where did you get it?'

'I bought a basic kit from a pawn shop in Cairns. Jerry's it's called. Got a real good deal for cash. Eleven hundred bucks. It was in such good condition, it must've been stolen.'

Jack consulted the case file. 'Was it a...Autel Robotics EVO II?'

Mitchell's eyes widened. 'Yeah. How'd you know?'

'We may not be as smart as you, sunshine, but we're not complete dummies.' He locked eyes with Mitchell. 'Where is it now?'

'The bottom of the Pacific Ocean.'

'What about the gun? What kind was it?'

'A Sig Sauer.' *Sour, exactly like Trevarthen said.*

'Model?'

'P365 9mm.'

'How many shots?'

'Fifteen round magazine.'

'Where did you get it?'

'Same second-hand store. Under the counter, of course. Semi-automatic weapons are illegal in this state, in case you weren't aware.'

'One more question before we take a break for tea,' said Jack.

'Sure.'

'Do you have any remorse for the atrocity you perpetrated?'

The lawyer held up a finger to interject, but it was too late.

'None,' said Mitchell. 'And I'd do it all again.'

Chapter Thirty-Nine

HE STOPPED his run along the esplanade to watch a yacht sailing beyond the rocky breakwater. Shielding his eyes from the sun, he recognised the vessel, its spinnaker billowing in the sea breeze. *Hammerhead*. It was impossible to identify the person who stood at the helm, but Jack figured it must be Michael Salesa enjoying his new toy. Jack would also be on the water soon. He'd scheduled a charter fishing trip with Trevarthen for tomorrow, a welcome chance to unwind after the stress of the Keenan murder case. They'd chased marlin together a while back, with both men landing and releasing a couple of whoppers. He couldn't wait to go again.

Jack resumed his jog, every now and then tugging on Daisy's lead as she lunged at unsuspecting people enjoying the autumn sunshine. *She's friendly. Don't be scared.* He was sick of saying it every two minutes. Obedience training jumped to the top of the to-do list. Well, almost. First there was the fishing expedition.

Run completed and perched on the tailgate of his

Hilux, Jack plucked a rubber collapsible dog bowl from the rear, filled it from a tap next to a public barbecue block. He smiled as Daisy slurped like she hadn't had a drink in a week.

As he wiped sweat from his armpits with a hand towel, Rick Astley started singing from inside the car. Skye calling from London. He frantically opened the driver-side door, grabbed his mobile. *Surely not?*

'Hi, sunshine,' he said in the most neutral tone he could muster with his heart racing like a steam train. 'You OK?'

'No, Dad. Mum's going downhill fast. You've got to come!'

A lump formed in Jack's throat, he forced it down with a hard swallow. 'I'll do my best, love.'

'Two weeks now,' she sobbed. 'I'm losing her...I can't...'

For once in his miserable life, Jack Lisbon was lost for words. Tears welled in his eyes, and he made no attempt to wipe them away.

'You there, dad?'

'Yes,' he gathered his composure. 'I'll book the flight today.'

'What about the case? I've been following it online. Don't you have to give testimony in court?'

'No, sweetheart. The man confessed and provided us with a heap of evidence. Plus we're dropping the attempted murder charge. Which means the trial will be a short formality and my presence won't be required.'

'Are you serious?'

'Yes, love. I'll be with you in a couple of days.'

'Please don't change your mind!'

'Not a chance. I'll call you again once I've booked everything, OK?'

'Yes. Mum will be pleased to see you. Not sure about Aunty Jocelyn, though.'

'Me too.'

A quick call to Micky Knox to ask about staying in his St Albans house was met with enthusiastic approval. As was the request to make a room available for Skye.

Showered and sprawled on his three-seater couch, ready to zone out and watch the rugby league match of the day, a text alert. Taylor. He hit the call return button next to her contact icon. 'Before you say anything, I can't make the committal hearing for Sabrina Keenan on Monday.'

'What, no hello?' said Taylor.

He turned the TV volume down as one particularly loud commentator started getting excited about the upcoming game. 'Sorry. I spoke to Skye earlier. Her mum's on the way out.'

'Oh, no!' Taylor gasped. 'Wasn't it supposed to be months?'

'Yeah, but you know how these things go.'

A silence punctuated the conversation until Jack said, 'Listen, could you do me a favour?'

'Anything.'

'Could you look after Daisy for me when I'm gone. I couldn't handle putting her in a kennel.'

'I'm not sure the landlord would be too happy about me keeping a big dog like her in my apartment.'

'I was thinking more along the lines of you staying here at my place. There's lots of room. You can make as much mess as you like.'

'I don't make a mess.'

Jack forced a laugh. 'You know what I mean.'

'I guess I could do that.'

Jack let out a sigh. 'You're a godsend, Claudia.'

'I'd need you to show me how everything works. Washing machine, oven, all that stuff.'

'Of course. How about you come over and we can run over everything.'

'When?'

'Now.'

'You sure?'

'Please, Claudia. I'd appreciate some company tonight.'

'On my way.'

He stared at the frantic action on the television, registering nothing. The sound of Daisy's paws clicking on the floorboards snapped Jack out of his stupor. 'Come here, girl.' The dog's head resting on his lap, Jack decided he didn't want to watch the football. He flicked over to YouTube, found the song, hit play. Frente's version of "Bizarre Love Triangle". As the singer's haunting voice filled the room, Jack curled up into the foetal position and cried himself to sleep.

BLAIR DENHOLM

Next in The Fighting Detective Series

vinci-books.com/movingtarget

When Jack witnesses a brutal murder on the city of Lisbon's iconic tram, his family getaway turns into a hunt for a deceptive killer.

Turn the page for a free preview…

A free prequel novella...

vinci-books.com/takedown-free

Get the explosive prequel to The Fighting Detective series, absolutely free.

Moving Target: Chapter One

THE DARK, brooding rain clouds that had been hovering over London for the last two days finally opened up. Light drops quickly turned into a steady drizzle. Fitting, Jack Lisbon thought, as he pulled his daughter closer to his side. His ex-wife Sarah, the reason they were all gathered here today, was always complaining about the English weather.

'Daddy, when is the funeral service going to start?' Skye sobbed. 'I just want it to be over.'

'Soon, love.' Jack clicked the little button that locked the top of the umbrella into place. 'I think the vicar's still waiting on a few people to turn up.'

'Who? Everybody mummy knew is already here!' She pointed at the large crowd of mourners huddled in the gardens and around the doors of St James Church in Croydon, South London.

'Just a couple more, sweetheart.' Jack estimated the crowd at around sixty people, not including the vicar, funeral director and attendant staff. An equal distribution of black and white faces, predominantly female. Sarah had been one of the most popular hairdressers in the area, her customers encompassing all ages. Handkerchiefs were in abundance as the mourners failed to hold back the tears. *Fair play to you Sarah,* Jack thought to himself. *You had the common touch and the people loved you.*

If Jack got a third as many punters turning up to his farewell gig it would be a miracle. He could count on the fingers of one hand those who truly cared. Claudia at work, a couple of the uniforms, Trevarthen in particular. Micky Knox here in London. Oh, and his dog Daisy. True friends were few and far between. But that never really bothered Jack. The one who cared the most for him – and the one he cared for the most – shivered under his wing like a frightened little bird; her mother cruelly snatched away by cancer way too young.

Now it was time to step up, to be a real parent, not just exist as Skye's abstract notion of a father. Or the image she held dear – the heroic detective who lived in the exotic tropics of Far North Queensland, Australia. He would earn her trust and love after the grieving and the healing was over. Given his shady work history in the UK – sprinkled with suspensions and reprimands – it had been a battle to prove he was worthy of custody. When the decision in his favour finally came through, his heart nearly leapt out of his mouth. It could have gone the other way, with a particularly nasty government bureaucrat arguing that Jack was a bad man with a record of absenteeism, alcoholism and aggression, and that Skye should remain in Britain under the care of the state. Even though past troubles in the UK were a black mark against him, Jack proved he was a changed man. His unblemished and stellar record as a criminal investigator in Australia – with a number of high-profile cases even making the news in the UK – certainly didn't harm his cause.

As they waited for the remaining stragglers to arrive, random people approached father and daughter, offered their condolences. Touching, Jack thought, since only a few of them knew Jack from Adam. And those who did, mutual friends of his and Sarah's from happier days, probably hated him deep in their hearts for abandoning Sarah and Skye when his own life started to spiral out of control. Running away from his responsibilities, they'd be thinking. An irresponsible wastrel of a man.

If only they knew the truth. Or perhaps it was better they didn't. In reality, Jack had run away from some serious trouble that could have seen him sentenced to life in prison. Outwardly, he'd fled the country because he was given an ultimatum by the London Met – resign with some dignity intact, or face being sacked for corruption. But the biggest motivation for his escape was the fear that someone would discover he'd committed a brutal murder. And stolen a shitload of cash from the victim's safe. Because if today's sympathisers knew that, they might not be extending their hands for Jack to shake.

'When are the rest of the people coming?' Skye blurted. 'I'm sick of waiting. I'm cold…and…I'm…' she burst into a flood of tears, Jack hugged her tight. 'Why did mummy have to die?' she wailed, her head snuggling into his chest.

'There, there, sweetheart. I know, it's not fair.' He stroked her mop of curly hair. 'It's just your cousins from Jamaica we're waiting on now,' said Jack gently. 'They won't be long, I'm sure.' He felt his breathing had become constricted, loosened his necktie. He hardly ever wore the damn thing; it usually hung out of sight in the back of the wardrobe, only seeing daylight for court appearances.

'I've never even met them,' she pouted and stamped one foot on the damp grass. 'Why are they so important that the whole funeral is being held up?'

'Come on, love. You're twelve years old, a big girl now. We have to be patient with other people. Maybe they were held up in traffic? Let's give them the benefit of the doubt.'

Lips pressed hard together, she looked up at him with moist eyes but said nothing. Her petulance was perfectly understandable. Jack had only heard Sarah mention these cousins once or twice in passing. Perhaps they were thinking there'd be an inheritance waiting for them? If so, they were going to be sorely disappointed. Sarah was known for donating far too much of her meagre beautician's wages to charity, but she always made sure there was enough left over to pay for Skye's needs. In other words, she died virtually penniless.

A black cab pulled up outside the church, sending a spray of water from a puddle in the gutter. Two people dressed head to toe in black alighted. 'Look, love,' said Jack, pointing at the latecomers. 'Here they are now.'

Ida and Lenny, daughter and son of Sarah's older brother Marcus, who himself died a decade ago from cancer, slowly made their way through the little graveyard towards the gathered guests. They must have recognised Skye from photos, Jack surmised, because Ida stopped mid-stride and the pair changed direction and made a beeline towards them.

A few words of introduction and sympathy were exchanged, Skye remaining the epitome of respect despite the harsh words she'd only moments ago said to Jack. The cousins, in fact, were friendly and gracious and came across as deeply sincere; Jack took back his unspoken words about the inheritance angle. Skye took an instant shine to them, too. She held out her hand to cousin Ida. 'Would you like to sit with me and dad at the front?' she said, the tiniest smile breaking out on her face. It was the first real positive sign in Skye's demeanour since Jack picked her up from a none-too-pleased Aunty Jocelyn and they'd gone to stay at Micky Knox's house in St Auburn. Jack's heart melted at the kid's sudden turn of generosity. Sarah may have been a temperamental hothead when it came to her relationship with Jack, but she always showed genuine compassion for others. It seemed Skye had inherited the caring gene from her mum. *Not a bad legacy to leave behind, old girl*, Jack said to himself.

'OK, everyone,' called the funeral director through megaphone hands. The bald, portly man waved his hand at the entry to the church. 'Let's all get inside now.'

JACK GLANCED down from the raised dais. It reminded him of the press conferences he'd run with Inspector Joe Batista, only the audience wasn't waving microphones and shouting questions at him. All the mourners' eyes were turned towards him expectantly. He singled out Skye, gave her a smile of encouragement and an awkward wave, mouthed the words "I love you." Giant teardrops rolled down her cheeks. He scanned the room: some folk were squinting disdainfully, knowing Jack only from the bad things Sarah had told them. Others wore more forgiving expressions.

The vicar had already spoken at length, a selection of traditional hymns and two rollicking gospel tunes had been sung. Sarah's sister Jocelyn, her best friend Ramona from the salon, a handful of women Jack didn't know, had all had their turn, saying glowing things about Sarah as a mother, a friend, a family member, a pillar of the community. Skye was praised as the perfect child, which drew some laughs.

Now, it was Jack's turn. As an ex-husband who hadn't enjoyed the most convivial relationship with the deceased, the job wasn't going to be an easy one. The room was so quiet, when he cleared his throat it sounded like a chainsaw starting up. He took a sip of water, then looked down at the piece of paper he'd written the speech on, which was totally unnecessary since he knew by heart all the words he'd composed on the plane from Dubai to Heathrow. Despite their years apart, and the knowledge that he and Sarah had been at each other's throats far more often than they'd spent in each other's arms, he put the best spin on it that he could. A joke here and there, recalling Sarah's volatile temper by mimicking her Jamaican accent but with respect, not in a mocking way: *You're guilty as a cat in a fishbowl! Dere will be hell to pay, Jack Lis-bon!* Skye could barely keep it together as Jack busted out her mum's favourite phrases.

Then, no words left to say, he took a deep breath and stepped down. He felt he'd done justice to the woman's best qualities and people weren't staring daggers at him. At any rate, it was a relief to have finished.

The burial ceremony was the hardest thing Jack had had to endure in his life. Watching his daughter's tiny hand tossing soil over the casket, streams of tears indistinguishable from the slanting rain, brought tears to his own eyes. Conscious of his chest rising and falling as the vicar spoke the eulogy, he prayed he wouldn't faint from the emotion of it all and topple into the grave and land on Sarah's coffin.

As everyone filed out of the churchyard on their way to the wake in a nearby community hall, Skye holding the hands of her cousin Ida and her dad, Bob Marley's classic "Three Little Birds" boomed out loud and clear from speakers inside the church. Skye sang along like it was a memory of her favourite nursery rhyme. No doubt her mum had The Wailers on a loop at home. Jimmy Cliff and UB40 were other favourites Skye would be well acquainted with. As they exited the gate and headed for Jack's rented Opel, the entire crowd was belting out the song, telling each other not to *worry 'bout a ting!* When they got to the reception, the atmosphere could tempt Jack into hitting the booze, but he would stay strong as ever and stick to coffee. Years of sobriety behind him, he would never return to his bad old ways. He had a kid to raise and be a good example for, after all.

As Jack opened the passenger door for Skye, he looked at her with the deepest affection he had ever felt for another human being. So many missed years, so much to make up for. In a few days, after a number of boring but necessary legal formalities had been taken care of, Detective Sergeant Jack Lisbon of the Yorkville CIB, Queensland Police Service, would be winging his way back to the warm tropics. This time, with the most precious thing in his world keeping him company. If he ever returned to the UK, he reflected, it would only be on the strength of an extradition order. Who knew? Maybe a dogged cold-case investigator might figure out the truth, that Jack had offed the despicable Alex Gallagher. But that would never happen because Gallagher was a piece of scum, and, unlike Sarah, mourned and missed by few. And certainly not by any cold-case investigators.

But before touching down in Oz, they were taking a side trip to Jack's ancestral home of Portugal, where his father was born and learned his trade as a mechanic before migrating to the United Kingdom. The little break would give him and Skye the perfect opportunity to grieve in peace. They'd take a well-earned rest for a couple of weeks, soak up some sun and see all the famous sights, and prepare for their life together Down Under.

And while they were there, Jack would meet a cousin of his own and do his level best to stay out of mischief.

Moving Target: Chapter Two

THE WOMAN WAITING inside the Humberto Delgado Airport terminal's crowded greeting hall held a cardboard sign above her head displaying the words "Lisbon welcomes the Lisbons!"

'*Bom dia*,' said Jack in the most appalling Portuguese. 'Nice touch with the sign. Very droll. Mirabella Coelho, I presume?'

'*Bom dia*, Jack,' said the woman, delivering a white-toothed smile that gleamed like a camera flash. 'You presume correctly.' Mirabella, who spoke English with only a trace of an accent, glanced at Skye, to be met with an expression of curiosity mixed with suspicion. 'And you must be Skye! Your father has told me *so* much about you in our little chats.'

Skye, wide-eyed, said: 'Only good things, I hope.'

Mirabella laughed. 'More than good, young lady. You've been through a lot, he tells me. A kidnapping a couple of years ago, for goodness' sake. And now this awful tragedy with your mum…' She reached out slowly to touch Skye on the shoulder, but the girl shrank back into her father's one-armed embrace.

'Oh, I'm terribly sorry!' said Mirabella, her hands cupping her reddening cheeks. 'I've said something wrong. I didn't mean anything by it.'

'No, no.' said Jack. 'I...ah...just a second.' He placed his carry-on bag on the floor. 'That thing's darned heavy.' It wasn't – the bag contained a paperback and a change of underwear. He needed time to regroup mentally. 'It's just that us Brits have a tendency to dodge the emotional stuff.'

Mirabella nodded, as if satisfied with the explanation.

Jack scratched the back of his head. He wasn't flustered merely due to the awkwardness of the unfolding situation. There was a more superficial reason. Mirabella, whom Jack had met online through a genealogy site but never seen before, looked like she could have been the twin sister of his work partner back in Australia, Detective Claudia Taylor. Mirabella's eyes were brown instead of Taylor's deep forest green, and her hair – tucked into a scrunchie, yellow like Taylor often wore – had more of a wave to it. She stood a couple of inches shorter than Taylor and weighed perhaps a kilo or two more, with a bit of extra padding on the hips. There were some minor differences in facial features, too, but overall the likeness was uncanny. He even wondered if Skye's initial standoffishness had something to do with the woman's close resemblance to Taylor, whom the kid had spoken to on Zoom calls. Skye had formed a kind of bond with Taylor, liked her a lot, even viewed her as her father's potential new girlfriend. And maybe Jack did too.

Jack took a deep breath. 'Like you said, she's been through a lot. We just have to give her some time, don't we sunshine?'

Skye peeled herself away from Jack's side, rubbed a

wrist under her nose and gave a little sniff. 'Yes.' She gazed up at their new friend, forced a smile. 'I'm sorry for my reaction, Mirabella. It's not your fault what happened.'

'No need to apologise, my dear.' She winked. 'Let's get to the car and back to my place. I have a couple of rooms set aside for you two. It's cool here in the terminal, but believe me, it's nice and warm outside. Feel like a swim?'

Skye nodded rapidly. 'Are we going to the beach?'

'No. I have a pool at my place.'

'Well,' said Jack, tossing the backpack over his shoulder again like it was empty, drawing a look of astonishment from Mirabella. 'What are we waiting for?'

THE OPULENCE of the woman's home took Jack's breath away. Located in a secluded pocket of the leafy Belém district, the three-level house contradicted the one thing he thought he knew about the local people. That they were dirt poor. With Portugal having one of the lowest per-capita incomes in Europe, he half expected Mirabella to take them to a modest little flat way out of town. The drive from the airport had already set Jack's expectations low: crumbling facades with tiles missing here and there, pathways and traffic islands overgrown with grass and weeds, graffiti prolific on the walls of all kinds of buildings. Yes, she had a nice car, but for some reason Jack assumed it was rented.

'Please, follow me.' Mirabella waved her guests into the brightly lit atrium, dotted with deep-green plants. They gawped around at their surroundings, cool air from a powerful air-conditioning system washing over them. Sparkly clean and tidy as a pin, the tile and glass interior put the airport terminal to shame.

Mirabella showed Jack and Skye upstairs to their rooms. Five-star luxury all the way: king size beds with expensive sheets, ensuites in both bedrooms, wide-screen TVs, bar fridges. As he was unpacking his meagre supply of clothes, Jack wondered if this lavish home could really be Mirabella's property. She'd be lucky if she was forty and, as far as he knew, the woman was single. Perhaps she inherited it? Or maybe she was renting in a share arrangement with some other people. Or was she some kind of protégé, like his mate Mickey Knox, the drop-shipper extraordinaire? When he and Skye had changed into their swimming gear and the dressing gowns that were laid upon their beds, they met up again with their host in the vast sitting room.

Jack fired from the hip. 'Have you owned this place for long?' It was a direct question loaded with an assumption. A classic detective's ploy.

'One year. Actually, not even that. I'd say nine months. And,' she dragged the word out, 'before you make any wild guesses, because I can see it all over your face, I'll tell you how I can afford it.'

Over fresh orange juice and a platter of walnuts, olives, sliced carrot and celery, Mirabella explained how her website had recently enjoyed a stratospheric rise in popularity, especially in the last year. Apparently, there were loads of millionaires in Brazil who were prepared to fork out lots of money to find out if they were related to a famous explorer from centuries ago. Having a lineage that goes back to Vasco da Gama, Ferdinand Magellan or even one of their crew, brings a ton of street cred in the backrooms of Rio's business enterprises.

Grab your copy…
vinci-books.com/movingtarget

About the Author

Blair Denholm is a born-and-bred Australian crime fiction writer whose previous jobs have been as varied as translator, debt collector, technology researcher, banking and insurance consultant, and even car-wash attendant. Over the years he has lived and worked in New York, Moscow, Munich, Abu Dhabi and Australia. His life-long love of sports is reflected in the plots of The Fighting Detective series.

Denholm's flagship series, The Fighting Detective, stars ex-boxer Detective Sergeant Jack Lisbon and is set in the steamy tropics of North Queensland, Australia. The series features heavy doses of noir crime with a vigilante justice twist. So far there are eight novels and one prequel novella in the series, with more in the pipeline.

Denholm's debut novel, *SOLD*, is the first in a noir trilogy featuring the detestable yet lovable one-man wrecking ball Gary Braswell. The book was long-listed for movie adaptation by Screen Queensland in 2019. The other books in this series are *Sold to the Devil* and *Sold Dirt Cheap*.

Denholm has also written two thriller novels set in Russia. Captain Viktor Voloshin is a hard-boiled investigator who has to fight the establishment in order for justice to be served in his own special way. The first in this series, *Revolution Day*, was published in 2021, with the follow-up, *The Defector*, released in 2024. One more book will round off this series.

In 2024, Denholm signed on with UK-based publisher Vinci Books.

Blair Denholm grew up in suburban Brisbane, Queensland. After two lengthy stints in Tasmania, he now resides in the relatively cooler climes of the Southern Downs region of Queensland with his partner, Sandra, and faithful dog, Bruno.

Acknowledgments

Well, here we are at book #6 in The Fighting Detective series. Getting this far and not throwing in the towel is largely down to my supportive partner, Sandra. Also, a big thanks to all my advance review readers and my proofreader, Jiver.